♥

Blood Ties,
Love Binds

♥

Blood Ties, Love Binds by Alexa Whitewolf

ISBN: 978-1-989384-08-4
Copyright ©2008-2018 Alexa Whitewolf

Second Edition
Cover design by Y. Nikolova at Ammonia Book Covers

This is a work of fiction.

Acknowledgements

A writer's life is never easy. Between many all-nights and juggling multiple things, it can be easy to get lost or overwhelmed. Which is why it's important to have a great support system.

I've been blessed with an amazing husband who understands that I'm not always going to be cooking dinner – especially when I'm working on a new novel. His support made this book possible, and Steven, my love, know that I appreciate it every moment of *every* day.

To my mom, a huge thanks for always believing in me! If you hadn't been the mom you've always been, I'd never have grown up to be the woman I am today.

To my two furballs, Zeus and Achilles… Thanks for all the times you knocked my laptop/tablet over so we could play, and so I could take a breather. Thanks for knowing me well enough that you could tell when I needed a break. And *thank you*, most of all, for the long walks in the moonlight that always spark inspiration!

A huge shout-out goes to my friend and fellow talented author Eldon Farrell (Descent Series & Singularity), who spent hours perusing the earlier draft. His feedback smoothed many hurdles in the long process of rewriting this story!

Massive, massive thanks to Y. Nikolova at Ammonia Book Covers for yet another awesome cover!

And as always, to my readers – thanks for sticking it through with me!

♥ *Prologue* ♥

The villa rose amid a colourful field of tulips and grapes. Three stories high, with a faded beige exterior and windows from the Renaissance Age, it painted a pretty picture. Vines covered the cracked walls, enhancing the structure's ancient feel.

Acres and acres of vastness surrounded it, with no soul to be seen for miles on end. The only security was a metal gate uniting the rectangle of cement blocks. Its lock lay discarded on the dusty ground, the rusted top broken off by force.

The area was picturesque, perfect for a vacation, were it not for the men lining the entrance to the metal gate. Like a human wall, they circled the outside periphery, their unwavering gazes glued to the villa and the person hiding within.

The rising sun casts a shade over their contingent, not obscuring them, but somehow emphasizing their sinister countenances.

♥∞♥

A screech of tires outside pulled Cassandra's attention from her phone.

"Shit."

She ran up the stairs and into the attic, heading to the small window for a better view. A thin lace curtain blocked the frame, and Cassandra moved it to the side, glancing below. Two other cars had arrived, bringing the total number to eight.

Her hazel eyes momentarily fell on the lake in the distance, now painted with the rising sun's amber glow. *Such a beautiful landscape...and such pity I'm about to die here.*

Cassandra kept herself out of sight, biting her lip. The vultures' numbers had multiplied, and it didn't look like they'd be leaving anytime soon.

From afar, it looked like a welcoming committee, the type any diplomat would get. The men wore dark, business suits, sunglasses and drove expensive-looking black cars. Some were pacing, others leaning against the vehicles as they waited.

The only problem with that assessment was that Cassandra was no diplomat – quite the contrary. Her trip to Italy was motivated by love, and a lack of survivor's instinct that would be her downfall, considering the heavy guns the men were packing.

As if on cue, the sound of a gunshot snapped Cassandra out of her ruminations and drew her gaze to the morbid spectacle below. Two of the men were busy wrestling a third, and a short argument ensued. It ended when the man received a gunshot to the head and dropped dead on the ground. Within seconds, the sandy grass was stained by his blood.

Cassandra tore her eyes from the morbid scene and forced herself to step away. Biting on her lip until she could taste blood, she felt for the gun strapped in the waistband of her jeans, drawing comfort from the small protection. *Good thing my parents thought to hide at least some measure of protection on this estate. Not that it'll do me much good despite my semi-decent aim.*

Not for the first time, Cassandra was reminded of the steps that had led her to that exact moment. The distrust, the betrayal, the love and the heartache. With the mounting danger, it was impossible not to imagine what would have happened if she had simply walked away.

As quickly as it came, the idea was repelled by another. *I wouldn't have done anything differently.*

The unwelcome thought crossed her mind that there was no escaping the final showdown…and she had no backup.

They know I'm here. I know they're out there. The question is how much reprieve do I have?

The ring of a cellphone cut through the oppressive silence. Cassandra dug it out of the pocket of her jeans, not even bothering to look at the caller ID.

"Hey, D!" She tried to keep a neutral tone, if only to hide her predicament, but her boyfriend's words quickly dispelled the notion she had succeeded.

"What the *hell* are you thinking, Cass?" She cringed at the anger in his voice, but held back a snarky retort. *He's worried, and if the situation were reversed, I would be too.*

Another car moved down the dusty road and her grip on the cellphone grew slack, even as her muscles tensed, intent on the men's reactions. *Is this it?*

Panic bubbled up Cassandra's throat, almost choking her. Damon's muttered curses on the other line faded in her ear, and she couldn't get a single word past the knot in her throat.

As she watched the latest newcomers exit the newest car, Cassandra reached behind with her free hand and pulled the gun out of her waistband, her knuckles whitening from the force of her hold.

With her life hanging in the balance, she couldn't help but think back to how the whole mess had begun…

♥ *Chapter 1* ♥

A few weeks earlier…

Damon turned from his spot at the bar, casing the surroundings while sipping a glass of scotch. With his free hand, he pulled at the tight collar of his white shirt, drawing in a proper breath despite its constricting hold.

"Was this penguin suit really necessary?" His lips barely moved as he spoke into the microphone embedded in his tie, addressing his team on the other end.

"You wanted to blend in, right?" Amy's voice held a spark of amusement, and Damon rolled his eyes.

"You're enjoying this."

His teammate was smart enough not to retort, and only silence answered him. Damon was about to draw her into another conversation, when movement by the elevators drew his gaze.

"Target confirmed on my 6. Navy suit and cropped hair."

A pause followed as Amy consulted with the rest of the team, then, "Confirmed. You're a go."

Damon downed the rest of his drink, and headed towards the elevator. He added a convincing stumble to his steps, keeping his face angled to the floor in order to avoid the cameras. When the beep of the doors opening sounded, Damon stumbled into the target with enough force to knock him into the elevator, separating him from his group.

"What the he—"

With the doors safely closed and the elevator moving up, Damon dropped the act and slammed the man against the wall, one hand gripping his throat. "Where were you last Friday night, between one and two in the morning?"

"Screw yo—" The curse finished on a wheeze as Damon tightened his hold.

"Do I look like I'm fucking around? I asked you a question, Dimitri Kovalski, and I expect an answer."

It took a few more seconds until he turned blue in the face for Dimitri to tap the wall, signalling submission. Damon eased off his grip enough for him to speak.

"I was at the *Five Gentlemen* club."

"And did you attempt to assault a young woman by the name of Rita Shakes?"

Dimitri's eyes narrowed and he struggled against Damon's hold, attempting to escape it. Damon's fingers closed around the man's thorax with the force of a lion's jaw. He stared him down until Dimitri slacked in his grip, and nodded.

"I need a verbal answer."

"Yes. I was drunk and –"

Damon dropped his grip, only to follow it with a punch to the gut. The target bent over in two, then dropped to the ground, coughing and wheezing.

"I'm not interested in your excuses. I've gotten what I came here for."

When the elevator doors opened, Damon walked out and straight to one of the hotel rooms. He checked around to make sure no one saw him, then swiped a key and entered.

The room was packed with computer monitors and people, all either on the phone or typing wildly. Amy, a petite redhead who had joined his team a year earlier, walked to him and held out her phone.

"I have the Polish ambassador on the line."

Damon nodded and took the call, already unbuttoning the collar of his shirt. With the first few buttons undone, he could breathe freely. "Mr. Ambassador, I apologize for disturbing you at such a late hour."

There was a brief silence, then the man's thick Eastern European accent came on the line. "What is the meaning of this?"

"We have proof one of your diplomats committed a violent act towards a British citizen."

Only silence answered him, and Damon's jaw clenched as he dropped all pretence. "I know you were aware of Dimitri's transgression, Marcus. It's time you strip him of his diplomatic status and let the authorities have him."

"You have no proof."

Damon turned to Amy and nodded. She lifted a small recording device to the phone, and played Dimitri's confession. Damon waited a moment before returning on the line. "Is that enough proof?"

"How did you get that?"

"It's what my firm does, Mr. Ambassador. Now, do we have a deal, or are we to go to the press with this information?"

There was a heavy sigh on the line, then Marcus said, "I agree to your terms. I'll draw up the paperwork first thing in the morning."

"It *is* morning, Mr. Ambassador. No better time than now."

After hanging up on the diplomat, Damon returned the phone to Amy and shrugged out of his suit jacket. When he felt her hovering nearby, he faced her once more. "What is it?"

Rather than her usual confident self, Amy shied away from meeting his gaze. "Something came up across our radars…"

When she didn't continue immediately, Damon arched an eyebrow. "Well?"

"Something you asked me to keep an eye on."

Damon's expression hardened, even as he pulled his jacket back on. "Show me."

"Are you all packed?"

Damon moved away from the window of his corner office to glance at the newcomer. When he'd last seen Derek Pennington, he'd been his boss, but before all that, his mentor and friend.

Gray hair cut short like a marine – despite his recent retirement – and dressed in a suit the envy of Armani himself, the old man had aged well. Yet the tight grip when they shook hands, and the solid pat on his back betrayed his strength.

"What brings you here, boss?"

A chuckle, and a wry smile. "It's been a while since I've been your boss, Damon. But word has it you're heading out on a solo mission."

Damon stayed quiet, unsure how much to reveal. Even in the tight-knit secretive groups, one could never be too safe. And despite Derek no longer calling the shots, his advice carried weight.

Before he could decide, Derek levelled his dark gaze on him pressingly. It lasted for a few seconds, before he nodded. "You're going back to her."

Damon's jaw tightened reflexively at being found out,

but after a moment of indecision, he inclined his head ever so slightly. "Yes."

Derek paced toward the window, keeping his own counsel. The air in the room brimmed, filled with tension. He turned after a few moments, his gaze no longer warm, but all business. "Why now? It has, after all, been over... what, ten years?"

"She's in trouble. Or will be as soon as certain pieces fall together."

Derek pursed his lips, his stare hardening. "You don't trust me?"

Damon sighed, holding up his hands. "That's not it, Derek. She means a lot. Too much."

Derek's eyes fell to his protégé's tightened fist, then back up. "I can tell. Ten years you were under my command, and not once did I see you lose your temper. *Iceman*, we called you. And yet here we are, barely two minutes of mentioning her, and you're wound up like a cord ready to snap."

Damon knew any answer was futile, considering Derek knew him better than anyone. He'd helped Damon when he applied to the special operations side of Interpol and pulled him out within a year after he started his own private security company. Within a few years, the reins had passed to Damon.

"You're right," Damon admitted, dropping into the closest chair. "She always got to me, even when we were younger."

"What made you leave back then? You never did tell me."

Another moment passed as Damon gritted his teeth. The scene was as familiar in his mind as though it happened yesterday. "Her father."

Derek tilted his head to the side in surprise. "You? Intimidated by a parent? I wouldn't have pegged you for the type, even as a teenager."

"It wasn't intimidation. The bastard was a manipulating prick." Damon's knuckles were white from clenching them so tightly. He could have hit something, but forced a deep breath instead.

Derek stepped closer and placed a calming hand on his shoulder. "Whatever happened, you are past that, lad. Nothing – no *one* – can stand in your way."

"You're right."

Derek looked ready to add more, but settled for a handshake, then walked away. By the door, he turned again. "Remember my number one rule: keep your wits about you. It would be a shame to lose you, now that you finally made it to the top."

Damon watched him leave, his words raking more than he wanted to allow. Then he glanced at his gym bag, packed and almost screaming with exuberance.

Time to go.

♥∞♥

Damon passed by airport security with a single sweep of his badge. The border agents knew enough not to contest it when his passport scan came back classified, and way above their pay grade. So even though he was packing weapons, they let him through.

On the airplane, Damon found a spot by the window seat. Unlucky for him, a busty blonde occupied the seat next to him. She took one look at him and practically panted.

"Pardon me, miss," Damon tried to say as politely as possible, while squeezing past her – without succeeding. A fact made even more impossible when she arched her back and brushed her breasts against his forearm.

He dropped to his seat in relief after long, agonizing moments, and turned away, rummaging through his backpack. Whether on purpose or not, his neighbour chattered away, attempting to engage him in a conversation he wanted no part of.

Despite himself, one question got through. "What brings you to visit Canada?"

Damon faced her fully, almost smirking at her expression when she took in the scar on the side of his face, near his hairline – an old knife wound. "My fiancée, actually. I'm going back to see her."

The woman's gaping mouth was a sight, but he turned away without outright laughing. A roll of his shoulders released some pent-up tension, then he plugged headphones in his ears and settled in for the ride.

Ready or not, Cass, here I come.

❤ *Chapter 2* ❤

A honk behind her had Cassandra jump, then quickly press the accelerator and take off. She'd been so lost in her own thoughts, dreading yet another work day, and she'd missed the green light.

As she turned a corner, a quick peak in the rear view mirror showed her the same black car following her. Cassandra frowned, wondering what kind of trouble she'd attracted again, when the dashboard of the car flashed red, white and blue.

"*Et merde!*" The French version of *oh shit* rolled off her tongue too seamlessly. Biting back a second curse, she engaged the signaller and pulled over on the right side. The cop car stopped mere inches away from her back bumper.

Cassandra bent over the passenger seat and rummaged for her license and registration, bemused at what might have triggered the random pull-over. When she straightened up with her ownership and insurance papers, the police officer was already at her door.

The window slid down with a push of a button, and Cassandra angled her profile to get a peek at the cop. "I'm sorry, officer, but why—"

The words died on her lips when the man squatted down, his face mere inches from hers. "Hello, Cassandra."

The dusty-blonde hair and strong jaw should have been appealing, especially when combined with the unique cerulean shade of his eyes. But all Cassandra felt was a need to get far, far away from the law officer who'd plagued her the last few months.

"Sean." His name passed through gritted teeth, though

she forced herself to remain calm. "Here are my papers. Mind telling me what you pulled me over?"

A smirk on his lips, Sean took the required documentation from her hand and pretended to look through it. *I would've thought he had it memorized by now, considering how many times he flagged me down for bullshit excuses.*

Cassandra forced another breath through her lungs, recalling old meditation techniques from her youth of practicing martial arts. After long moments, she got her heart rhythm to slow down – at least until Sean squatted back down.

"Your sticker is overdue."

"My what?"

"License plate sticker, Ms. Di Cavalier." He paused for a breath, then grinned. "You were supposed to renew it two weeks ago after your birthday, yet our records indicate no such action was taken on your part."

Are you freaking –

Cassandra bit back the string of curses running through her mind, and instead forced a neutral tone. "I apologize, officer. It slipped my mind, but I'll take care of it today before heading in to work."

Sean tilted his head, lips pursed as if considering her words. Then, a dejected look on his face, he said, "I'm afraid I can't let you off with a warning."

Of course you can't, asshole. And it's not the first time.

"Fine. How much?"

Sean pulled his notepad out of his back pocket and wrote something, then ripped the paper off and handed it to Cassandra. She glanced at it, then did a double-take. "Four hundred dollars!?"

His widening smirk told her it was the exact reaction he'd expected, but Cassandra was past trying to be reasonable. "This can't be right."

"Are you defying an officer of the law, Ms. Di Cavalier?" His eyes glittered dangerously, yet it was not enough to deter her.

"Not defying, officer. Merely wondering how in hell the fine *tripled*. As far as I knew, it was one hundred forty or thereabouts."

Sean's gaze became hooded and he leaned into the window frame. "Would you like to contest this with my superior?"

Cassandra bit on her bottom lip, fighting back a scream of rage. She couldn't, because doing so would mean paperwork, and her legal name on said paperwork, open to the public – and that was more of Pandora's box she didn't need to open. Unfortunately, Sean was more than aware of the little nugget of information.

With a satisfied smirk, he pulled back. "Didn't think so. Of course, there are other ways to pay off the fine… Or even make it go away."

Cassandra's glare would have incinerated him, if only superpowers were real. As it was, it did manage to make that infuriating smirk slip off. "Still playing hard to get, I see. Very well, see you next time."

And with an infuriating wave, he was gone. Cassandra listened to the sound of his engine in the distance until it was gone, then looked in her lap where the fine had fallen. Tears of resentment hit the back of her eyelids, but she blinked them away.

With a deep inhale, she pulled down the mirror and checked her meagre makeup. The mascara hadn't run over her cheeks, and though her eyes looked glazed, she could always blame it on allergies. Pursing her lips, she resolved not to let the idiotic cop get to her and instead got the car back on the road, heading to work.

♥∞♥

Cassandra poured herself a cup of coffee, trying to ignore the guy hovering at her back. When his presence lingered, she glanced over her shoulder – only to catch him staring at her ass.

"Can I help you?" She couldn't keep the bite out of her voice, especially after the morning run-in with Sean.

When he noticed her addressing him, the guy blushed a dark crimson and moved away, mumbling something under his breath. Cassandra sighed into her cup, wishing he'd either come outright and say something, or stop being creepy.

Shaking her head at the crap day that was unfolding, she went back to her desk and sipped her beverage, scrolling through the news. Working at *The Gazette* had the benefit of always being in the midst of the action, and yet never having time to enjoy it.

After a few moments of respite, Cassandra opened a new document and started typing.

"Cass!" Someone called to her not even moments later, and she snapped her head up from the document she was working on to look into Renzo's gentle brown gaze.

Her best friend had a casual look going, from the faded dark jeans to the navy shirt he wore, and the ruffled hair. Cassandra cracked a smile at his expression, until his next words made her frown. "What are you still doing here?"

"Still? It's only –" A quick glance at the clock confirmed it was way past four, and she'd been in earlier than seven. "Whoops."

"Lost track of time again?" Renzo – short for Lorenzo – chuckled, then leaned over her shoulder to read. "You *do* know the deadline for the piece on the lobbyists isn't until next week. Always ahead, when you should be getting some sleep for a change."

"Can't," Cassandra rolled her eyes. "And it's not the lobbyist piece I'm working on, but my resignation letter. I told you I was quitting, remember? Besides, once this is done, I'll have enough time for resting and relaxing."

Renzo's smile slipped off and he crossed his arms over his chest. "I thought you were joking about that."

Cassandra snorted, then turned to her computer. "Of course you would."

Noticing her tone, Renzo pulled a chair and plopped down on it, closer to Cassandra's desk. "What's gotten up your butt today?"

"You mean besides the jackass cop that won't leave me alone and the stalker in the eating area here?" She glanced at him, then sighed and turned his way. "I can't, Renzo. I thought this was what I wanted to do, and I mean the internship was cool at first. But I want to feel part of something."

"And the freedom of speech, the sharing we do here, is not enough?"

Cassandra threw him a look. "You know full well it isn't. I've liked it, sure, and you know I'm as good a wordsmith as any of them. But I'm not in it for the social climbing… Plus,

| 19

I can't help feeling that the longer I'm in the media zone, the more there's a chance of someone finding out about me."

Renzo's expression softened, having captured the quiver in her voice. "I get that, Cass, I do. But you can't live in fear of your family's drama being splashed on front page news… It's no way to go about your life, or making decisions."

"Maybe." Cassandra turned back to her screen, and the half-completed resignation letter. "But it's what I'm feeling right now."

Renzo was quiet for a moment, then he touched her shoulder, waiting until she faced him once more. "What about the volunteering? Do you want me to come with you to another soup kitchen?"

Cassandra laughed at that, recalling the last time he'd joined her and alienated everyone with his questions. Subtle about his money, her friend was not. "No, thanks," she finally managed to get out. "Maybe around Christmas, but for now, I really want to focus on me."

Renzo stared in her eyes for a beat longer than necessary, then stood. "All right. I know nothing will change your mind, but I hope you know what you're doing."

"I do."

He was about to leave, but turned at the last moment. "You're still coming tonight, right?"

Renzo's dad owned a club in downtown Montreal, and it was summer opening night. Cassandra grinned, thinking of the fun awaiting them. "Need you ask? I wouldn't miss it for the world."

Once Renzo left, she focused her attention on the letter. Less than ten minutes later, Cassandra printed her resignation letter and headed into her boss' office. *The Gazette* was a fun enough place for a career, but all good things eventually come to an end.

Time to go home.

♥∞♥

The drive to her neighbourhood in northern Montréal was non-eventful, and Cassandra breathed a relieved sigh when she parked in front of her small bungalow. Though nothing like the villa in Tuscany her birth parents had called home, it was cozy and met her needs – it also helped her keep a low profile. Amid the young couples and students renting in the area, Cassandra didn't stand out.

Some would say twenty-one was too young to own a home, but Cassandra had been nothing but careful with her inheritance money. At the end of the day, it had come down to need: an absolute, essential *need* to have her own place and not answer to anyone but herself.

Like most days, the first thing she did upon getting in the house was swap her flats and jeans for running shoes and shorts, then hit the road. After the stress of the day, the only way she could relax was with a good jog around the neighbourhood.

One leg in front of the other, the music blasting in her ears, Cassandra let the stress of yet another pathetic day pour out of her. But even as she jogged, her mind kept going back to the events of the past hours, and frustration rose like a tidal wave, making her breathing choppy. She tried to control it and think about something else.

Renzo's sympathetic expression flashed through her mind, bringing an uneven smile to her lips. *Why can't I find a guy like him, instead of attracting idiots?*

As if on cue, her music was interrupted by an incoming call. Cassandra pressed a button on her smartphone to answer. "Renzo?"

"Hey, gorgeous." Though his tone was smiling, Cassandra knew he meant nothing by it. Their instant connection had been of the sibling variety, not the passion type. "Just wanted to hear how the notice went." A pause, then, "Bad time?"

Cassandra coughed up a laugh, then halted in the shade of a tree. "I'm out running, smartass. Only you would think of something perverted."

Renzo's good-natured laugh vibrated through her headphones, and Cassandra grinned in response. On top of being kind and generous, Renzo was strong when needed and always lent a shoulder for crying. He'd even managed to make hanging out at a club fun – something she was actually looking forward to for that night.

"It went as expected," she answered his previous question. "Editor-in-chief didn't want me to leave, then when I wouldn't budge he switched to threats that I wasn't giving him enough notice and he'd pursue it in court."

Renzo cursed something unintelligible in the phone, then said, "What did you tell him?"

"To shove it up his bumhole." Cassandra recovered from her giggle, then admitted, "No, seriously, I told him he can't stop me from leaving and that I'd heard enough dirt to put him out of a job. He quieted enough after I gave a few examples, and let me be on my way."

There was a silence for a beat, then Renzo said, "Maybe I should talk to him."

"Uh, no!" Cassandra winced at her loud tone and brought her voice down. "Renzo, your last name is about as famous as mine is. If the boss hasn't yet made the connection, what's the point of pushing it? You really want the paparazzi on your tail, too?"

Renzo sighed on the line. "You're right, as always. I know my dad's ways weren't always legal, but he's still my dad and I'd rather not have him dragged through the mud again." Another pause, then, "But you're coming tonight, right?"

"I already said yes," Cassandra rolled her eyes. "But for the record, yes, I am. I wouldn't miss getting tipsy and a night of dancing with you for anything! Is your dad coming?"

The only thing that made their usual hangout nights better was Fabio Moretti's stories – and the dramatic Italian flair he delivered them in.

"He didn't say, but maybe. I'll let the security guys know, so see you in a few."

Before Cassandra could say bye, Renzo hung up and her playlist restarted – with a love song. She scowled at her phone before shuffling through the list until she found a good enough beat.

It wasn't that she wasn't interested in dating – only that she wasn't interested in love, or sex. A broken heart at a young age was enough experience, as far as she was concerned. Plus, most guys – the ones that weren't outright cretins – found her personality too strong and intimidating. And if that wasn't it, they had an issue with her no sex policy and didn't stick past a few dates.

Shaking her head, Cassandra tried to clear it of relationship ideas and instead picked up her pace. As she ran around a corner, her smile slipped off, and she hesitated for about a millisecond. A group of four teenagers, probably only sixteen, were laughing and joking in the distance, blocking the way. They looked exactly like the kind of guys to appreciate the sight of a girl running… More than they should.

Mentally, Cassandra scanned her outfit – decent jogging shorts, tank top, sneakers. She'd dressed out of habit, but was rethinking it as she passed by them. Awareness crept up her back, notifying her she had ventured outside her neighbourhood, and with kids their age, they were only interested in one thing: showing off to their buddies, which always led to stupid decisions.

And she wasn't looking forward to being the object of their attention. Cassandra had learned the hard way to be realistic as far was her life was concerned.

If those kids are dumb enough to try anything, I can easily take them on. Father's aikido training might just come in handy. The thought did nothing to reassure her, but Cassandra pushed past her misgivings and kept her pace.

She heaved a sigh as she got closer, trying to jog past the teenagers. No sooner had she moved near their circle that they nudged each other and turned to face her.

"Hey," one guy's lips moved and he grabbed Cassandra's elbow when she was passing him. "Where are you going, chérie?"

Why can't they ever keep their hands to themselves? The thought rushed through her in an angry blaze.

Renzo always maintained that all a guy had to do to get a girl to notice him was be nice. Clearly, he and the teenagers belonged to different planets. Cassandra breathed in and turned the music off with her free hand. Though she tried to speak as calmly as she could, her eyes narrowed on his hand. "Let go of me."

It was her best attempt at being civil and Cassandra willed herself to make it work. If her mood had been angry before, the kid's reaction sparked a new fuse.

He smiled, then looked to his buddies for approval while tightening his grip. *Great. That's going to leave a bruise. But then again, so will I!*

Cassandra gritted her teeth and drew her free hand back, about to punch him. Before she could follow through, she was side-tracked – a rare occurrence. But in the particular situation, it was unavoidable.

The moment she moved, a black, sleek muscle car stopped right beside them in a squeal of tires. If she had known at the time who was driving, Cassandra would have run away as if the devil himself was chasing her.

Or she would have thrown an explosive at it – either option was as feasible as the last.

However, she had no idea what was coming her way.

♥ *Chapter 3* ♥

When Damon's plane landed, he thought it was the worst of the flight. Despite his military training, flying was not something he particularly enjoyed. Yet getting out of the Montréal airport turned out to be hell, and not only because of the flag on his passport. Canada kept an eye on foreign operations being handled on its own soil, which meant as soon as someone scanned his papers, he was stuck.

Despite the urge to storm out, Damon forced himself to stay calm and surrender placidly. He submitted to a full line of questioning and inquiry by a constable of the Canada Border Services Agency. After three hours of checking his credentials, it was a call to Derek that quieted everyone down.

The old man had enough wiggle room and power left that he placed a call to British ambassador in Canada, who in turn contacted the superiors of the CBSA and had Damon released. This after strongly emphasizing he was to check in should he leave Québec to head on to another province.

It was all Damon could to keep the impatience from showing until he was free, carry-on bag and all.

His team arranged to meet him by the Vieux Port, so he headed over in a taxi. When he asked the driver to drop him off in front of an abandoned warehouse, the elderly man took one look at his bulky frame and the tattoo on his neck and reversed out of empty parking lot so fast, Damon had to keep from laughing.

The area was deserted despite mid-afternoon. Containers littered the ground as far as the eye could see. Ugly industrial buildings with their paint falling off and broken windows completed the décor.

Despite the calm appearances, Damon scoured the surroundings to make sure no one had followed him. Occupational hazard or paranoia, the case could be made for either. Satisfied he was alone, he started walking towards the darkest of all warehouses – it had a red X painted under a window, a signal earlier agreed upon.

He barely passed the rusted entrance when metal by his temple pulled him to a complete stop. Judging by the round object pressed against his temple and its sheer weight, he guessed it was a gun.

"Identify yourself."

The voice was more a growl, and out of the corner of his eye Damon could see another built guy, a head shorter than himself, but muscled like the a bodybuilder. Despite words he could have interpreted as panicked, the man's hand didn't shake.

The soldier in him scanned his opponent's attire. Jeans and simple white t-shirt, commando boots, shaved head and taut posture – it was easy to recognize a comrade.

"I'm Damon Voight, from Pennington Securities."

The man paused for a beat, then asked, "Got any ID?"

Damon nodded and lifted his palms a little at a time. "I'm reaching for it, don't shoot."

Once he pulled out the ID and the man had a closer look, he lowered his firearm. His previously tense posture relaxed into a semblance of regular civilian. He even cracked a grin and clapped his back.

"Welcome to your base, boss."

Damon let out a sigh of relief and turned to him, only

then noticing his shadow. In the background was a younger man in his late teens, with glasses and a freckled face. His reddish hair stood in contrast to the darkness of the place.

"And you guys are?"

"Zak, and this here's Paco," announced the bulkier of the two.

"No last names?" Damon hid his smirk, knowing full well it was operational procedure to keep those away from senior agents. After all, he'd implemented the rule for protection of secondary assets in the event primary ones got captured.

Zak threw him a look that implied he knew as much. "Just following instructions."

Damon followed them past the entrance into a corner of the warehouse where they had set up a table with multiple monitors. "Your work area, I take it?"

Paco nodded, and Damon turned his gaze to the remaining space. Most of it was filled with crates, barrels, and tools lying on the ground. "Alright, so I have my muscle and brains, but where are my wheels?"

Zak pointed to a corner behind him, and pulled out a pair of keys from his back pocket. "You'll like this, boss."

Damon caught the keys mid-air and glanced at the logo. He turned and walked to a tarp-covered area that seemed to hide a monster underneath. With one tug of his hand, he pulled the cover off and let out a low whistle.

The sleek beast of a car was beautiful, if ostentatious. Muscled front, barred well-enough to walk unscathed from an accident. All curves on the outside, leather on the inside, silver rims with dark red endings… "Damn."

"Boss, you look shocked," Paco laughed at his expression.

Damon could only shake his head, bemused. "Let's just say I'm used to shitty wheels in my ops." He'd let Amy arrange for his travel, but why would she pick such a noticeable transport? *A question for another day.*

"Yeah, but I mean now that you're the boss, isn't that the point?"

Zak glared at Paco to shut up, which the kid did promptly. *Guess they weren't supposed to reveal how much they knew about me.*

Damon caressed the car one last time, then turned his attention to his team. "All joking aside, what do you have for me?"

Paco bounced away and came back carrying a folder – *on Cass, no doubt.* "All the info's in there," he said, confirming Damon's suspicions. "Personal, professional, hangouts, etc."

He grabbed the file, flipping through it. Pictures of Cassandra at various locations were spread through, along with lengthier reports of her activities. He walked to the car and threw it inside the car, impatient once more. He'd had a high-level summary version on the plane and read most of the file on his tablet, but whatever remained he intended to devour at the earliest opportunity. For the time being, he had a girl to see.

With a wave to the guys, Damon promised to stay in touch, and got in the car. It purred to life, and he couldn't resist the temptation to rev the engine. Zak grinned on the sidelines, and Damon took off with a last salute.

He had originally planned to meet Cassandra at her workplace, a neutral enough location. All plans of doing that got shot to hell by the lovely border officers doing their job. The clock on the dashboard indicated it was well into the afternoon, meaning he could still catch her at home.

As Damon drove through Cassandra's neighbourhood, his alert green eyes scanned the area – more out of habit than any real threat he perceived. The houses were the usual white-picket-fence type, secure enough apparently for kids to be walking their dogs alone. He passed Cassandra's bungalow, stopping only long enough to realize she wasn't there.

Figuring it would be best to move than stay still, he took off again towards another street. *Might as well get to know the surroundings while I can.* After a few turns, he ended up a bit farther off into an area with townhouses.

As he drove under speed limit, a woman jogging on the sidewalk caught his eye. Her dark brown ponytail swished from side to side, earphones in her ears. As an active military guy himself, he'd seen wacky jogging outfits, but hers was on the scale of more sporty than eye-catching. Despite the well-worn tank top and shorts, her tanned legs and curves held his attention.

The woman came to an abrupt stop, her gaze narrowed onto a group of kids further down the street. And as his car pulled up closer, he realized what had caught his attention.

On some level of his mind, Damon had known it would be hard, but he wasn't prepared for the reality of seeing Cassandra. From where he had stopped, across the street from her at an intersection, he had a perfect view of her face – heart-shaped, tanned, button nose and lips that were much more kissable than he remembered.

The fire in her eyes had only sharpened with time. Long

gone was the girl from before, the one he'd known in their youth. Here stood a woman – and his body warmed up in response.

Damon shut the impulse down immediately, knowing it was too soon, and he had too many amends to make. Cassandra was more likely to kick his ass before he even had time to explain, at least if he went by what her file said.

He opened the glove box and shoved said-document in, locking it up. For the time being, she didn't need to know everything. It was time to stake the land and see what her role was in the mess her father was involved in.

Damon reached for the door of the car but before he could exit and grab her attention, Cassandra was on the move – and heading straight for the kids.

More than interested to see how events would unfold, Damon ignored the part of his brain that advised against it and settled in for the show.

He lasted for all of two seconds until one of the teenagers grabbed Cassandra. Before Damon's brain caught up to curb the impulse, he was already flooring the gas and aiming for them. His body coiled at the sight of Cassandra's puzzled expression, and he barely restrained the part of him that wanted to go full-on military.

♥∞♥

The goose bumps at the back of her neck should have been a warning. Over the years, Cassandra had learned to trust the gut feeling predicting something was heading her way. Yet the anger unfurling in the pit of her stomach, fuelling her blood, overpowered her sixth sense.

She heard an engine revving, then tires skidding as the

car came to an abrupt stop nearby. Cassandra spared a glance over her shoulder, taking an extra second to admire the sleek beast of a car.

An insistent pain snapped her back to her captive wrist, and the teenager about to get his ass kicked. Gritting her teeth, Cassandra met his confident gaze and opened her mouth to say something, but movement behind distracted her – again.

Rather than respond to her glare, the teenager's eyes shifted to the car. Something akin to fear flashed across his expression, nudging Cassandra's attention back to the newcomer. The angle of her body increased the pressure on her wrist, but she paid it no attention, focusing on the license plate.

NOMAD.

Though lately there'd been more custom-made license plates in Montréal, English was not a language one saw often. Especially not in the pure francophone area she had settled in. It was akin to social suicide and attracted the French cops like moths to a flame.

Of course, like any town, Montréal had its rebels. *I even knew one of them – once.* Cassandra pushed away the fleeting thought in favour of focusing on the teenager. Would she rise to the challenge and retaliate, or be an adult and let it go?

The time for deciding passed in a flash, around the same time someone stepped out of the car. A *male* someone. She had been about to think *boy*, but that was definitely not the body of a teenager clad in a pair of dark blue jeans and a dark t-shirt that showed off nicely-defined muscles.

It had been a while since she'd seen such a fine specimen, and her hormones weren't unaffected – quite the opposite.

"I do believe she asked you to let go," the newcomer announced in a voice smooth as dark chocolate and whiskey combined. A faint accent lined his words. *Australian? British?* Distracted by the whole package he presented, Cassandra couldn't place it.

There was an underlying threat in the man's voice, something that sent shivers up her back even as it piqued her interest. *A gentleman, in this day and age? Kind of hard to believe.*

After delivering his threat, the man leaned against the car, folding his arms across his chest. Her weakened female mind was quick to notice the way his arm muscles bulged. His predator-like stance struck her as familiar, quickly followed by the lingering sensation she had heard his voice before.

Drawing in a shaky breath, Cassandra's eyes roamed from his torso to his face, hoping that his eyes, much like for everyone else's, would betray him. To her dismay, sunglasses covered them, and she only saw her reflection.

Figures.

Despite his nonchalance, the slight tilt of his head was a dead giveaway that he was watching her. That realization nagged at Cassandra, amplifying her anxiety. That sixth sense she'd ignored before pulled at her thoughts, trying to warn her once more.

Annoyed at portraying the damsel in distress to this stranger, Cassandra yanked her wrist out of the teenager's grip, hissing at the stab of pain. He'd held on too tightly, and already she could see a slight reddening of her skin.

Under her breath – but loud enough so they'd all hear – she muttered, "Thanks, but I was making myself clear enough without your help."

Her tone came out a tad sharp, and years of good manners being drilled into her attempted to trigger a semblance of remorse. Yet all Cassandra felt was annoyance and a tell-tale flush spreading across her cheeks.

Now free from restraints, she moved to walk away. Before she could take a second step, the same teenager wrapped an arm around her waist, pulling her into him.

Shock rushed through Cassandra with all the subtlety of an icy shower, but instead of cooling her off, it incensed her further. *This guy is either incredibly brave, or incredibly stupid!*

Her jaw clenched in reaction, even as she tried for one last bit of self-control. Then the kid snickered, and she noticed the stranger move forward, cold fury radiating in the tight line of his mouth.

Enough is freaking enough!

Cassandra didn't stop to think about why the mystery man was so angry, or why he had so quickly stepped around the open door of his car to get to her. Or even why he wanted to help her in the first place.

Her mind was a blank slate, fuelled by rage and acting through muscle memory alone. Aikido lessons from the past ran through her mind at flash speed, and her body moved into striking position.

Cassandra elbowed the teenager in the gut, satisfied when he half-bent over and groaned in pain – releasing her with the movement. Before he could straighten up, she whirled around and delivered a knee between his legs. Mouth gaping, the teenager gurgled some semblance of a cry of pain and collapsed on the ground, his palms now cupping the rather sensitive area between his legs.

"How about you think twice next time you want to put your hands on a girl without her consent?"

His friends stepped up and Cassandra shifted her stance, keeping one foot slightly in front of the other even as she angled her hips to the ground. Whatever their move, the position ensured she had perfect reach and balance to react.

Yet rather than the full-on confrontation she expected, the remaining teenagers helped their buddy up and walked – almost ran – away, glancing back several times as if not believing their eyes.

At least someone learned their lesson.

Movement to her side made Cassandra even more conscious of the stranger, who'd been observing the entire altercation. The goose bumps on her neck intensified, and she took a minute to compose herself.

Once her breathing turned regular, she turned around to see the stranger biting back his laughter, trying – and failing – to keep a serious face. Her previous annoyance resurfaced. "If you'll excuse me…" She walked past him with her head held high, refusing to meet his eyes.

For the third time in less than ten minutes, she was stopped by a hand grabbing her wrist. She glanced up at him in slight shock – hadn't he witnessed her pummel the other guy?

Muscles reacted before her brain fully caught up and her free fist rose menacingly, aiming a punch straight for his jaw. Before she could make contact, the man's hand came up and grabbed her wrist, gently but firmly.

It took Cassandra a moment to realize he was smiling –

sunglasses be damned! As though to press her buttons, he angled her wrist in a way that had her pressing closer to him to alleviate the pressure on her bone.

"You–" Cassandra gritted her teeth, trying to hold back the string of obscenities she wanted to shout. Something must have shown in her expression, as his grip grew lax on her wrist.

"Easy, gorgeous, I'm not hitting on you. I was trying to flag you before you dashed off." A pause, then his tone changed. "You seemed rather eager to escape my presence."

Was that a hint of bitterness in his voice? Cassandra couldn't be sure, but the explanation seemed plausible enough and she relaxed. She also concluded his accent was definitely British, since he'd spoken more than a few words at a time.

The man let go of her wrist, and she yanked the unused headphones out of her ears, stuffing them in the pocket of her shorts. When she looked back up, his head was tilted to the side once more, watching her. Cassandra could feel his gaze through the sunglasses, and despite the sun a shiver ran up her spine. In an effort to hide her discomfort, she forced her chin up and returned his stare.

The sunglasses hid enough of his face to make it hard to read his expression. However, she had no trouble noticing his clenched jaw and the roughness that seemed to permeate his entire presence. It was more than just the way he held himself, like a proud young lion. And it was definitely more than pure strength, though his build indicated he was not someone to mess around with.

The quick second Cassandra's body had been pressed up against his had confirmed he was all muscle, and a different shiver ran through her at the thought.

Her gaze roamed over him, trying to figure out what it was about him that tugged at her attention. His hair was cropped on the sides, and a tattoo peeked on the side of his neck. That same side had a scar that ran down his cheek, but rather than break the symmetry of his face it enhanced his rough appeal. Though he was attractive, he was nowhere near her type.

Yet when he shifted from his stance and moved a step closer, Cassandra didn't back down.

The stranger jerked his head towards the guys disappearing at the end of the street. "We ought to leave while we can."

She held back a scoff – barely. He was sorely mistaken if he thought she'd been in any serious danger, considering she could have gotten out of it without so much as a scratch.

Once more, Cassandra felt her expression giving her away when he smirked knowingly. "I suppose you could have fought those wankers, if you so wished. But I reckoned you would prefer a quiet dinner instead of a night explaining to the police why you beat four teenagers up."

His soft-spoken words stopped her thoughts in their tracks. *Quiet dinner? Hopefully not with him!*

"Yeah, I suppose so." Ignoring the dinner comment, Cassandra tried for a semblance of politeness. "Thanks for standing up for me, by the way, though it was hardly necessary."

"Oh, I know," the stranger's smirk deepened. Something was amusing him, and by association annoyed the hell out of her. "You never needed my help, Cass, though I always offered it. That offer still stands, no matter how much time passed."

She froze at the mention of her name, suspicion creeping

up her spine. "How do you know my name?"

"It's been a long time, Cassandra..." This time, his British accent completely disappeared, and instead his intonation turned more Canadian. A softer smile tugged at his lips, replacing the cool expression from seconds earlier. "Do you really not remember me?"

As he spoke, the man took off his sunglasses, revealing eyes of the deepest emerald. Cassandra stumbled back a few steps, willing herself to look away even as she recognized the truth standing before her.

She could put a name to that face, unbelievable as the thought was. The realization dried up her throat, and her defensive walls shook to their foundations as it echoed in her mind.

A name she had tried to forget with all her might in the last years, and never quite managed. A name that still sent shivers down her spine as he had. *As he still did.* The only guy she had loved, trusted with her heart, only to have it shattered.

Damon Voight – a ghost from the past.

❤ *Chapter 4* ❤

Damon watched in slight satisfaction as realization dawned on Cass. Playing the dashing stranger had its appeal, but nothing compared to the recognition drifting in her eyes, even as her lips parted in surprise.

His delight turned to growing frustration when it seemed like she would bolt any minute. He understood the knee-jerk reaction, especially considering their history, but before he could speak Cassandra drew her hand back and slapped him.

Damon stood still for a moment, processing the hit. Her hazel eyes sparked outrage, and a delightful flush stained her cheeks. He forced himself to look past that. "What was that for?"

It was the wrong question to ask, judging by the way she clenched her jaw. When she spoke, Cassandra's voice was tight with reined-in emotion. "You dare ask me that, after ten years? Ten *freaking* years!"

"Cass, I –" Damon tried to take a step closer, but Cassandra moved back, holding her palms up to ward him off and shaking her head.

"No. *Hell*, no! I trusted you, and you broke my heart, pretending to feel the same. I was only fourteen, Damon." Her voice broke on his name, but her eyes only reflected the anger within, their cold glare daring him to contradict her.

Damon knew he had his faults, but pretending he had feelings for Cassandra had never been it. He'd been only seventeen, fresh out of a stint in juvie and interning at her adoptive father's law firm. Their relationship was practically written in the stars, as innocent and forbidden as it had been,

| 39

and heartbreaking to the end.

"I didn't pretend," was all he could settle for, hoping the truth of his words would ring through.

"Really? 'Cause my father was quick to point out you'd left at the first smell of money, to follow some grand career overseas."

Shock coursed through Damon, rendering him speechless. *That bastard!*

Viktor Beauchamp might have once been a good man, but this confirmed there was nothing worth saving in him. *If he could lie to his own daughter like that… What else did he do?*

Flashes of how he'd met Viktor ran through Damon's mind. The cops, arresting him for punching his mom's boyfriend when he was abusing her. The court, where a judge not too fond of *young hooligans who disrespected authority figures* wanted to make an example out of him. The trial, where Viktor had been a more than adequate defense lawyer, and gotten him paroled early. The man had a private practice but occasionally took pro bono cases. It had been both a blessing and a curse to have him as mentor, and intern at his law firm.

While it had turned his life around and helped him focus, not to mention meet Cassandra, the job had also been the reason he'd lost the most important person in his life. *Viktor will pay for this, one way or another.*

Damon met Cassandra's gaze once more, and held it. Something in her expression shifted, but she wasn't running away. *Yet.* He pounced on the chance while he still could. "That's not the full story, actually it's not even *a* story. I left, yes, but not for the reasons you think."

"Sure you did." Cassandra's eyes shifted from his,

avoiding the truth.

Before she could stop him, Damon reached for her chin and forced her to look him at him. "You used to be able to tell when I was lying. Tell me, am I now?"

Flashes of the girl he'd known crossed her expression, though Cassandra did a good job trying to hide it. He could still see the girl he'd helped out with homework, the tougher yet vulnerable side of her he'd fallen in love with…

How can she think I'd leave her? It stung to think that all she recalled of him was his ambitious streak.

It took Damon a second to realize Cassandra had frozen at his touch, and the look in her eyes had changed. When he tuned in to the change in her, he picked up on her quicker breathing, nostrils flaring as if inhaling his scent. Up close, he could now smell the vanilla perfume emanating from her skin, and he wanted nothing more than to sample her lips.

Cassandra's eyes widened, the anger set aside by the pure chemical reaction they had to one another. The blazing glare, so eager to put him in his place, dimmed now to a sense of assessment.

Damon had been used to girls throwing themselves at him in the military, but he'd never been interested in more than a night. Only one woman had occupied his thoughts, and she was now so close every instinct in him screamed to make her his.

My little spitfire.

While Cassandra sized him up, Damon looked his fill as well. She had grown into a beautiful woman, something he never doubted. Those hazel eyes that changed color with her mood were a startling smoky blue at the moment, almost a pure reflection of the darkening sky. Her long, wavy brown hair fell out of her ponytail, and he had an insane urge to tuck it back behind her ear.

Her breathing was erratic as she ran through a multitude of emotions – all showcased on her face, despite how much she tried to conceal them. Damon's gaze skimmed over her top, which up close did little to hide her considerable assets. Her trim waist and hips were inviting, to the point his hands itched to hold her.

Shit.

Damon stepped back, letting go of Cassandra and attempting to readjust his thinking. He'd been able to control his fear and disgust in the missions he participated in, yet mere seconds in her presence and his control flew out the window.

He chose to focus instead on the one thing that didn't fit from his first-hand assessment: her wariness. Cassandra's reaction to him, he could understand, especially given the lies she'd been told. But she was an open book, or at least had been. Yet there she stood, looking at the world not with the rosy glasses of a pampered princess, but rather with the knowing eyes of someone who had *seen.*

One thing at a time, the rational part of him warned, and Damon retreated mentally. Whatever else happened that wasn't in her file, he would find out. And if anyone had hurt Cassandra, he would make it his life's mission to turn theirs hell.

Keeping close to her would be no problem at all. His mind was already in the gutter, and all he could think of was spending the rest of his life making up for leaving, and showing her his love.

Because no matter what she thinks, Cass was made for

me, and I for her. One way or another, I'll make her understand... Especially once I take care of her bastard stepfather.

The thought alone made his blood boil.

♥∞♥

No way. Just...hell to the no.

Cassandra's flight or fight instinct stopped working the minute Damon touched her, looking at her with truth in his eyes and swearing he hadn't left for fame and glory. She'd locked the pain away, swearing high and low that she was over him.

Yet there she was, staring at him for what felt like hours, unable to stop. His touch had brought back that one, innocent kiss they'd shared, before he'd vanished the next day. And all she remembered was the guy she'd known in her teens. He'd been everything a foolish girl could wish for. Everything Cassandra knew she could never have again.

"Damon..."

The name was dragged from her, almost as if she was testing it. The taste of that kiss, long ago, was almost on her lips and she couldn't help her gaze from falling to Damon's mouth. It was as if some force of destiny had drawn them together yet again, and their involuntary reactions were beyond either of their control.

The more she stared in his eyes, the more Cassandra wanted to run and never look back, despite how cowardly that was. In complete contradiction, another part of her wanted to stay and talk to him, ask him what had happened, and reconnect. Deep down, she wanted to believe him when he said he hadn't left for money.

That unyielding faith in him, more than anything, scared

the hell out of her and she instinctively took another step back. Ignoring Damon's narrowed eyes, Cassandra kept a cool voice as she addressed him. "What are you doing here, Damon?"

"Montréal has always been my first home. I was bound to come back, don't you think so?" His tone, in contrast, was casual and the smile never left his face. Yet there was nothing genuine about it, rather it seemed forced and impersonal. The coldness of his expression struck her in a very unfamiliar way, at odds from his warmth so long ago.

This man in front of her had little to do with the boy Cassandra had once known. Gone was the openness, the frankness, replaced by a stoic composure and inscrutable mask. It was more proof she should have nothing to do with him – ever.

With that in mind, she turned around and was about to stalk off without another word. Damon was quicker, as if having read her mind. In just a few steps, he blocked her path, his arms folded across his chest.

The way he towered over her by a head raised Cassandra's hackles even further. She tilted her chin up to stare him squarely in the eyes and raised one eyebrow in what she hoped was a polite enquiry. "It's great you came back to your roots, Damon, but I don't see what that has to do with me. Was there something you needed?"

He seemed unsettled for a fraction of a second, a tiny flicker of something flashing in his eyes. *Good.*

Cassandra's small victory was short-lived, as a mask slipped over Damon's face, and he became the stranger yet again. *What happened to you?* The question was on the tip of her tongue, but she bit it back – barely. It was not her business what he'd been up to for the last few years, nor did she want to know why he'd stayed away for so long. She inhaled sharply, resolved not to let Damon see her reaction.

"As a matter of fact," Damon started suavely, "I wanted to offer you a ride home."

"Thank you, but I prefer running to riding. In any car." Cassandra stepped to the side in an attempt to walk around him, but yet again he moved with her.

"Cass, let me drive you home. I'm in the neighbourhood, anyway. It's better than having you run into even more trouble." He had the nerve to chuckle at that. "Some things never do change, do they?"

When she glared up at him, genuine amusement glittered in his eyes, but Cassandra refused to bite. "And yet, some *do*. I'm capable of taking care of myself, thank you very much. I'm sure you can agree, after what you witnessed."

With each word, each glance, Cassandra heartbeat increased. *Too fast.* She needed to leave before she said something she would regret. *This is too much, too soon.*

Damon's eyes raked over her body, and she flushed angrily when he still refused to move. "Get out of my way, Damon. I don't need you to drive me home." She paused for a beat, glaring. "I said, *move*."

The warning tone – and the anger behind it – would have unsettled more than one adult. All Damon did was stare at her, immovable, and say, "I insist."

She was about to *insist* for him to step away when a definite challenge surfaced in his eyes.

"Unless, of course, you're afraid." The words passed

Damon's lips, and it was too late to bite them back. He knew he was baiting the little spitfire, but she was making it too easy.

Shock flared in Cassandra's eyes, enough to part that pretty mouth. All he wanted was to bend lower and have a taste – just one – but he held back.

"Afraid?" Disbelief collared her tone. "Of *what*?"

A few things came to mind, but none Damon could point out in the moment. It hadn't escaped his notice that Cassandra was too busy being mad at his return to question whether there was more going on. If her attitude to him was a prelude to what would follow, he was in for a hell of a ride – and he intended to enjoy each moment in her presence.

Instead of warning her and revealing things she was not ready to hear, Damon opted to continue for the current tone. "You tell me."

Though it came off more challenging than intended, the words had the desired effect. Cassandra bit her bottom lip as though to stop from screaming at him. Then, she scoffed and stomped towards his car, stopping only once she reached the locked door.

"Are you coming or what?"

Damon didn't bother answering, instead striding closer to her. By the time she realized how close he was, she was stuck between the car and him, and her eyes widened. "What are you–"

Damon lifted his hand as if to caress her cheek, watching her eyes widen. Her breathing picked up again, and he hid a smug grin. *At least your body reacts to me, Cass. The rest, I can conquer little by little.*

He moved his hand and the car keys appeared as if by

magic. While beeping the car to unlock it, Damon watched Cassandra closely. She tried to hide it, but the disappointment in her eyes was unmistakeable.

After a beat of stunned silence, Cassandra slid through the open door and into the car, almost dropping into the leather seat in relief.

"Buckle up."

Ignoring her scowl, Damon headed to the driver's side, keeping his satisfaction under wraps.

♥ *Chapter 5* ♥

The leather was smooth against her backside, cool after the heat of the outside. Yet Cassandra still felt flushed, and she had an inkling it was tied to the man driving the powerful vehicle.

Out of the corner of her eye, she sneaked a glance at Damon. She wanted to resent the way he still knew which buttons to push, but something about seeing him, having a chance at closure... *And then risk him breaking my heart again? No way.* Cassandra pushed all thoughts firmly away from anything resembling feelings, and instead focused on his features.

Damon's jaw was set, eyes fixed on the road. There was a hardness to him now that had erased all trace of the boy she'd known. Even more so, he had a certain haunted look about him, evident in the way he inspected their surroundings yet never lost control of the car.

On some level, Cassandra wondered what had brought him back. *And where was he all this time?*

Theorizing kept her busy and she didn't realize they had entered her street until they were pretty much at her house. And then it hit her – she'd never given Damon her address.

Cassandra whirled to him, determined to get answers. "How the hell did you know where I live?"

Damon took his time turning off the engine, rolling a shoulder as if to ease unseen tension, and finally met her gaze. "Well, that's a loaded question, and it requires a rather long answer." He glanced out the window to her small bungalow. "Invite me in?"

Cassandra's jaw went slack at the innocuous question. While she tried to get over her shock, the silence grew deafening in the small space of the car. Through it all, Damon maintained his stare, unapologetic.

"How *dare* you?" The words tumbled out of Cassandra's mouth in an angry hiss, more spitting than a hellcat ready to fight.

To his credit, Damon barely blinked at her tone, and the tirade that followed.

"You come waltzing back in here after ten years and expect to just catch up and do small talk? I damn well don't think so!"

Trembling with rage and hurt, she jumped out of the car and stomped her way over to the door. When she reached for the keys in her back pocket, they slipped out of her shaky hands. *The nerve of him!*

Before she could reach down, Damon's voice washed over her. "Let me."

In one fell swoop, Damon picked up the keys and inserted them in the lock, then opened the door. Cassandra held out her hand in silent demand for her keychain, but he only shook his hand. A heartbeat later, he broke the silence. "I know I have a lot to explain, but now is not the time."

"And why not?" Cassandra folded her arms.

Damon grimaced in response, rubbing the back of his neck. "It's a really long story, Cass. Some of it, you may not even believe. I owe you the truth, you're right, but–"

A loud ring made Cassandra jump, and Damon trailed off. From deep in the hall of her house, her landline was obnoxiously demanding her attention. No one ever called it –

except Viktor. And his sudden reappearance predicted nothing good.

Cassandra scowled at Damon. "Come in, but don't make yourself comfortable. I need to take this."

It didn't escape her notice Damon still had her keys, but another ring turned her focus to the matter at hand. Stomping inside, Cassandra growled into the phone, "Yes, father?"

"Is that any way to greet your old man?" Viktor's raspy voice seemed to get worse every time he called, but Cassandra felt none of the usual concern. *If smoking kills him, that's his deal.*

"Sorry." The excuse was half-assed, but the slight guilt she felt at her tone was quickly washed away by the certitude he'd barely register her words anyway.

As if on cue, Viktor said, "Is it true what I heard? You quit your job at *The Gazette*?"

For a moment, Cassandra could only gape at the phone. *How the hell did he know?* It was true that Viktor had always had an uncanny way of finding out things, but this, out of nowhere after not talking to her for four months?

Only one explanation remained.

"Are you having me *followed*?" Cassandra's hiss was meant to be only for Viktor's ears, but Damon was close behind, not even attempting to conceal his eavesdropping.

As her adoptive father sputtered on the phone, Cassandra cut him off. "You know what? Doesn't even matter. I can't talk right now, bye."

She slammed the phone down on the counter, glaring as if it would bite her.

"Was that Viktor?"

Cassandra faced Damon, resuming her folded-arms stance. "And if it was?"

To her surprise, he only frowned, eyes shining with worry. "What did he say?"

She considered not answering for a minute, but it would have been petty. "To know why I quit my job today."

"At *The Gazette*?"

Again, her jaw dropped. "Seriously, what the *hell* is going on?"

♥∞♥

Damon debated how much he could tell her, already guessing by the fire in Cassandra's eyes that he had to be truthful. A lie would only build more distrust, and the gulf between them was already filled with half-truths and betrayal. Yet his military training and years of experience whispered to tread carefully, and not jump into trusting she was fully innocent in the entire mess.

"We think your father is involved in some shady dealings."

To her credit, Cassandra didn't seem shocked or upset. After staring at him for a long moment, she spun on her heels and headed into the kitchen. Bemused, Damon followed and watched as she poured herself a glass of water, holding one out for him as well.

He accepted the drink with a nod and downed it in a few large gulps. After setting the glass in the sink, he waited while Cassandra digested his words.

When she finally lifted her gaze from the ground, it was to ask a single question. "Who's *we*?"

"Me and my team." At her frown, Damon shrugged. "I

own a private security company. To keep it short, we stop bad things from happening, and do our best to correct them when they do." A pause, then, "Word got across the ocean of a group being involved in nefarious dealings and Viktor's name came up once we dug deeper."

He kept out the part where he'd had Amy specifically scour the underground networks for snippets of drama concerning Viktor Beauchamp. Damon might have left ten years earlier, but he hadn't forgotten *why*. It had been only a matter of time until the excuse he'd been yearning for had presented itself.

"And that's what brought you here?"

Cassandra's tone dragged his attention away from the past. She was keeping her facial expression neutral, but was that disappointment he heard in her tone? If it was, Damon counted it as a step forward.

"Yes," he admitted, not technically lying. *But now might not be the time to reveal the full extent of the issue.*

"What kind of dealings?"

Damon hesitated, watching her closely. She met his eyes without trying to shy away, tilting her chin just so in defiance. He held back a smile at the flash of a challenging younger version of her popping in his head.

That image was shattered when the air around them shifted. Awareness crept up his back, and his body reacted to their mutual staring contest. He hadn't expected the reunion to be easy, but the way Cassandra kept challenging him only cemented his belief in their future. *I'll get through to you, Cass. It may take me a while, but those walls will crumble and I'll make you see you can trust me again.*

Damon cleared his throat and shifted his stance, in an effort to reroute his wayward thoughts into a semblance of order. Despite all he'd been trained to see, Cassandra didn't fit the accomplice profile. And, deep down, Damon knew her moral code couldn't have changed that much.

When Cassandra dropped her defensive stance, there was nothing deceptive about her body posture, and Damon chose to go with his gut feeling. "Drugs, cars, illegal stuff."

His attempt at being vague didn't pass unnoticed, but Cassandra didn't press. If he had his way, Damon intended to make sure she never saw the horrors from their files.

After another few minutes, she said, "Ok, what do you need from me?"

His stunned expression must have been clear, as Cassandra smiled, though it didn't reach her eyes. "Come on, Damon, there's a reason you sought me out, and it's obviously not to mend fences. Which is just as well, because I've moved past whatever it is we had ten years ago."

"Why offer to help, then?"

Cassandra shrugged and moved to the fridge once more. This time, she pulled out a bottle of red wine and poured herself a glass. "You missed a few things while you were gone, D."

She laughed, but it sounded harsh and bitter. Damon moved closer, but one glare from Cassandra rooted him to the spot. She picked up the glass and drank it in one shot, her knuckles gripping the countertop with enough force to turn them white.

"Talk to me, Cass."

She slammed the glass back on the cold granite surface, whirling to face him. "Didn't you wonder why I believed you so easily, just now? I know better than most what Viktor's capable of. Why do you think I don't live with my over-possessive, verbally abusive adopted father anymore, hmm?"

A knot formed in Damon's stomach, even as he forced words past his dry throat. "What did he do to you?"

She held his gaze for a moment, then sighed and leaned her hip against the counter. Shoulders curled inwards, all fight seemed to have gone out of her. "Nothing. And not for lack of trying. I left as soon as I could, and he only calls me every once in a while now. As for your earlier question, I offered because I can't stand by and let Viktor ruin people's lives. Not like he did his own wife's, and not like he attempted to do with mine. So regardless of our history, how can I help?"

Damn. Damon hadn't expected the reasoning, nor Cassandra's revelations. He was torn between wanting to wrap her in his arms and protect her from the world, or going after her adoptive father with the viciousness of a rabid dog. Since neither option was feasible at the moment, he settled for second best. "Let me crash here for a few days, a week at most."

A pin could have been heard falling in the silence that followed. "Come again?" Cassandra's voice broke on a squeak at the end, betraying her panic.

Damon held up his palms as a gesture of good faith. "I could use the time to gather intel on Viktor, and anything you tell me could help, because it's obvious I missed quite a lot." He paused for a beat to judge her expression. Since Cassandra wasn't yelling – yet – he continued, "Plus, I didn't book a hotel. With it being prime Formula One season and festivals, there's nothing free to rent in the area. Trust me, I looked." A small white lie, one that made him cringe internally. He used the guilt to project his best vulnerable expression. "Unless you want me to sleep in the car?"

For a second, Damon thought Cassandra would refuse outright. Her mouth opened as if to refute him, but good manners seemed to overtake everything else. She shook her head, muttering, "I can't believe I'm doing this, but…you can have the couch."

♥∞♥

Cassandra pushed away from the counter, vaguely gesturing to the wine bottle she left behind. "Feel free to have some."

She couldn't stand the look in Damon's eyes, as if he could tell everything she'd been through and wished nothing more than to take it all away. Fury streaked through her, fuelled by the alcohol in her blood and her own annoyance at her ever-changing emotions.

Exiting the kitchen, Cassandra threw her sneakers to some forgotten corner of the hallway, then went to the supply closet. She picked up pillows and a blanket and made her way to the living room, avoiding the kitchen area.

Letting Damon stay the night was one thing, but it didn't mean she had to enjoy his company. Jaw clenching, she muttered some decidedly unladylike words under her breath, then turned to go upstairs to have privacy.

With all the drama, she only had a few hours left to get ready for the night with Renzo. On a regular basis, she was fairly quick as far as getting pampered went. Yet after the interactions with Damon, Cassandra had a feeling the mental part of things – calming down from being around him – would take much longer than a few minutes.

Privacy seemed to be wishful thinking, as she ran into Damon not even seconds later, at the bottom of her stairs this time. He was leaning against the wall, a leg stretched out to stop her from moving past.

"In a hurry?" Damon's cool assurance was back, more infuriating than ever in the wake of their conversation.

Cassandra's palm itched with the desire to smack him, but she pulled in a deep breath, adamant not to let him get to her. Speculation made its way to her clouded brain. If he thought she was involved, would he leave? Or maybe back off enough to give her time to breathe and pull herself together?

The words were out of her mouth in an impulsive move that was all of her own making. "Yes, actually. I have to be at Renzo's club in an hour." She didn't specify who Renzo was, nor what he was to her. *Let Damon wonder.*

After the initial fire that lit his eyes, Damon's expression grew once more unreadable. "Club? I didn't know you hung around those, Cass. It used to be the place you'd avoid at any cost. Trouble magnet, remember?"

Cassandra scowled at him, taking a step closer and keeping an icy tone. "As I mentioned before, a lot of things have changed."

"Clearly." The sharp edge to his voice caught her attention, and she had the odd feeling it concealed something else. Before she could dig deeper, Damon spoke again. "Can I come?"

Of all his nerve...

"No." Rather than let out the tirade on the tip of her tongue, Cassandra took a deep breath. "It's a closed party, sorry. Only friends allowed. But there's food in the fridge if you're hungry, and everything you need on the sofa for sleep. I'm sure you're tired from your flight."

Ignoring Damon's ever-shifting expression – the side smirk he had on hinted at his amusement – she broke eye contact and stepped over him, moving up the stairs. Despite the nagging sensation of being watched, she didn't look back.

As soon as she got to her bedroom, Cassandra closed the door behind her and leaned against it, trying to calm down her breathing. On the outside, she may have managed to not show much, but inside, her emotions were more mixed up than ever.

Damon's departure had been a huge blow for her, and it had taken a long time for her to function properly. It wasn't only that she missed Damon, though she couldn't stop thinking about him. She craved his company, his laugh, his smile… Everything about him.

But even more, she missed being herself. Because with Damon, she could talk about anything, without having her opinions thrown away as if they counted for nothing – as Viktor was prone to do. Or without having to be told who to be, or which way to act.

With Damon, it had been simple. So simple she should have thought twice before giving her heart to someone so intent on destroying it. But she hadn't, and the consequences of never doubting Damon had shattered her.

I won't make that mistake again. With Damon, or anyone else.

Cassandra sighed and straightened away from the door, heading to her private ensuite. For once, she was grateful of the luxury. *At least I don't have to worry about running into Damon with nothing more than a towel to cover me. With my luck, it could happen.*

♥∞♥

Damon tore his eyes from Cassandra's locked bedroom door and headed back to the kitchen. He poured himself a much-needed glass, letting his thoughts wander as he sipped it.

He'd gotten entrance into her home, and a leave to stay. Cassandra may have drawn her own conclusions about his presence there, but she was further from the truth than she knew. Yes, stopping Viktor played into his plans, but it was only the tip of the iceberg. *All things in their due time.*

Damon gulped the last of the wine, then headed to his car. After a quick glance around the, he pulled out his carry-on bag. It looked like a regular gym bag, but once inside the house he started pulling out its contents: motion sensors, alarms the size of his thumb, and a gun he tucked in his waistband.

Taking off his shoes for ease of movement, he set about securing the house. Damon moved to the backdoor, leading onto a large yard. There were no back neighbours, but that didn't necessarily mean the area was safe. He set up infrared alarms around the door, then headed to the windows.

The front door would be left without alarms, as he planned to keep watch on it all night. The windows, however, were another weak point. He couldn't make them bulletproof, but that didn't mean he couldn't at least set up minor reinforcements.

After the windows, Damon moved to the basement door and added another alarm to its base. The size of half his pinkie, they were unnoticeable to the eye and their chameleon coloring ensured they blended in the background.

As he moved about, Damon kept an eye on the upstairs

area. The shower was running, but he wouldn't put it past Cassandra to come check on him. It was imperative to at least secure the perimeter, in the event something happened when he was not around.

Flashes of his past life hit him, of the ops he'd been a part of. His military squad hadn't always been in the right, and he'd seen his share of horrors. Especially vivid in his mind was the recollection of subduing civilians, and how easy it had been to infiltrate compounds more secure than the White House.

Damon reached for one of the windows, his hand clenching into a fist. His body bowed over the glass, tension straining past his control. The thought of Cassandra with a bullet in her head filled him with despair, and his heart squeezed.

That's what I'm here to prevent. He scowled, shaking off the unease. *Time to get my shit under control. But first, supplies.*

Damon walked back to the living room and the gym bag, pulling out an encrypted cellphone. He pressed one button and it rang twice, then a familiar voice answered.

"Yes?"

Damon nearly sighed in relief at Derek's voice. Though he'd been in missions on his own since his time in the military, he always kept contact with his former mentor. When shit needed to get done, Derek handled it better than anyone else. He was also the only man Damon fully trusted.

"I made contact and confirmed Viktor is on the move."

There was a pause as the old man registered the information. "Is the asset secure?"

Damon glanced up the stairs, then nodded, "Yep, with

me. And I don't plan to let her out of my sight."

"You might have to." A pause, then, "I received your encrypted email, and you were right. We did receive report of a source, but it's a bit out of your way."

A tinge of unease hit Damon's stomach. "I'll take it."

"Are you sure about this, Damon? I've read the file, and what's in the database. None of this is easy, and may not be worth it if you end up leaving your skin in the game."

Damon didn't hesitate as he answered. "I'm sure. Give me the name and address, Derek."

"Very well." The elder man's crisp British accent became more pronounced in his annoyance, but he rattled of a series of numbers – coordinates to a location.

Damon repeated them back, then filed them away for later. "Got it. And, Derek? Thanks."

"Good luck."

Once he heard a dial tone, Damon went to the kitchen sink and held the gadget above the garbage disposal. He broke the cell phone in half, then dropped each part in, watching them shatter under the powerful grind.

Then he put on his shoes, scribbled a note and grabbed Cassandra's keys from the entrance table. A spare dangled on the keychain and he ripped it off, using it to lock up.

The errand would take less than an hour, then he could be back to watch over Cassandra. *Nothing will go wrong in the meantime.* Despite the mental reassurance, Damon's stomach curled in a knot as he gunned the car's engine, taking off in a screech of tires.

♥ *Chapter 6* ♥

An hour later, Cassandra took one last look in the mirror, biting on her lower lip and assessing her image with a critical eye.

A black halter dress hit mid-thigh, the gauzy material draping her body in a mist of mystery. Red highlights in the fabric caught the light as she moved, and the four-inch stilettos made her legs appear longer, wrapping around her ankles with thin satin bows. In sum, the whole outfit was more than eye-catching.

Cassandra's makeup was kept to a minimum: black, smoky mascara emphasized her eyes and lip gloss to give her lips a soft shine. A soft rose-like fragrance surrounded her every move, and her hair was down, curly and chic, reaching mid-back.

Perfect.

Hand on the knob, Cassandra hesitated for a tiny second. She hadn't heard a word from Damon while getting ready, which somehow amplified her anxiety. Shaking her head, she opened the door and headed out. The click-clack of her heels resounded on the hardwood floor as she walked down the stairs, but no one seemed to be around.

A peek in the living room confirmed the sofa was empty, and a glance outside revealed Damon's car was also gone. Cassandra tried to tell herself it was relief she felt at the sudden departure, not disappointment. But too many things were left unanswered, with the prime question being: did Damon intend to come back?

While she pondered the matter, Cassandra ended up in

the kitchen. A small piece of paper stuck on the fridge caught her attention. There wasn't anything special about it, other than its color: bright, neon pink.

Considering Cassandra hated pink, having always deemed it too much of a girly color, seeing it in her kitchen attracted her eye. She moved towards it, almost hesitant to touch it. A scribbled message had her attention until she noticed the signature. *Damon. It figures.*

Afraid her knees would give way, Cassandra pulled a chair and sat. Allowing a simple note to sway her so easily was beyond stupid. But it was more than he'd left the last time and raised buried old feelings.

With shaky hands, Cassandra read the actual note, taking in Damon's fine handwriting, almost unrecognizable from the messy printing from the days when they were friends. She'd always made fun of it, though her writing wasn't much better.

A rush of memories threatened to overflow, but she ignored them and focused on the words.

Cass,

Sorry I took off without a word. Business called in town. It probably won't take long, but I wanted to leave something behind. I know I have a lot of explaining to do, and you don't want to hear half of it. I'm talking about what happened ten years ago, Cass. We need to talk about that.

But it will wait. I wish you'd wait for me to come back tonight, but I know it's too much to ask. So I'll only say this: be careful at the club and stay out of trouble. I know you'll find it, so my warning isn't filled with empty words.

Damon.

P.S.

I know you hate pink, but it was the only quick way I could figure out so you wouldn't miss my note. After all, I don't believe I'm allowed to come upstairs…

Cassandra stared at the offending slip for a long moment after reading it. If a simple note like that one made her knees buckle… She didn't even want to think about what the next days would bring.

She stood and ripped the note to pieces, then grabbed her purse and keys with gritted teeth. Damon would remain off her mind tonight, *coûte que coûte. Whatever the cost.*

The car was a smooth ride – one of the best Damon had driven for a mission. Though getting to the location on his GPS was easy, his mind was on Cass and what he'd left behind. He hated the thought of her so close to danger, especially at Viktor's hands.

Damon kept one hand on the steering wheel and with the other unplugged the GPS machine when it warned he was close to reaching his destination. A few buttons ensured all data was erased, corrupted to the point no hacker could fix it. A glance behind him confirmed no other cars were on the road with him, and he wasn't being followed.

A touch of a button, and the passenger window slid down. Damon pulled over on the gravel, then threw the GPS device out the window as far as he could. He heard a splash and drove back onto the road, his mind at ease that he'd protected his source – so far.

His thoughts shifted back to Cassandra. Desperate times called for desperate measures, and if he was to protect her, he needed all the information at his disposal. It was the only reason he'd elected to pursue this lead, thin as it could turn out to be.

Stepping on the gas, he took a corner and ended up on another dirt road, arriving at a secluded house within minutes. Two stories high, with cracked paint and windows that had seen better days, the building looked near collapse.

Damon exited the car, inspecting the surroundings once more to make sure he was safe. Dogs barked in the distance, but as far as he could tell no one else was around. He approached steadily, locking the car behind him with the key fob.

Years of military training and his time with Interpol had taught him awareness and to always expect the unexpected. Even as he approached in stealth mode, Damon was ready to draw his weapon at any sign of danger.

His time working for Interpol had put him in the path of the world's most wanted serial killers and criminals. He'd seen horrors he wouldn't wish on his worst enemy, and to this day had nightmares.

Once he reached the door, Damon knocked three times. Noises came from inside, but they were too faint to identify. A heartbeat later, the door opened, and a blonde girl in her teens appeared, dressed in pyjamas.

"Err," Damon hesitated, wondering if he had the right house. A quick glance at the number confirmed he did. "Is your dad in?"

She frowned, looking him up and down with narrowed eyebrows. He repeated his question in French, and her expression turned even more confused.

"Je n'ai pas de père." Without a backwards glance, she returned back inside, leaving the door ajar. *I don't have a father,* she'd said.

Damon stood aghast, trying to understand her response when a male shape entered the hallway instead. The kid was fifteen at most, but one look in his eyes confirmed he'd seen much more than most others his age.

He murmured something to his sister, then headed towards Damon and closed the door behind him. "C'est toi, Damon?"

Damon inclined his head at the question, pulling out his badge. After a quick inspection, the young kid moved to the corner of the patio. One foot bounced uneasily off the ground, and his eyes darted around.

"You're Christian?"

The kid gave a curt nod, avoiding his eyes. He wrung his hands for a few seconds, crossed and uncrossed his arms, then finally settled for leaning against the wall.

He nearly jumped out of his skin when Damon placed a hand on his shoulder. "You're safe with me, kid."

His firm voice got through the nerves, and Christian met his eyes. "Who told you to find me?"

Damon shrugged. "I have my sources. Interpol, remember?" He flipped the badge once more to reassure Christian, then put it in his back pocket. It was expired, but Christian couldn't know that. And Damon had meant what he'd said: he *was* safe.

He turned his unblinking gaze to Christian, silently willing him to speak. After a brief moment of hesitation, Christian inhaled deeply.

"A year or so ago, I had a friend in high school. He, um, he got really into drugs, and lost control. Started gambling, selling stuff to pay off huge debts." Another big gulp of air, and he continued, "He landed in juvie a few times, but Viktor Beauchamp always pulled him out. I didn't know why, at first. Then my friend told me he dealt drugs for Viktor. I'm not sure what happened after that, but a few weeks later he was dead."

Damon pondered the information, hesitant to ask the obvious question. Christian appeared to have been through enough, but he had to know. "Why didn't you go to the cops?"

"They're paid off in this town, man." He grimaced, eyes darting around again. "I wouldn't even have talked to you, if you hadn't tracked me down. I don't want to be involved!"

Panic echoed in his raised voice, and Damon tightened his grip on him. "You won't. Nothing you just told me will go to court. I only needed confirmation I'm after the right guy." Damon reached in his back pocket, pulling out a piece of paper with a phone number written on it. "Call this number. The guy who answers is named Derek, and he'll make sure you and your sister are escorted somewhere safe."

Christian reached for the paper, jaw agape as if not believing his eyes. His hand shook, but he pulled back before taking what was offered. "What's the catch? I can't testify, man. If I do, they'll kill me like they did my dad, and Gen'll be all alone."

"I promised you'd be safe, Christian." Damon squeezed his shoulder, emphasizing his statement. "Derek will make sure of that, and you don't have to testify. I swear, there's no catch to this."

"So what, you're just a Good Samaritan?" There was wariness in the kid's voice, but less than before.

Damon sighed, wishing he could take his pain away, but knowing there was nothing he could do about it, other than ensure Christian had a future and didn't end up another dead teenager. "You could say that, yeah. I also happen to hate criminals like Viktor, and young kids getting hurt. He'll get his due."

Christian searched his gaze, lower lip trembling. In that moment, he finally looked his age, and Damon's chest tightened. "Take it."

With trembling hands, Christian reached for the paper. Damon nodded and moved away, heading to his car. "Take care, kid."

"Wait!" Christian called out. "How will you get this guy, when he has all the cops in his pocket?"

Damon grinned as he answered over his shoulder, "Because I have a personal stake in this."

♥∞♥

A chuckle escaped Cassandra once she pulled in the parking lot of the club. Downtown Montreal was always packed, and *Fire & Ice* was one of the most outrageously popular clubs in the province. Still, what her eyes registered was something straight out of a movie.

A long line of people stretched from the entrance down the block, and disappeared around the corner. She'd passed the line-up on her drive, and it went on for a few kilometers.

She recalled the first time she'd come with Renzo, on the club's opening night. He hadn't revealed the club was his until a few drinks later, complaining instead about anything and everything from the size of the tables to the uncomfortable bar stools.

When he'd finally been honest, Cassandra had offered to help him redecorate and it had been the beginning of a great friendship. The club's popularity had only grown over the last winter months, and it seemed the summer season would be very profitable.

Renzo must be hiding somewhere inside, poor guy. He tended to avoid the public as girls latched onto him, attracted by his charm, good looks and money. Much like Cassandra, he was a slave to his fortune and last name.

Cassandra got out of the car and walked to the entrance where Benny, the main bouncer, was attempting to manage the crowd. He had two junior bouncers with him, not that it seemed to help with the bells and whistles that were vibrating through the mass.

Benny took one look at Cassandra, recognition flashing in his expression, then turned to one of his assistants. "Let her through, she's a regular." He offered one of his rare smiles. "Nice to see you could make it, Cassandra. Renzo mentioned you'd be coming tonight."

She returned his grin, squeezing his arm as she passed by him. Tough-looking but with a heart of gold, Benny had grown on her since her first time at *Fire & Ice*.

"Looks like you'll have a busy night," Cassandra nodded to the crowd.

Benny rolled his eyes. "You're telling us. Summer's definitely here."

She waved goodbye, then stepped in the club. The indignant voices outside faded as soon as she was inside. Cassandra inhaled the perfume-laced air, then wrinkled her nose and followed the lit hallway.

After a few seconds, she emerged onto a balcony that offered a view of the entire club. Set on two levels, it had a general population area, and a VIP section off to the second level. It was only last winter that Renzo's dad had added another level to the club, and she now understood why.

Bodies occupied every inch of the dance floor below, moving to the fast-beating rhythm, no worries on their minds. When a quick head scan confirmed her friend was nowhere to be seen, Cassandra followed another path that led to the upper level where all the regulars VIPs were.

Unlike last time she'd been there when they'd had a semblance of privacy, the secondary level was also packed that night. Upon her entrance, two men from the bar turned their attention to her.

Not good, but it's not like I didn't expect it.

"Cass!"

❤ *Chapter 7* ❤

The voice came out of nowhere, and before Cassandra could scan for it, someone engulfed her in a hug. After a moment of surprise, she hugged back, recognizing the arms around her – and the cologne of the person.

Any other male touching her without permission would have gotten injured for their effort. But Renzo was pretty much family. Cassandra might've missed her romantic happy ending, but at least she had a brother. Even if they weren't blood-related.

She inhaled Renzo's scent, then smiled and pulled back. His arm stayed around her shoulders, enough of a deterrent for the guys at the bar, who turned their attention elsewhere.

"I didn't think you'd miss me so!"

Renzo rolled his eyes at the teasing, then grabbed Cassandra's hand and led her to the only empty booth left in the area. "Are you kidding me? Everyone at *The Gazette*'s missing you, and it's barely been a few hours. When the boss realizes what he's lost, he'll come begging at your door. Man, what I wouldn't give to see that!"

It was Cassandra's turn to roll her eyes. Renzo and the editor of *The Gazette* were like cats and dogs. His lack of leadership skills aside, the boss had poor hygiene and leering eyes. As far as Renzo was concerned, the man needed a long vacation on a very deserted island – permanently.

"Honestly, Renzo, I don't even get why you work. It's not like you need it."

He shrugged, meeting her gaze in that disconcerting direct way of his. "For the same reason as you, Cass... Something to do."

She nodded at his honesty, understanding more than words could express, but ready for a change of topic nonetheless. "So, any conquests tonight?"

Renzo burst out laughing, leading Cassandra to raise her eyebrows. "Not yet… But I bet it won't be long. There's a huge crowd outside, did you see it?"

"Yup! Benny has his hands full tonight. Maybe your dad should consider adding another level… Or building a second club next to this one. You'll have a hell of a clientele this summer."

Renzo grinned. "That's what I'm counting on to find the girl of my dreams."

Cassandra avoided his gaze, reaching for the water glass a waitress had set in front of them. Renzo's words only made her think of Damon. He'd been the guy of her dreams, once. *And look how that turned out: an epic fail, as far as choices are concerned.*

She'd underestimated Renzo and his perceptive skills. Even as she looked around the club in a vague attempt at hiding her thoughts, he wasn't fooled. He leaned over, catching her chin with his index and forcing her to meet his gaze. The gentle brown eyes widened as he read through her.

Cassandra sighed and pulled out of his reach. "Ok, spit it out. My eyes betray me, right? You've only mentioned it about a thousand times by now, as you did your Italian grandma's precognitive skills. So?"

Renzo narrowed his eyes, all trace of humour gone. "Cass… Did you… Is there someone in your life?" His voice was soft, but the booth muted some of the noise, at least enough so she could hear him.

"No," was Cassandra's deadpan answer. "Why?"

Renzo's frown deepened. "There's something different about you. I'd say it's just that you had a bad day, but it's so much more than that. It looks like you have things to think over... Am I right?"

Touché, was what she wanted to say. Instead, Cassandra expelled a breath and whispered a small, "Yeah, Renzo. As always."

Concern shone in his eyes, and she nodded at the unspoken question. "Don't worry, I'll be ok. Like you said, I need to think. But first, I also desperately want to relax and forget this pathetically bad day."

Renzo tilted his head to the side, a half-smile tugging the corners of his lips. "Dance?" Things were always so easy with him.

Cassandra grinned her answer, then Renzo whisked her away on the VIP dance floor. In a matter of minutes, girls dragged him away and she ended up partnering with strangers. Not that she minded, as long as the guys kept their distances. The music surrounded her, its deep-set vibrations thrumming through, unwinding her body.

Even as she moved to the beat, Cassandra found her thoughts drifting to Damon, wondering what had lured him away – or whom. An unfamiliar hand on her hip had her whirl around. The guy was young and handsome, but nothing about his easygoing smile appealed to her.

Shaking her head, Cassandra moved away and to the side of the dance floor. She caught Renzo's questioning expression and smiled in what she hoped was reassurance, then walked away. For the time being, he seemed to accept her change of mood.

Yet Cassandra had no doubt that once he got bored with the sirens surrounding him, he'd be more persistent than ever. And this time, he would want answers.

Her gaze raked through the club, still looking for a distraction, and it settled on the bar. Renzo would definitely approve of his best friend getting wasted for the first time in ages. A nagging voice at the back of her head whispered it was a bad idea, but Cassandra ignored it and made her way through the crowd.

The bartender, Sam, smiled at her. All staff and most of Renzo's friends knew her around the club. She was his best pal, the one who always got his ass out of trouble... And hers into plenty.

"Cass!" Sam shouted over the music, waving her over. "Want a drink?"

"More like need one!"

Sam held a finger up, then disappeared for a few moments. When he reappeared, he pushed a glass filled with an orange concoction towards Cassandra. She scrunched up her nose at it when a strong smell of fruits and alcohol assailed her senses.

"Really, Sam? This is girly as all hell."

His boom of a laugh washed over her, and a few heads turned in their direction. "Try it first, then talk."

Cassandra scowled at the drink as if it had personally offended her, then shrugged. "Goodbye stress, hello hangover."

She tipped the small glass and gulped down the whole thing. At first, all she could taste was a mix of peaches and raspberries. Then fire burned a slow path down her windpipe and into her stomach, where it seemingly exploded into smaller flames.

Cassandra coughed violently, trying to calm the irritation in her throat. She was vaguely aware of Sam laughing at her.

"Hell, woman. Drink it slow!"

Shaking her head, Cassandra swallowed a few more times then met Sam's gaze again, raising her index to show she wanted a second one. When he seemed doubtful, she scowled. "Don't argue!"

He rolled his eyes, and served her a refill. This time, she drank it sip by sip, and the cough wasn't as bad. Within moments, the liquid spread like wildfire through her veins, creating a pleasant buzz.

"I must say, you learn fast." The voice was deep, silky and faintly accented.

Cassandra turned on the stool and met warm, black eyes, in a very European face. The guy could have been a model with his aristocratic cheekbones and fine-chiselled features. Everything in him screamed money and ease, from the tip of his designer shoes, to the starch white that was clearly made of fine material, hugging his muscles like a lover.

"It's sort of my motto," Cassandra said while taking another sip of her drink, refusing to be impressed by his choice in style. "Never make the same mistake twice."

"Ah, but how old are you?" The stranger smiled. "Young in body, old at soul?"

His grin was engaging, and Cassandra responded despite her usual reservations about strangers. Still, a sense of unease settled over her, though she couldn't pinpoint it.

This man didn't seem to have any bad intentions. A French intonation tainted his accent, marking him as out of place among the regular clientele with their Quebec dialect. Without her good ear for languages, Cassandra never would have noticed.

He was handsome, well-built, young – roughly her age – and interested in her. Add to that a great sense of style and the cutest dimples when he smiled, and you got a full picture of Prince Charming himself.

So why the awkwardness?

The answer dawned on her with all the grace of a cold shower. His confidence, the way he towered over her and the glint in his eyes… It all reminded her of Damon.

The realization made Cassandra choke on her next sip, and she coughed again. *For Pete's sake, am I going to die because I can't stop thinking of the most stubborn guy I've met in my life!?*

Luckily, it didn't get to that. The Frenchman gave her two strong pats on the back, and she inhaled air with the desperation of the drowned. When her teary eyes met his, the newcomer was smirking.

"Think you need some CPR?" His innuendo couldn't be missed.

"I'll survive," Cassandra retorted, feeling more confident as she threw back the last of her drink. She signalled Sam for another refill.

Before he could lecture her as his disapproving face warned, a different voice echoed behind her. "Cassandra, but what a sight you are for sore eyes!"

Cassandra whirled around with wide eyes, her drink

forgotten. "Uncle Fabio!"

A full six feet tall, with sleek black hair, olive skin and dressed in the latest-fad suit money could buy, Fabrizio Moretti was still a striking man in his forties. Cassandra had only ever known him as Uncle Fabio since Renzo introduced them.

Sliding off the bar stool, she moved into his arms, chuckling at his overdramatic entrance. Fabio hugged her tight, lifting her off her feet and placing her back down. His cologne was overpowering – more the type to turn one's head quick. It didn't help the devil had a silver tongue.

"What are you doing here?" The question escaped her when she pulled back, but Fabio kept an arm draped over her shoulders.

"I'm paying a visit to the place," he murmured, glancing around until his gaze sharpened on the bar. His next words made her cringe like a little girl caught at fault. "Having fun?"

Cassandra knew he was referring to the empty glasses, and her unsteady feet. Before she could do otherwise, he snapped his fingers towards Sam. "Take that crap away and don't serve her another one."

There was a steely tone to his order she wasn't used to, and she tried to move again. His arm only tightened. "Where did your friend go?"

Go? Cassandra turned around at that, but sure enough the Frenchman was gone. *Odd...*

"He's not, um… I'm not sure exactly who he was."

Uncle Fabio met her eyes, his expression unreadable yet intense. "You should be very careful whom you associate yourself with, my dear."

Then, as if he hadn't just delivered a cryptic warning, he

kissed her cheek and let her go. "Say hi to Lorenzo for me, I have to go."

"But I thought you came by to see the place?" Her question fell on deaf ears, as Fabio was already disappearing down the stairs.

Shaking her head, Cassandra decided to hop back onto the dance floor. She'd barely made it a few meters when a muscled chest blocked her way. Before she even looked up, a whiff of his cologne warned her it was Damon.

"What do you want?" She tried to scowl, but his dark expression made her waver.

"Interesting company you keep." Before Cassandra could answer, Damon reached out and grabbed her elbow. "We need to talk. *Now*."

"I don't think so." Cassandra yanked her arm out of his grip, shouting to be heard over the music.

Damon's jaw clenched, and in the dim light his eyes reflected the cold tinge of neon. "I insist." When Cassandra still didn't move, he glanced to where Renzo was dancing away. "It's about your friend."

His words took her by surprise, enough so to wear down her resistance. When Damon sensed the shift in her body, he grabbed her elbow once more and dragged her away. Cassandra had to give in, or risk falling down.

Damon walked as if on a mission, going down to the lower level and into one of the hallways that led to a back exit. Just before they got to the door, he pulled them into an alcove and pressed Cassandra between him and the wall.

"You're impossible!" Cassandra's shout got lost in the music, but Damon's face darkened enough to confirm he'd heard.

She tried to move past him, unwilling to sit behind and listen further, but his grip on her wrist caught her by surprise. In full reaction mode, Cassandra lifted her free hand to hit him. Damon caught it, too, then pressed both her hands against the wall, the movement bringing his body flush against hers.

"*I'm* impossible?" Even in the dim light, his glare pinned her as effectively as iron hold. "Since I've come back, all I've tried to do is make amends. But you're so damn wary of me for reasons I don't know, that you don't even realize how much danger you're in!"

Cassandra opened her mouth to retort but Damon's was on hers in the next breath, and she lost all air in her lungs. It was nothing like the kiss they'd shared as kids. Fierce, possessive, his lips moved against hers with urgency, filled with years of held back passion.

Her mind pushed her to fight it – evidently, she wasn't as inebriated as she'd thought. Instead of listening, her fingers curled into the hand pinning her, and her body arched towards his. Even as Damon continued to plunder her mouth, her brain stopped working, analyzing, and all she could do was surrender to the feel of his lips against hers.

Tasting her surrender, Damon let go of one wrist and used his now free hand to place on her hip, pulling her against him. Cassandra moaned softly into the kiss, but Damon kept going.

When he finally pulled away after a long moment, he rested his forehead against hers. Before Cassandra could say anything, shadows moved behind Damon and he froze, all senses on alert. Cassandra glanced behind, but already Damon moved, facing the newcomers and shifting his body to protect her.

"How nice. Sorry to interrupt the reunion."

A flash of metal glinted, and Cassandra dug her hand in Damon's. *He's got a gun!*

He squeezed back in reassurance, then said, "What the hell do you want?"

"You know what we're here for."

Damon curled his fist, unwilling to believe he'd been so careless and let them become exposed, all for a damn kiss.

"Let them take my cash," Cassandra's soft whisper came.

"It's not money they're after." Even with the dim light, he could tell by their stances the men were trained.

Damon waited until the closest one took a step forward, opening his mouth to say something. The gun in his hand was close to Damon's chest, enough so that an accident was waiting to happen. Damon smacked the man's wrist, and at the same time shifted his body to the side, pulling Cassandra with him. The gun didn't leave the attacker's grip, but once Damon let go of Cassandra, he was free to wrestle him.

He elbowed his opponent in the nose, and felt the bone give way. The man howled in pain, loosening his grip on the gun enough for Damon to take control. He followed with a punch to the jaw, slamming the guy against the wall.

Damon whirled around, eyes scanning the darkness for more attackers. Shuffling from behind reached him despite the loud music, and he turned to Cassandra. He'd expected to see her under cover, not wrestling the gun from the second man – in heels, to boot.

"Cassandra!"

His shout passed unnoticed by both, and he started to head over. Cassandra dragged herself out of the man's hold, stumbling backwards. Despite her inebriated state, she caught herself and moved with impossible speed in her getup.

A swift kick caught the guy in the knee with the heel of her four-inch stilettos. As he lost his balance, she grabbed his wrist with both hands and moved forward, ducking under his arm. Half-wobbling, half-falling down, the manoeuvre worked. The man went flying over her head and landed on the ground, unmoving.

Cassandra straightened up with his gun in her possession, smoothing her dress and tossing her hair back. Catching Damon's bemused stare, she smirked. "What? You can't have all the fun. Now what's this about me being in danger?"

Damon crossed the last of the distance separating them and wrapped an arm around her waist, pulling her to his chest. For a brief moment, Cassandra allowed the contact, breathing in the safety his hold provided. Then her eyes fell on the two unconscious men, and the adrenaline high she'd been in slipped away.

She took a few steps back and met his gaze. "Talk to me, Damon."

He ran a hand over his face, then pointed to the two men. "They weren't here for money. They were here to kill me...and get you."

Cassandra's gaze shifted from him to their attackers a few times, then she pursed her lips. "Who do you think sent them?"

Damon's jaw clenched and he shook his head. "No idea, but I will find out. I swear to you." His expression shifted, melting into something softer as he took a step closer, hand extended. "Cass, about before –"

She held up a hand, stopping him. "Not right now, Damon. *Please.*" Cassandra looked down at the gun in her hand, then wrapped her arms around her middle as the reality of the situation sank in. "Let me get my head around this first."

Damon caught on to her mood change, and his extended palm clenched into a fist. So many apologies and half-truths threatened to spill off his tongue, but he bit them back. He closed his eyes for a brief moment, and by the time he reopened them, he was back in control. "Got it. But, there is something we need to talk about, and that's your safety."

Cassandra met his gaze then, biting her bottom lip. She straightened from her stance with a heavy sigh. "I need a drink before I hear the rest of this."

Damon nodded and took her elbow, moving them back towards the safety of the club.

"What about them?" Cassandra asked.

"They won't be stupid enough to stick around." He took the gun still in her hand from disarming the attacker and tucked it in the waistband of his jeans, hiding it under his shirt.

As they walked back into the throng of people, he glanced at her out of the corner of his eye. "By the way, you have an interesting way of getting drunk."

Cassandra shrugged, her unfocused gaze seemingly miles away. "I could always hold my liquor, remember?"

They stepped up to the bar and Damon moved down to order a drink. He made the mistake of letting go of Cassandra's hand. When he next looked behind him, she was gone.

♥ *Chapter 8* ♥

They'd warned him Cassandra was a target, but Damon had no idea where the danger would come from. As he scoured the surroundings sipping a whiskey sour, he kept himself under check. No point giving in to panic, when it could be a simple case of the flight instinct kicking in.

Still... His gaze sharpened on the exit areas, wondering if he'd missed a third attacker that could have forced Cassandra to follow him with some threat. He was about to give in and call his team to order they track Cassandra's cellphone when a flash of black and red caught his eye in the mass of bodies.

Cassandra was moving of her own accord through the crowd, heading anywhere but near him. Apparently known by many, she stopped by two groups and spoke with a few people, only to be dragged onto the dance floor by an overeager youngster.

Damon reasoned she needed space, that it was her silent wish. He tried to put himself in her shoes, having just had to defend her life after he'd practically forced a kiss on her. How many challenging emotions could be swirling in that pretty head? And how much longer until she gave in, and heard him out?

He sighed, and voted against going after her. *I can allow her some space, at least for now.*

Keeping an eye on her in the mass of people was easy. Harder than he thought possible was keeping his hands from strangling every guy that neared her. Damon slunk by the edge of the bar, keeping a wary eye out.

He saw him too late.

Derek had been correct in assuming his proximity to Cassandra would affect his view of the world they lived in. First he'd missed the guys following them and put them in danger, and now there was another looming threat.

With his background, it was easy to spot the hitman. He was too well-put together, his smile a little too cold, his walk too determined as he approached his prey.

It didn't take him a long time to engage Cassandra. Damon's grip tightened on his drink, a growl building in his throat. He was familiar with the man and his work, if one could call it such.

He was known under many aliases, but his team had dubbed him Wraith. Much like the mythical spirits, he roamed from country to country, snuffing out lives. He loved to create chaos wherever he went and was on Interpol's most wanted list for a variety of bombings that had taken place all over Europe – and the string of bodies he left lying around.

Wraith sold his services to the highest bidder, with no loyalty or code. Women and children were not a problem for him either. But seeing him in person, close to the woman he loved, changed the game. Someone was very willing to afford him. Not to mention, how the hell had he entered Canada, when he was on every watch list possible?

Damon vowed to find the answer. *But first things first.*

He observed from afar as Wraith danced with Cassandra, knowing he wouldn't dare anything too risky. Not in public. After a few minutes of engaging with him – and it didn't seem to be their first time talking – Cassandra was approached by another young man.

From the file pictures, Damon recognized Lorenzo

Moretti. Apparently, so did Wraith, as he changed directions and swiftly vanished in the crowd.

Damon frowned at the odd disappearance. Lorenzo had none of his father's imposing stature, nor his reputation. Why would a man like Wraith be running unless... He straightened off the bar stool. *Could it be he's after both Cass and her friend? And if so, why the hell would Viktor or whoever's paying Wraith want the kid dead?*

Damon wanted to whisk Cassandra out of there, but the chance to find out more about Wraith's presence there was too good to pass on. With one last longing look at Cassandra, he followed the assassin out the back.

Wraith didn't even bother to slip past the exit door. In a corner of the men's washroom, he pulled out his cellphone, and Damon heard the tell-tale sign of a call being made. He headed to the urinary, going about his business and staggering, pretending to be drunk.

"Da," Wraith spoke into the phone. "This is Anton."

Damon picked up the faint Russian accent, which the assassin no longer bothered to hide. The guy was a pro, a chameleon that had learned to dispose of the one trait they had to identify him time and time again. Yet here he was, leaning against the wall and making no move to hide himself.

Soon followed a conversation Damon had trouble understanding – Russian had never been his forte – but he caught a few phrases about *contacted the mark* and *more to follow*.

Whatever instructions Wraith received from the other end caused him to smile eagerly. "It will be my pleasure."

He hung up, and Damon moved away from the sink

where he'd been washing his hands. When Wraith passed near him, he made a show of stumbling into him.

"C'est quoi ton problème, bordel!" Wraith shouted, cursing at him in French.

What the hell's your problem, man? Damon translated mentally and moved back, shaking his head and muttering a slurred apology. "Pardon, pardon."

Wraith threw him a look of disgust, then left. Once he was gone, Damon ducked in the last stall, and pulled out the cell phone he'd pick pocketed off the hitman. It was an old school flip phone, not even password protected. *Bastard's cocky, too.*

Gritting his teeth, he flipped the device open and scrolled to the call log. A single number with its caller ID glared back at him, making his blood run cold: Viktor Beauchamp.

"Son of a bitch."

"Indeed."

Damon glanced up, freezing when he noticed Wraith there. Smug as the bastard was, he was also cunning like a fox, and his hooded eyes were focused on Damon, assessing him.

Shit.

To the untrained eye, Damon would have passed for a regular person. He'd had to blend in enough times that taking on an undercover persona was second nature to him. But would the façade hold with a trained assassin?

Before Wraith could inquire further, Damon held out the phone. "You dropped this."

The man glanced at the gadget, then picked it up. "Thanks, mon ami."

He turned away, and for a moment Damon thought he was leaving. But the next second, his fist caught him square in the jaw, and rammed him into the wall.

Wraith pulled him out of the stall, then proceeded to deck him again. Damon allowed the second hit, falling into the cement this time.

"Who sent you?" Wraith hissed, towering over him.

When Damon didn't answer, the assassin reached down and wrapped his hand around his throat, pulling him to his feet and slamming him against the mirror. The strong scent of alcohol rolled off him, and still Damon fought his urge to react.

He had a simple decision to make. Blow his cover, or pretend something else. The image of Cassandra chatting with Wraith, unaware of the psycho hiding under the surface, was enough to decide for him.

He broke the chokehold with a ferocity that stunned Wraith, and followed it with a punch to the right temple. Taking advantage of the ringing the man was probably experiencing, he grabbed him by the neck and slammed him head first into the tiled wall.

A satisfying crunch echoed, but rather than fall to the ground, Wraith got up with a savage grin. Blood trickled down the side of his face from a cut in his forehead, but he didn't seem bothered by it. "You're not new to this," he stated with certain vigour.

This guy is definitely psycho. The glint of a blade only reinforced the assumption, and they danced around each other, each man trying to find a breach.

The door opened and someone walked in, freezing when he noticed what was going on. Wraith's eyes were on Damon, his expression taunting him to do something to stop what would inevitably happen.

Before Damon could warn the man off, Wraith turned to the newcomer and stabbed him in the gut. The guy dropped with a groan, blood pooling out of him. The assassin took off, cackling, and Damon ran to the poor guy, taking his shirt off to staunch the blood flow.

Calling the cops should have been out of the question – too many issues would arise, namely about his presence there at the time of the attack. Yet as the stranger grew pale, his breathing laboured, Damon did it anyway.

"911, what's your emergency?"

"Ping this location and get your asses here. Someone got a knife wound to the stomach, and he needs immediate attention!"

The wound was non-fatal, at least if help arrived in time. Damon was still there when paramedics strolled in about ten minutes later and took over. With the man too unconscious to tell them who stabbed him, he needed to leave before he drew too much attention.

Damon stepped to the exit, ready to disappear in his usual way, but a burly cop blocked his way.

"Going somewhere?" he asked, plainly intending to make sure he didn't.

♥ *Chapter 9* ♥

Her mind miles away, Cassandra moved to the beat echoing in her ears. She was dancing, and for all intents and purposes should have been enjoying herself. Yet the memory of the two assailants, and what Damon told her, made it hard to do so.

Her lips still tingled from the memory of their kiss, and the ardour he'd been holding back. Cassandra had thought it an easy feat to avoid their chemistry, but when faced with the choice, she'd actively made the decision to kiss Damon back.

And that, more than anything, scares the hell out of me.

She was pulled out of her thoughts when the Frenchman from earlier reappeared and danced with her, then Renzo came to check on her. Both left shortly after, probably picking up on her distraction and unwillingness to entertain.

Despite feeling Damon's eyes on her, Cassandra didn't make a move towards him. She needed a break from being around him after what had happened, and was grateful he seemed to understand and kept his distance.

The last of the alcohol wore off with the final notes of the song, and her brain jumped into overdrive, thoughts invading her mind. *If my own father is responsible for this…*

Cassandra noticed Renzo dancing a few feet away, keeping an eye on her, the other on the girl gyrating against him. When she met his gaze, he pushed his partner away, then walked over.

Without a word, Renzo grabbed her hand as a big brother would – even though he was younger than her by eighteen months – and dragged her up the stairs and to the corner booth, their earlier hangout. He waited until she sat down, before sliding in next to her.

A wave of dizziness hit Cassandra, potent enough she had to rest her head on the leather seat. When she opened her eyes, Renzo was watching her, eyes narrowed in concern. "You ok?"

She hesitated to answer, wary of the string of questions that would follow. The tell-tale crease in Renzo's brow could only mean he was annoyed – and he rarely got so with her.

Cassandra finally nodded. "Yeah, just had a few too many drinks."

"It was more than one, the way Sam told it," Renzo muttered, now scowling. "Not that I don't approve you having fun for a change. But getting wasted when you obviously have a lot on your mind might not be the best idea."

"Maybe I just needed a blank slate for a few hours." She glared back, but gave up when it made her head hurt.

"Looks like you got that," Renzo said. He waited a beat, then asked, "So, are you going to tell me what's going on?"

Cassandra only shut her eyes again, hoping her pitiful demeanour would be enough to deter him from questioning her further. To his credit, Renzo gave her another few moments of respite before his impatience got the best of him. "Is it the guy Sam saw you with?"

Sighing, Cassandra faced her best friend. "Not exactly." The Frenchman's face flashed briefly in her mind, before being replaced by Damon's inscrutable eyes.

Renzo's intent expression didn't break, and Cassandra knew it was time to come clean. *Besides, maybe he can figure a way out of this mess that's eluding me.*

With that in mind, she motioned the waitress for a glass of water and started speaking. "Do you remember when I told you the reason I wasn't looking for a steady relationship?"

"Yeah," Renzo's voice was gentle, no more reproach left in it. "You said a guy crushed your dreams of a happily ever after. What about it?"

His non-judgemental tone, in that moment, made Cassandra love him all the more. Their friendship had an unspoken agreement of permanent honesty, but it wasn't always easy when one feared reprisal. With Renzo, Cassandra didn't.

It was that, more than anything that confirmed she was doing the right telling him at least part of the story. As her silence lengthened, Renzo reached for her, but let his hand drop halfway when she spoke again.

"What did I tell you about my parents, once we started becoming friends?"

Renzo seemed confused at the question, but thought back to that first time he'd brought Cassandra to the club, and the night of chatting that followed. "I remember we talked a bit about your birth parents, and you mentioned they were of French and Italian ancestry... That your dad was heir to an estate in Italy, rich but unhappy in life until he met your mom, a countess. Or was she a duchess?"

Cassandra shook her head, whispering, "Countess. Neither wanted to marry someone of their station because of how superficial that aristocratic world is, but they fell in love with each other at first sight despite their fortunes and upbringings."

Renzo sighed dramatically, lifting his free hand to his heart. "If only I could get so lucky!"

It got a chuckle out of Cassandra, which soon died out recalling how her parents hadn't had their happily ever after. "When, um, they died…"

She paused, taking another deep breath. Renzo glanced around their area, which had emptied out as more of the VIPs went to the lower level to dance. "Do you want me to take you home? We can continue this later."

"No, it's fine. I'm good. I made peace with their death a while ago, but I can't forget what they taught me."

"Nor should you…"

"It's not what my adoptive father said." Cassandra pursed her lips, but try as she might the bitterness flowed in her words. "When my parents died, they left me everything. I don't even know what the fortune amounts to now, since I've barely touched it and left it to an accountant to handle. But Viktor, for adopting me, received five million American dollars…yearly."

Renzo gaped at the figure, though he was used to rather copious sums of money himself between the club and his father's own investments. "Damn, girl. That's a nice bonus as compensation for raising you. So why would he tell you to forget what your parents taught you?"

"He wanted to mould me to his image, and that meant forgetting everything that was European about me, and turning North-American." Flashes of more than one fight flitted through her mind, but Cassandra pushed the painful memories away. "He was verbally abusive, enough so to make me doubt everything about myself. While that may have worked on his wife, it didn't on me. And that's when Damon walked in."

"Damon?" Renzo leaned in, catching the hitch in her tone that revealed how relevant the name was to her story.

"Yeah. He interned for Viktor and ran errands for him. We got to know each other after a while, and he sympathized with me having to get used to an entirely different way of life in Canada. He had a way about him that encouraged trust, and I fell head over heels for him."

Renzo opened his mouth to say something, but seemed to rethink it as he asked in a softer voice, "How old was this guy?"

"Three years my senior. And on my birthday one year, we ended up kissing. We allowed ourselves be at our most vulnerable point and I stupidly thought it would always be like that. That every bad thing in my life was finally replaced by a good one. And that, for once, it would last."

Cassandra took a deep breath, blinking back the tears that threatened. "You have to understand, it's not like I used to go around falling in love. My birth parents, they taught me the value of love from a young age, and I've always been looking for that."

Renzo grabbed her hand in his, squeezing it. "What happened, Cass?"

She shrugged, wiping at the corner of her eye with her free hand. "The day after the kiss, Damon vanished without a word, without so much as a goodbye. Viktor told me he left to pursue a great career, and I shouldn't be holding him back. So…I let go. But I never forgot, nor allowed myself to get so close to another man."

"Cass…." Renzo's eyes weren't full of pity, but rather of comprehension. He let go of her hand and opened his arms, wrapping them around her when she buried her face in his neck. "You didn't deserve that. You've been through so much, you didn't need more."

No words moved past the lump in her throat, so Cassandra only nodded in his chest. More tears stung her eyes first, then the sobs followed. For long moments, Renzo held her and allowed her tears to soak his shirt. He kept silent, patting her head and whispering soothing words until she regained control over her emotions.

When she tried to pull away from his arms, he shifted his weight so she rested against his side, leaning her head against his shoulder. With his free hand, he gave her a handkerchief.

A laugh bubbled out of Cassandra, as surprising as a unicorn appearing in that moment. "Old-fashioned much, Renzo?"

His shoulder lifted in a shrug. "What can I say? Some girls like old-fashioned guys."

"And the right one's waiting for you, somewhere."

Renzo made a noncommittal sound, then cleared his throat. "So... This Damon guy's back?"

Cassandra sat up at that, biting on her lower lip. "Yeah. And he's not in town just for kicks, apparently."

Renzo's expression turned even more suspicious. "Meaning?"

"Damon says Viktor's involved in some shady dealings, and he's here to try to stop him. I, um, might've offered to help."

Since they were close, Cassandra felt Renzo's body tense, even before his tone gave away his incredulity. "You *what*?" He searched her gaze, shaking his head when she only looked away. "I don't believe this. Why torture yourself, Cass? No offense, but this Damon guy seems like a dumbass, from what you've told me. A *manipulative* dumbass. The most dangerous kind. Why–"

Cassandra interrupted him. "Because I have a score to settle with Damon, questions I want answered. Plus, running away would be useless. It would only give Damon false ideas about feelings I may have."

There was a short silence as Renzo assessed her expression. "Do you?"

"Do I what?"

"Have any feelings left for him."

"No!"

Cassandra's reply was sharper than intended, but Renzo didn't take offense. If anything, the slight widening of his eyes hinted he saw something in her reaction that was definitely concerning, and to a deep degree.

"I swear, Renzo, Damon is a part of my past."

Despite her convincing words, she was aware of the fact that the past could haunt, and even come back. Damon Voight was living proof of that.

Renzo, to her surprise, let the matter slide, true to form. Instead of lecturing her, he hugged her, then flashed a smile that didn't reach his eyes. "Alright, Cass. I'm going to call my dad, see if he knows anything about Viktor's supposedly illicit activities."

"Oh, speaking of! Your dad was here earlier."

"He was?" Renzo looked around as if expecting Fabio to materialize. "Where is he now? Maybe I'll just ask him in person."

"Not sure, he kind of took off... Maybe a phone call would be best."

Renzo shrugged, then headed to the exit staircase. Before leaving, he turned back one more time. "If you need me, you know how to find me." With his face in shadows, she couldn't read his expression. However, his tone was full of undertones as he said, "Take care, Cass."

In the next heartbeat, he left and she was alone with her thoughts.

Cassandra sighed, knowing she didn't fool him, just as she couldn't lie to herself. But she was a survivor, always had been, and she resolved to act as one. *Damon can go to hell.* His return wouldn't ruin everything she had worked for in the last years.

Pressure in her bladder turned her musings inwards, and to the immediate need to use a washroom. But as Cassandra followed in Renzo's steps and went down the stairs, a familiar tingle raced up her spine. She stopped in her tracks at the bottom of the stairs, sure of one thing: *Someone's watching me.*

Taking a page out of a movie, Cassandra pretended to stumble and bent down. Her hair fell around her face like a curtain, and she darted a quick glance around her, then out in the crowd. No particular person stood out, which only left more questions. Yet the feeling was still present, an eerie warning that seemed to echo Renzo's last words.

It can't hurt to be more careful than usual.

Straightening up, she slipped out of the booth and headed to the bathroom located at the back.

On her way there, the commotion by the men's washroom caught her eye. Cops swarmed the entrance, and inside it, some paramedics were working on an unconscious man. But it was the guy in a white shirt stained with blood that caught her attention, and her heart beat faster.

"Damon?"

The devil of her thoughts turned around, a flash of something crossing his face. Behind him, she saw the last face she wanted to, and attempted to keep her expression neutral.

"Cassandra."

Sean's oily voice raked her, as did the way his eyes traveled up and down her body. But even more so was the way he stood close to Damon, hand on his gun as if he was a threat.

"What the hell are you doing?" Cassandra stomped over, glaring at Sean and forgetting all about her lady needs.

Damon's arm wrapped around her waist, stopping her from going further in. "No need for you to see this."

She glanced up at him, noticing the tight jaw and flashing eyes. When Damon didn't elaborate, she turned to Sean. "What's going on?"

"You know this guy?" Sean narrowed his eyes.

Cassandra didn't like where he was going with the question, nor the way he kept looking at Damon – like he was one step away from arrest. Behind him, the paramedics were loading the unconscious man onto a stretcher.

"I asked you a question, officer," she glared back. At the reminder of his rank, Sean finally snapped to.

"Someone stabbed an unidentified male in the men's bathroom. We're looking at all options, but right now your friend is a person of interest."

Cassandra glanced at Damon, noticing the apologetic look in his eyes.

"Well, I find that hard to believe," she retorted, tearing

her gaze from his. "Damon was with me this entire evening, and if you need further confirmation you can ask Renzo, who manages the club. You know, Lorenzo *Moretti*, Fabrizio Moretti's *son*."

Sean paled at the thought of going around a Mafioso's spawn. Like all cops in the area, he was well aware of Fabio's past as an enforcer for the Italian mob. Despite his now rather more legal dealings, no one wanted to mess with him. Plus, he still had the chief of police in his pocket, something Cassandra was well aware of.

"Now, are we done here?"

When Sean grunted something about not leaving town, Cassandra grabbed Damon and pulled him through the exit door. It was only once they were outside, in the semi-privacy of a badly lit alleyway, that she turned around to face him.

"What the *hell* happened?"

❤ *Chapter 10* ❤

Now how the hell am I supposed to tell her what happened, without scaring her shitless?

Damon took to pacing to avoid Cassandra's sharp gaze. He ran a hand over his face, trying to figure the least damaging option in the long run. Judging by the tapping of her foot, he was running out of time and Cassandra was losing patience.

As though hearing his thoughts, she muttered, "Anytime now."

Damon stopped moving, out of options. "Why did you run off, after what happened with those two guys?"

Cassandra blinked at him, then broke eye contact. "Does it matter?"

"It does to me."

"I needed space, ok? Is that what you wanted to hear? That despite how well I handled myself, the fact remains two people tried to attack us. And according to you, they meant to kidnap me and kill you."

Damon frowned at the way her voice broke on that last bit of information. "I wouldn't have thought you cared, from the way you've been acting."

Cassandra met his gaze then, and something in her expression softened. She gave no answer, instead cocking her hip and folding her arms across her chest – and looking sexy as hell.

Damon got side-tracked by her stance, but when she cleared her throat in irritation, he snapped to. "They didn't find you by chance, and I've already mentioned that you're in danger."

If he expected that would be enough to pacify her, he was dead wrong. Cassandra only arched an eyebrow, plainly expecting him to continue.

"They knew enough to realize you'd be here, Cass. Probably have a file on you that gave them all the details, including your closeness with the club's owner."

"Why would you say that?"

"Because I've got one, too." Damon stepped closer, getting tired of the space between them. "How are you, after what happened?"

"I'll live." Cassandra's eyes narrowed with each step Damon took towards her. "But if you want to ease my mind, answer me this: why did I find you with cops, and what the hell does all this have to do with Viktor?"

Damon cringed. "The cops, that's a different story. As for Viktor, I wish I knew." Cassandra didn't immediately refute his evasive answers, so he changed tactics. "Why would you come here, a club, of all places?"

The question destabilized Cassandra enough to answer. "It's a form of therapy. The loud music stops me from thinking, and at least I'm not at home wallowing." She bit her lip on the last confession, as though she hadn't meant to say as much.

"Is that all it is?" When Cassandra frowned, Damon stepped closer still. "Or is there more to it?" He was near enough that she had to tilt her head to look at him.

"What are you going on about now?"

"Lorenzo, your buddy. What's he to you?"

Cassandra's mouth fell open as if she couldn't believe her ears, then she snapped it shut and tossed her hair over her shoulder. "Really? You have a right to ask that?"

"Cass, I –"

"No, don't you even freaking dare." Lips pursed, she lifted a hand to shut him up. "It is none of your business what Renzo is or isn't to me. Your precious intelligence should have told you as much. But what I'd like for you to do is stop dancing around the subject and tell me why the hell Sean was about to arrest you. Then maybe I can figure out how much trouble I got myself into by lying for you!"

With her little rant, Cassandra ended up closer and they were almost chest to chest. Her soft fragrance wafted and it was all Damon could do not to give in and kiss her until they both got on the same page. Instead, he latched on to the easiest thing she'd said.

"Why *did* you lie?" When her eyes flashed, he hastened to add, "Answer me that one thing, and I'll tell you the rest, I swear."

Cassandra stared at him for a moment, and in the dim light Damon couldn't quite make sense of her expression. Then she sighed heavily and looked away. "I don't know. It's just… I'm acquainted with Sean, and he's not the best cop around. Maybe I didn't want you at his mercy."

She looked backed at him then with a wry smile. "Though somehow, I have a hard time imagining you at anyone's mercy – ever."

The moment was too good to pass up on, so Damon seized it and closed up the last of the distance. Cassandra was surprised, arms falling to the side, and swayed on her heels. It gave him the perfect chance to grab onto her elbow to hold her up, pulling her body into his.

"There is only one person I'm interested in giving that

power to," he whispered while staring in her eyes, "and that's you."

The faint light of a street lamp shone on Cassandra's face and he had a front-row seat to her shock. Damon's eyes drifted down to her lips, and leaned his forehead closer to hers.

Cassandra's breath hitched, and his heartbeat sped up. Time was suspended for that one moment. But rather than take what she might willingly give, Damon reluctantly tore himself away and let her go, stepping back.

"A deal's a deal," he stated. "Thank you for covering for me, though you are right – your buddy Sean couldn't touch me even if he wanted to."

"He's not my buddy." Cassandra's adamant mutter had Damon bite back a chuckle.

"I'm not guilty of anything he wants to pin on me. To be perfectly honest, I assumed you'd be safe here, considering the people who own it. I've evidently been wrong, but originally I figured someone would have to be a fool to try anything."

"So you know about Renzo's dad?"

Damon's jaw tensed at the question. Renzo's name alone was enough to get his blood boiling, considering Cassandra's unwillingness to confirm their relationship. The kid's ties to the Mob were another reason for his discomfort. "If you're referring to Fabrizio Moretti being the old cleaner and enforcer for the Montréal Mafia, then yes, I'm well aware."

He paused, trying to fight off his next question, but the curiosity was too much. "It doesn't bother you what he was involved in?"

Cassandra tilted her head to the side, pondering his words. After a moment, she shook her head. "No. I've learned not to judge people. And besides, I've only ever known Moretti as Uncle Fabio, and he's always been nice to me."

Damon snorted at that. "I bet."

Cassandra stopped smiling then and went back to questioning him. "You said you assumed I'd be safe, implying that's no longer the case."

"Yeah." Damon ran a hand through his hair, glancing around to confirm their surroundings were still alone. "You aren't, not here and not anywhere in this damn town. Because someone *did* try something, and that's what landed me in hot water with the local cops."

Cassandra frowned, but didn't interrupt as Damon continued, "I was minding my business when I heard noises in the bathroom and walked in to the guy getting stabbed."

"And what makes you think this has anything to do with me?"

"Because the person who did the stabbing was at the bar earlier. Add to that the two goons who attacked us and something tells me this isn't a coincidence."

The frown never left Cassandra's face. "And you just so happened to hear the noises, huh?"

Damon shrugged, trying to keep his face blank. If Cassandra figured out how much he knew, she would press for more information. Until he put a few pieces together, it was best she stayed in the dark, rather than seek vengeance for something she didn't quite understand.

His cellphone rang, saving him from answering. Damon held up a hand to Cassandra to indicate he needed a moment, then shifted away from her. "Yeah?"

Derek's voice on the end was a

surprise. "You contacted the hitman?"

"Maybe."

"Damon, he's a valued Interpol target. Do not underestimate Wraith when he's on everyone's wanted list."

"I figured as much."

Cassandra inched closer, trying to catch pieces of the conversation, and he once more noticed her perfume. The man in him wanted to act on the impulse of pulling her in his arms, comforting her, but the soldier was aware of the unspoken line in the sand she'd drawn and tried to respect it.

Derek's next words demanded his full attention. "I need you to do something, and you won't like it."

Damon bit his tongue at his former boss' tone, as it broached no argument. But his next words lit a fire in his blood.

"You have to let the Wraith approach Cassandra. If she's his new contract, it may give us enough of an opportunity to finally catch him. Keep a tight surveillance, but we need to catch this guy with enough evidence to put him away for life."

"Absolutely not!" Damon hissed, aware of Cass freezing at his tone.

"Damon, be a soldier. Set your personal feelings away from this. Not only is this man an assassin at the behest of people who do unthinkable things, but he has hurt innocents. Ruined families. Broken wills until people were unrecognizable. You've seen the pictures of his victims."

Damon's hand tightened on the phone, knowing full well Derek was right. Images of the corpses Wraith left behind kept him up at night. But could he risk Cassandra's life?

"We need this. The victims need this." Damon grimaced at the words, knowing why Derek used that angle of reasoning.

Damon's time in the special ops showed him unspeakable things, and it was one reason he was quick to leave. To have another monster out there, one he could catch if he played his cards right, was a chance to set something right in this world.

There was no way to avoid it, and he surrendered.

"Two weeks." Damon's mutter was low enough for Cass not to hear. "If I don't have enough in two weeks, then I'm taking him down – permanently. My way."

"Agreed. And, Damon?"

He paused, having been about to hang up. "What now?"

"You shouldn't tell Cassandra, especially if half the things in her file are true. The more she knows, the more she will be in danger. We both witnessed the after effects when the Wraith likes to play games."

Damon hung up on a curse, barely holding back from throwing the phone against the wall. Only one thing was clear in his mind: *I won't allow that bastard to hurt her.*

Something in Cassandra's chest wilted when Damon faced her again. In the few moments he'd been on the phone, he'd once more transitioned into the frigid stranger. His green eyes were unreadable, his expression blank, and no amount of pressing for answers would get through to him, that much was clear.

Guess the soldier's back, again.

"Nothing's changed, has it?" Cassandra's mutter had him frown.

"What do you mean?"

Damon's eyes begged her not to, but she still spoke what

was on the tip of her tongue. "At the end of the day, I'm a disposable commodity to you." There was no other way to explain his disinterest in her emotions, or the way he didn't seem to care how much chaos he was bringing back into her life.

Pain crossed Damon's features, and he opened his mouth to deny it, but couldn't. Cassandra shook her head and was about to pass by him, having had enough of his spy games for the night.

Before she could, Damon grabbed her elbow and spun her around. She had a brief glimpse of his flashing eyes before his mouth descended on hers almost bruisingly. There was nothing tender about it, only a need to communicate what he could not say in words.

And boy, did she feel it. The way he cupped her head gently was at odds with the force of the kiss, but nowhere in there did she try to stop him. This grown up kiss was nothing compared to what they'd shared earlier.

Cassandra's entire body zinged from his nearness, almost melting in his embrace the longer it went on. As though sensing it, Damon pulled her tighter against him, until the only thing keeping her upright was his strong frame.

When he pulled away, lips hovering above hers, his eyes were menacing glitters. "You still think I don't care? Think again. The only reason I'm here is because of you."

Cassandra tried to read his eyes, sensing the truth in his words. *Why would he lie then, pretend he's here for a job? Why —*

The slam of a door snapped her to, and Renzo came around the corner. "Cass, you around here? Sam saw you go around the back."

He stopped dead in his tracks when he found Cassandra in Damon's arms. In a futile effort, she tried to step back, but it only resulted in Damon's arms tightening around her.

"Let me go."

"Nope," was the unequivocal answer to her hiss. The entire time, Damon's gaze didn't leave Renzo's. "We were not introduced. I'm Damon Voight." To her surprise, he offered his hand.

Renzo glanced at Cassandra, then stepped closer and shook it. "Lorenzo Moretti." He left out the, *Friends call me Renzo part*, she noticed.

"Do you mind letting Cass go? She seems uncomfortable."

Damon switched his attention to her, and by his smirk she predicted she wouldn't like his answer. "She didn't seem that uncomfortable before you interrupted us."

Before she could reconsider, her right hand lifted and connected with his cheek. The slap echoed in the alley, and Damon let her go out of shock.

"That's what you get for being a pompous ass." Cassandra's infuriated gaze locked with Damon's for a heartbeat, enough to see his answering annoyance. Then she turned on her heels and stomped away with her head held high. The last thing she wanted was to be a prize in a pissing contest.

Renzo was biting back a laugh when she passed him, but she ignored him in favour of the entrance door. Cassandra intended to get out of there and as far away from Damon as possible – before she did something stupid again like let him kiss her.

♥∞♥

"You really should try more tact if you're trying to win her over." Renzo's tone was amused, even as he eyed Damon's reddening cheek.

Damon glared at him, annoyed at the interruption. He'd been getting through to Cassandra, and Renzo's untimely appearance had ruined his plans. "And you should consider staying out of people's business."

Instead of backing down, Lorenzo widened his stance and folded his arms across his chest. While Damon could appreciate him trying to protect Cassandra, the job was his by default.

"This coming from the guy who was out of Cass' business for the last ten years?" Lorenzo taunted, and Damon stilled.

He gritted his teeth, even as he attempted to find some of that long lost control he'd gained in his special ops training. Kung Fu-ing Lorenzo's ass would not win him Cassandra's good graces, rather set him off a few steps. It surprised and irked him how much Lorenzo knew about their situation.

Emotions must have been easy to read on his face as Lorenzo then saw fit to elaborate. "Cass told me. Which begs the question, why exactly did you return when you're clearly not needed?"

"Again, I don't see how that's any of your business."

"Listen, bud," Lorenzo stepped closer at that, arms by his side clenched in fists. "I've had my share of meeting pricks and seeing Cass push them away. Something about you gets to her and I don't want to see Cass in pain. If you care about her at all, you'd leave."

Damon got up in his face at that, clenching his fist – but

holding back. "You don't understand what you're talking about," he growled. "It's because I care that I'm here, *bud*. So you'd better stay the hell out of my way."

He moved past Lorenzo to leave, but the guy was not giving up. He stepped in front of Damon, blocking his path.

Damon's nostrils flared in anger, and it was all he could do to keep a lid on it. His knuckles were white from the force clenching them. When their eyes met, Lorenzo barely flinched.

"You may be all hot shot and trained, but I've known this girl for long enough to realize she's special. Hurt her, and you'll pay in ways you haven't even imagined."

The threat was real enough, and again, Damon forced himself to remember Lorenzo was acting out of good intentions, and because he was legitimately interested in Cassandra's well-being.

Holding back the rage he wanted to unfurl, he simply nodded, "Duly noted." Then shoved Lorenzo aside and walked to his car. He intended to make sure Cassandra got home safe, no matter how long it took him.

♥ *Chapter 11* ♥

The next morning, Cassandra woke up to an empty household. Since she had nothing planned and no job to go to, she showered quickly and picked up a book, heading to a café down the street.

With the sunny day, she picked a spot on the veranda and ordered an iced coffee, then settled in for a quiet afternoon. An hour later, she was lost in the latest adventures of the spy novel, when a shadow fell across her table.

"I'm ok, I don't need a refill."

A chuckle had her glance up and her jaw dropped. The sun hit him from behind, but the aristocratic features were hard to miss even with the light causing her to squint.

"I'm terribly sorry to interrupt what seems to be a great book, but I was walking by and couldn't help but notice you. I realized not introducing myself last night was poor manners…" The Frenchman trailed off, and a tentative smile spread on his face. "Would you allow me to join you for a bit?"

After a beat of hesitation, Cassandra set her book down on the table. "Only if you tell me your name this time."

The smile became a full-blown grin. "Alain Valois."

Cassandra was even more charmed when rather than plop down on the seat after the introduction, he stood by the table, waiting for her acquiescence to sit next to her. "I'm Cassandra DiCavalier."

Alain took her hand in his and kissed the top of it, then let go. She beamed at the old-school gesture and gestured for him to sit.

"I do hope I'm not disturbing you," Alain said.

"Personally, I find it incredibly rude of people who engage in a conversation with me as I'm reading."

Cassandra chuckled, familiar with the feeling. "Not to worry, it was about time I take a break. This novel's getting a bit too intense."

Alain's eyes shifted to the cover and chuckled. "I suppose it is. These spy books tend to have so much drama. I much prefer mine cutthroat and concise."

Cassandra nodded, though something in his tone implied a private joke. She let it slide, interested instead in finding out more about him. "So what brings you to Montréal?"

"Business, for one." He ordered a cappuccino and the waiter disappeared, reappearing within moments with a fresh cup. Alain removed his sunglasses, inhaling the aroma and taking a sip. "Perfect."

"I love this place. The coffee is always amazing, and the fresh croissants could have you easily thinking you're in Paris."

"Really?" Alain held her gaze for a moment, then smiled. "I suppose then I should try one."

As if on cue, the waiter reappeared and Alain ordered a plate of croissants for them to share. Cassandra watched his movements, intrigued despite herself. He spoke with the ease and confidence of someone used to commanding attention.

This is a man who gets what he wants. Much like Damon.

The thought was an unwelcome one, especially considering her company, and Cassandra willed it away. She smiled at Alain instead. "So if you're here on business, what were you doing at *Fire & Ice*?"

"Looking for you, of course."

♥∞♥

Across the street, Damon shifted in front of a stand of newspapers. He'd been watching Cassandra for the last thirty minutes, after getting Paco to track her cell phone. When he'd returned from his morning jog to find the house empty, he couldn't fight the panic any longer.

Seeing Wraith take a seat at her table, and Cassandra's open body language, did nothing to ease his anxiety.

Inhale, exhale, he willed his body with each breath of air. His eyes were glued to Cassandra and the hitman. Every muscle wanted to take him down, but considering the lack of evidence, he doubted the cops would be on his side.

Especially considering he'd had a tail since he left the house. Behind his sunglasses, his eyes shifted to the side parking, where a marked cop car was parked. Its driver was the same cop from the previous night, Sean. He flicked another cigarette out the window, and it fell on the sidewalk, joining the used butts that were piling up.

The policeman was keeping an eye on him from the sidelines, probably still investigating the club stabbing from the previous night. Damon's jaw tightened at the surveillance, and he was half-tempted to call Zak to run interference.

He reached inside his jacket, noticing Sean's attention zeroing on him out of the corner of his eye. *Idiot probably assumes I'm planning to pull out a gun.* Damon purposefully took his cellphone out slowly, then waved it in his direction with a massive grin.

Sean scowled and gunned the engine, taking off in a squeal of tires. *Did he really think he was being slick?*

"I wouldn't annoy the local cops if I was you," someone

said from behind.

The voice was familiar, coming off his left side, but not enough to pinpoint it. Damon was about to turn, but something poked his lower back.

"I also wouldn't turn around. It would not do for people to see us chatting. Are we understood? Nod if you agree."

Damon gave a small nod, glancing to the café on his right to confirm Cassandra was safe. "Who are you?" His lips barely moved, and his tone was low enough that only the other man could hear. With the street empty in their corner, and no clients in the open-aired newspaper store, there was a semblance of privacy.

"Fabrizio Moretti." When Damon only responded with silence, the poke in his lower back disappeared. "I take it you know my name."

"I was well briefed on you, sir," Damon said. His fingers curled around the metallic grid of a row of papers, clenching it tighter. It took all his will not to reach for his gun. What the hell was the Mafia's enforcer up to?

"*Bien*. It will save us some time. What branch are you with?"

There was no point in lying, especially if Fabrizio was close enough to shoot. "I was Interpol special ops. I'm private security now."

It was Fabrizio's turn to be silent for a beat, then he said, "And what is your business with Cassandra DiCavalier?"

Damon frowned at the question, then connected the dots. Last night, Fabrizio had spoken with Cassandra, and he was Lorenzo's father. Evidently, he was well-enough acquainted with Cassandra to care about her well-being. *I hope that's all it is.*

"I'm here because she's in danger," Damon responded. "And I care for her."

"Care, or love?"

Damon fought the urge to turn around and see if Fabrizio was playing him. "Isn't that an odd question to ask, for a Mafia enforcer?"

"Maybe… But if you love her, you'll do anything for her."

Not entirely sure that he wasn't digging his grave, Damon sighed and admitted, "I love her. Have since we were young, and I'd put my life on the line for her any day, anytime."

"Good, because it may come to that. Do you know the man she is having coffee with?"

"Yes." The newspapers rattled from the force he was gripping the stand with, and Damon let go. It wouldn't do to have them tumbling down in a noisy mess and raise attention to himself.

"And you are familiar with his work?"

Damon nodded in response, not trusting his voice.

"When I was with the Mafia, I had a code. Men like him do not. I tried to warn Cassandra last night, but she is stubborn."

"I realize as much."

"Then you need to do a better job at protecting her."

Silence followed, then only the slightest shift of the air announced Fabrizio's departure. Damon's eyes landed back on Cassandra and Wraith, and he expelled a breath.

Enough is enough.

Cassandra blinked, her mouth falling open at Alain's

proclamation. She searched his gaze, expecting him to laugh, but his expression was neutral.

"I, um…" She trailed off, at a loss. *Is he a reporter?*

Alain laughed at her distress, then flashed a grin. "I'm joking, pretty lady. Though I have to admit meeting you was the highlight of my night."

Cassandra sighed in relief, then eased back in her chair and took another sip of her coffee. "So what did bring you there, then?"

"I'd had a particularly bad day – business deal gone sour. The valet at my hotel read my mood and suggested the new hip place in town for some relaxing. I wouldn't have gone, but I discovered much sparse energy. Dancing is always a good way to get it out of my system."

"And yet you were at the bar when I first met you." Cassandra's wicked grin seemed to throw Alain for a loop, but he recovered with an easy-going shrug.

"I needed some liquid courage, especially if I was to speak to the most beautiful woman there."

Cassandra blushed at the reverence in his tone, and looked away. As fate would have it, her gaze landed on none other than Damon. He was crossing the street, stalking towards them with a murderous look in his eyes.

"Damon?"

Alain's head whipped around at the name, and he also noticed the approaching thunderstorm.

"What are you –" Cassandra was interrupted when Damon only reached for her hand and pulled her to her feet.

"We need to go."

"Um, no." She yanked her wrist out of his grip, rubbing

the reddening skin. "And you need to learn some manners. I'm enjoying a nice cup of coffee with a friend, and I intend to stay."

Damon blew out a breath and deigned to notice Alain. He angled his body between Cassandra and the other man, clenching his fists. "Nice *friend*." When those fiery emerald eyes turned their full force back on Cassandra, she felt it from the tip of her toes to her head. "Come with me, now."

"I don't think so."

Alain stood at that point and threw some bills on the table. "Perhaps it might be a good idea to hear your friend out, Cassandra."

Ignoring his suggestion, she shoved Damon out of her way and took a step closer to the Frenchman. "I'm really sorry for this." Swiping her book off the table, she ripped a piece off the back page and jotted down her number. "Give me a call sometime? I'll take care of my *issues* in the meantime."

Damon didn't flinch at her glare, but Alain seemed amused. "Take your time." He lowered his head to kiss her cheek, then strode away whistling.

Cassandra whirled on her heels to face Damon, but already he was tugging on her wrist.

"Damon, let go!" she ordered, but his grip only tightened.

"Sorry, Cass, but we have to go. *Now*." Something in his tone of voice and in the gleam in his eyes warned her not to make a fuss, unless she wanted to cause a scene.

She let Damon drag her two blocks down the street, in the opposite direction Alain had disappeared to. When it seemed he wasn't about to stop, Cassandra dug her feet in and refused to budge further. "Enough!"

A couple passing nearby threw them a look, and Cassandra lowered her voice. "I don't want to get you into trouble considering the cops are probably following you, but you have to stop acting like a caveman."

Damon snorted, but glanced around to scan for police. When he noticed nothing out of the ordinary, he met Cassandra's gaze once more. "I think your buddy Sean got the message earlier."

"Earlier?" His tone confused her. "What are you talking about?"

"Sean's been tailing me since this morning when I went for a jog. He took off after I made it clear he's not being subtle."

"Damon..." Cassandra shook her head. "You need to watch your back with him. This isn't ten years ago, and you're not a boy who can get away with stuff. Be careful where Sean is concerned."

"Oh, like you're being careful?"

Cassandra didn't like his tone. "What the hell is that supposed to mean?"

"Do you even know who that guy is?" Damon's question, and the loaded emotion behind it, took her by surprise.

"Why do you care?" She shot back, pursing her lips.

"Cass, don't play games. Do. You. Know?" Damon's voice was bleak with anger, and something else.

If she had been on a calm mindset, Cassandra probably would have backed away a few feet. Instead, with her own temperature mounting in frustration, she took a few steps towards him.

"Honestly, Damon, how am I supposed to know? All you've done so far is showed up in my life, trying to take control, acting like I'm yours to protect after all this time, yet not delivered on the answers you promised me. So rather than ask me if I know who Alain Valois is, how about you tell me who the *hell* do you think you are?"

Damon mimicked her movement, inching closer. "You've asked me that question before, and I'll be damned if I don't answer it now. You seem to think I'm the enemy here, when I made it clear I want to protect you. And to make it *crystal*-clear, I'm what you don't seem to realize you need right now. As for your so-called Alain, you need to stop listening to your hormones and stay away from that guy!"

Cassandra's slap resounded in the street, causing more than one pair of eyes to turn to them. It surprised her because it hadn't been a planned reaction, yet Damon seemed to bring out the worst in her.

"I must be setting a record," Damon muttered, rubbing his cheek.

His expression had gone blank, but Cassandra was only getting started. She jabbed a finger in his chest, rising to her full height. "You may be some big shot security guy now, Damon, but this has to stop. I'm not going to let you control my life, I had enough of that growing up. And I'll do as I damn well please. So if you want to keep staying at my place, I'd suggest you keep your nose out of my business."

She stalked off, not even sparing a glance back.

Damon watched her go for a bit, then started to follow in her steps. No way did he plan to let Cassandra out of his sight, pissed or not. *She'll be the death of me.* His wry amusement was only outweighed by the seething anger at Wraith, and the games he was playing.

❤ *Chapter 12* ❤

Noises downstairs woke Cassandra up. She'd gone on a jog shortly after the confrontation with Damon, and when she'd returned had gone straight to shower.

I must have fallen asleep after... She got up from bed, stretching her muscles. A loud growl from her stomach stopped her mid-stretch. After a quick scan, she concluded around twenty-four hours must have passed since her last meal, and it was high time she ate.

Cassandra brushed her teeth, pulled on a pair of sweatpants and a sweater then headed downstairs. Enticing smells of pasta and meatballs caused her stomach to contract, and she increased her pace.

Peeking around the door to the kitchen, Cassandra was startled by what greeted her. Damon was moving around the stove, dumping some ingredients into what was her largest pasta pot. He stirred for a bit, then seemed to sense her eyes on him and turned.

"You're awake."

Cassandra glanced between him and the pot, torn between wanting to stay mad at him for his rude behaviour earlier, and the hunger clawing at her intestines.

She was saved from having to decide when Damon set down the wooden spoon he'd used to stir. "I'm sorry, Cassandra."

Taken aback by his raw, sincere tone of voice, she looked into his eyes. There was no effort to hide his feelings, and she got lost in the depth of his gaze. A long time ago, they'd had something. Could have had more. Was it so late, were they so removed from that time, that it had become impossible?

Cassandra bit her bottom lip. She couldn't get the sarcastic reply meant for Damon past her choked throat. Instead, she said, "It's not an apology I want, but an explanation. Why were you being so rude and overbearing earlier?"

"Viktor. I meant to tell you last night, but with the attack, we got side-tracked."

Cassandra frowned, trying to think what could have been so important. Then it dawned on her. "You were gone earlier in the night, just before I left for the club. Your note said something about information on Viktor."

Damon nodded, and some of the tension eased off him. "I went to see a source outside of town, and he confirmed we were on the right track. Everything he said already had me on edge, and the night only turned worse after."

Cassandra folded her arms across her chest, arching an eyebrow. "Still doesn't explain your jackass behaviour."

Damon ran a hand over his face, pinching the bridge of his nose. His neck was corded, and something about his stance made Cassandra want to take back the line of inquiry. Before she could, Damon met her eyes once more.

"You've obviously guessed, even more so than what I told you, that I've got some military training."

"I'd say it's pretty much a given."

He flashed a smile, gone just as fast. "Well, the one thing they don't teach you there is showing emotions. Protection comes second nature, and everything I see as a threat to you, I want to remove. But you don't make it easy. And I've been so used to taking command, being in charge, that it's not something I can shrug off easily. Plus, I didn't expect you to be so…" Damon trailed off, then shrugged. "So *you*."

"Meaning?" Cassandra asked.

"Meaning you're gorgeous, independent, and so damn used to having your way that it makes me want to take you away from all this craziness, just to keep you safe. But," he held up a hand when she opened her mouth to protest, "I know you'd never agree, and it would be crossing a line." Damon paused, searching her expression. "I *am* sorry, for earlier."

Cassandra stayed quiet, soaking in the apology and the truth of his words. She'd come to think there was nothing soft left in Damon, but this new side of him was making her rethink it.

A more pronounced growl from her stomach broke the heavy silence. Cassandra stepped around Damon, peeking over the pot to see if she'd been right. Pasta and meatballs swam in a dark sauce, and the smells wafting off it had her salivating.

"Is it almost ready?" She hated the whiny sound of her voice, but it did the trick as Damon relaxed and gave her a tentative grin.

"Yeah, a few more minutes. Why don't you set the table, and I'll do the serving."

Cassandra held his gaze for a few more seconds than necessary, then nodded. "You're not quite forgiven, just so you know. But this is a step in the right direction."

Damon chuckled, "I'd expect nothing else."

Cassandra grabbed plates and cutlery from the cupboards, and a bottle of wine from the fridge. By the time she was done setting up and adding two glasses, Damon returned from the stove with the pot. He served them both generous portions, then took a seat at the table.

An uncomfortable silence reigned for a few moments as they chewed through their food, then Damon reached for the wine bottle at the same time as Cassandra.

His touch was like a spark and she quickly withdrew her hand, focusing back on the food instead. Undeterred, Damon poured the wine and handed her a glass.

"To old friends reuniting."

His raised glass was both a challenge and peace offering, and Cassandra hesitated. Under all the possessiveness and blank expressions, this man had parts of the boy she'd known. Would it be the end of the world to try their hand at friendship, especially if it meant Viktor would get what was coming to him?

I guess not.

Cassandra sighed and clinked her glass with Damon's, offering a tentative smile. "To old friends."

They got through the rest of the meal in silence, though it wasn't as uncomfortable as before. And to Cassandra's surprise, Damon was a more than decent cook.

With the dishes away, they moved into the living room, now each nursing a second glass of wine. As she took another sip, Cassandra figured it was past time to poke the beast. "So, plan to fill me in anytime soon?"

"Fill you in? About what?" Damon took a seat opposite her on the couch.

Despite the ambient temperature in the room, Cassandra was aware of the heat radiating off him. Part of her wanted to get closer, soak it up and forget the world existed. The other part realized she was only reacting so because it'd been much too long since her last relationship.

The alcohol gave her a slight buzz, but she had to make

a conscious effort to redirect her thoughts to safe ground. No matter what her muddled feelings were trying to communicate, Cassandra vowed not to fall back in Damon's arms. It would only bring complications she didn't need.

"Cass?"

Damon's voice brought her out of her ruminations, and she blinked, focusing on him. "Hmm?"

"You're staring."

His blunt statement caused her cheeks to flame. She couldn't decide if it was due to embarrassment or annoyance, but he definitely didn't lack self-confidence.

"Don't flatter yourself." After swallowing another gulp of wine, Cassandra met Damon's gaze, letting her voice grow as sweet as possible. "You may have an incomplete file, but let me fill you in. There are men far more interesting than you out there. Ones who *want* to date me."

It took her a few seconds to realize Damon had grown silent at her words. When she darted a look at him, his emerald eyes were blazing.

"Oh, I'm sure there are men out there who just can't wait to date you." There was something hidden in the tension behind his words that raised Cassandra's hackles.

"What the hell is that supposed to mean?" Her voice was inflicted with not only hurt – they'd been doing so well – but also a hint of challenge.

With his free hand, Damon rubbed the back of his neck and sighed. "I'm sorry, that came out wrong. I only meant that I'd hate to see you hurt, and I can still easily recall what the dating scene is like in Montréal… Especially at clubs."

"How nice of you." Now that she'd started, Cassandra

couldn't keep the acid out of her voice. "And did you think about how hurt I'd be when you left ten years ago?"

Damon stared back, all emotion drained from his expression. There was something in his eyes, similar to that haunted look that implied he cared about something…About her.

Still, the words continued to come out, with Cassandra powerless to stop them. "Or are you saying that leaving me behind doesn't count as getting me hurt? You're being a hypocrite, Damon, don't you think?"

When Damon finally met her glare, his voice was soft. Before her defensive walls could rise again, Cassandra found herself listening to another apology she hadn't asked for, but that was long overdue.

"You're right," Damon said. "What I did back then… It wasn't the best decision I've ever made. I thought it was for the best, you have to believe me."

"How could it be for the best, when it caused that much pain?"

Damon set aside his glass, and reached for hers. Removing it from her numb fingers, he placed it on the coffee table then took her hands in both of his. His gaze was earnest, at its most vulnerable that she'd seen since his return.

"I need you to believe me when I said there was more to it, and I will tell you. Like I've told you other things. I'm not here to lie to you, or betray you, just to protect you. Please, Cassandra, if nothing else, believe that."

Her heart tugged, feeling like it was being split in two. There was so much Cassandra wanted to say, but the words that came out were as disillusioned as the rest. "Believe you?

Damon, that cost me more than I was ready to lose, once upon a time. Do you honestly think I'm about to risk more?"

Damon's eyes turned wary, but he didn't let it go. "Cass, what you've been through–"

"Don't!" The harsh reply left her lips unwillingly, as she got up to her feet. "Don't even pretend you know what I've been through in these past ten years, because you don't!"

On some level, Cassandra was aware she was overreacting, especially considering he'd apologized. But this was a conversation they hadn't had yet, and all the hurt of the past years bubbled underneath the surface.

To her surprise, it wasn't just her demons that rose to the surface. Damon shocked her by getting up to his feet, storming to her until they were nose to nose. "And don't imagine *you* know everything, because you don't! I've been through hell and back trying to survive leaving you behind, and I'm still there, Cass!"

Damon's words froze Cassandra on the spot. There was something about his determination, the raw pain in his expression, that got through her walls quicker than anything else had.

She tried to keep in mind that words didn't mean a thing for Damon. He'd promised her the moon and the stars, the world, and then disappeared without a backward glance. She didn't plan to fall for that song again. *Once was more than enough.*

"We're getting off track." Cassandra attempted to keep her voice calm, even when Damon's intense glare didn't cool off. "I didn't come down to pick a fight with you, but to give you whatever information you need on Viktor. The sooner I do, the sooner you can get him and be out of my life."

Something flashed in Damon's eyes, but he seemed to bite back the words on the tip of his tongue. He kept his distance, crossing his hands over his chest. "I'm listening."

"I don't know what you already have on him, that's why I asked you earlier to fill me in. And keep in mind I left Viktor's house the minute I turned eighteen, so what I know may be out-dated."

"Tell me anyway."

Cassandra fidgeted, uncomfortable under his too-intense gaze. "Viktor was a control-freak, enough so that he's kept records of everything in his house. When I left, we had a big blowout over him finding me in his office. He raised his hand to me, and I took off, never returning."

The string of curses that left Damon's mouth would have put a sailor to shame. After a few beats of watching him pace, he faced her once more. Something about his stance warned Cassandra that he was close to snapping.

When he spoke, his tone was equally tense. "Where in the house?"

"His office, there's a hidden safe behind the library. I once saw him hide a burgundy notebook there, and I'm pretty sure it held his dealers' contacts."

Damon blinked at her revelation. "You knew he was dealing drugs?"

"Everyone at my school knew," Cassandra snorted. "They used to come to me expecting me to hook them up."

Damon nodded, filing the information away for future use. "What else?"

"Viktor's business contacts. He met or defended a lot of

his dealers, so you'll probably find connections to a fair amount of money laundering in his financial records. With his gambling habit, I doubt he saved any of the money he got for raising me."

The only indication of Damon's rising ire were his narrowed eyes, and the clenching of his jaw. "Anything else?"

"Yeah. I'm pretty sure he had something to do with his wife's death. A year after you left, they separated and she threatened to take him to court for all he was worth." Cassandra bit on her lip, recalling the fight that had kept her up all night. "Two days later, she was in an accident. Dead on impact."

"Fuck." Damon turned away and pulled a cellphone from his back pocket. He dialled a number, then spoke briefly into it. It was too low for Cassandra to hear, but after a minute or so of silence Damon growled louder. "Just get it done. Tonight."

Then he hung up, and turned to face her. "Good, now that's dealt with."

Cassandra narrowed her eyes as Damon took another step closer, forcing her to retreat. "What are you doing?"

Her backing away was stopped short when she felt cold metal against her backside. She'd hit the refrigerator, and the predator glint in Damon's eyes warned he realized as much.

"I'm finishing what we started. You trusted me once, Cass," Damon said, all the intensity having left his eyes. The vibrant green was a touch more dull, his expression sad and pained. "And I want to be the one you trust again."

"Good luck with that." She raised her chin to glare at Damon, hoping it was convincing enough and wouldn't betray the fast-beating of her heart. "Would you mind moving, now?"

An amused gleam flickered in his gaze. The instinct to

smile was strong, but she fought it. This was not the best of times to let herself be swept away by Damon's dangerous charm.

"Yes," Damon's voice was silky as he leaned his head lower towards hers. "I mind moving, very much."

Cassandra's next breath hitched in her chest as Damon moved the last inch, and his body was pressed to hers – everywhere. One hand came up and lifted her chin, keeping Cassandra immobilized even as his lips got closer.

She avoided his eyes, wanting nothing more than to fight him – or so she told herself. But underneath the fire fuelling her annoyance, underneath the fear of losing something she'd never truly regained, there was a chemistry that pulled her to Damon with all the force of a magnet.

"Keep dreaming, golden boy." Cassandra's words sounded weak even to her ears. But it was when she made the mistake of looking up into his eyes, and her pulse fluttered, that she knew she was lost.

Oh... shit.

♥ *Chapter 13* ♥

Damon's lips were moving closer to Cassandra's, and she could only stare wide-eyed. She managed to drag her eyes away from his and pushed against his chest.

"Damon. *Move!*" Her voice rose slightly, but she didn't care if he could read her emotions, as long as it would get him out of her way.

With each smack against his chest, Damon only let out a chuckle, and refused to budge. "Why would I move, when I'm so comfortable at the moment?" His crooked smile earned a flutter in her stomach, and Cassandra bit on her lip.

Damon's gaze zeroed in on the movement, and something changed in his expression. His eyes darkened, nostrils flaring as if the last shred of control he had was slipping away.

Cassandra refused to be impressed by the hardness of his body pressing against hers. She clenched her teeth, considering using self-defense to get Damon at a safe distance from her, when the phone rang.

"Saved by the ring," Damon's eyes glittered as he eased himself off, allowing Cassandra to run into the hallway.

As she answered the landline, Cassandra noticed Damon leaning against the door of the kitchen, close by, to hear her conversation. She was about to turn and ask for privacy, when the familiar voice on the line made her eyes widen in shock.

"Cassandra?" The French accent was recognizable in the very pronunciation of her name.

She leaned against the wall opposite Damon, smiling like the proverbial cat that ate the canary, and switched to

French. "Oui, Alain. It's me. How are you?"

The answering flare of jealousy in Damon's eyes was satisfaction enough. It was obvious he knew who the caller was, and was none too thrilled about it.

"I'm well, thank you. And you?" Alain's voice brought her back to the conversation.

"Good. I'm sorry for yesterday. My friend has very bad manners."

Alain chuckled on the line. "So I gathered. Has he been…taken care of?"

Cassandra thought back to what had almost happened in the kitchen and held back a grimace. "Not quite, but I want to make it up to you. Will you let me?"

"Actually, that's why I called."

"Oh?" Cassandra kept her voice casual, but her eyes darted to where she saw Damon's fists clenching, as if he ached to grab the phone from her. "Interesting development."

"Yes…" Alain was saying. "I was wondering if you are free tonight? For a dinner and dancing, if that's all right with you."

The faint uncertainty in his voice had her smile. "I'd love to! Tonight, nine o'clock?"

"Perfect, I will pick you up." There was no more uncertainty there, only a deeply satisfied tone of voice.

Still smiling, Cassandra gave Alain her address, then hung up the phone. Damon's entire body was rigid with fury when she turned to face him again.

Head held high, she took a few steps, wanting to get to the kitchen. After all, she was still hungry. But before she could cross him, Damon's arm shot out, blocking her passage.

His voice was tense when he spoke, as if he was making a huge effort to control his pitch.

"Why did you agree to go out with him?" That was definitely anger vibrating with every word. "I don't like him, Cass, and you shouldn't be anywhere near him!"

"Didn't we have this conversation already?" Cassandra narrowed her eyes, hands on her hips. "You can hardly tell me what to do, Damon. I'm an adult now, not a little girl. I'll go out with whomever I damn please, and I don't need your approval. And if you must know why I agreed, it's because he's a charming, uncomplicated guy."

She ducked under his arm and walked to the kitchen, but couldn't resist one last dig. "Plus, he and I don't have any history. Yet."

Damon stood frozen for long moments as the meaning of her words sank in. Cassandra kept her eyes on his back as he took in a few breaths, then joined her at the table.

His eyes were guarded again, but traces of frustration rolled off him in waves. "I was out of line, you're right." Damon's sheepish smile made him look young, and something tugged at Cassandra's heart.

His silence as they continued eating peaked her curiosity, as did his intense expression. It was almost as if he'd come to some type of conclusion, and Cassandra reasoned that her curiosity had more to do with how it would affect her, than anything else.

"What are you thinking about?" she asked, swallowing the last remnants of her wine, and filling another glass.

Damon watched the amber liquid pour for a moment, then locked eyes with hers. "I was thinking about what you'd said. That when it comes to you, I should forget it. You've pretty much said the same thing to some extent or another since I returned. It all implies that I'll never get another shot, correct?"

Damon's question took her by surprise, and Cassandra took a gulp of wine to buy some time before answering. The liquid trickled the wrong way down her throat and before she knew it, she was coughing. She walked by the sink and got a glass of water, gulping it down until the irritation in her throat calmed down.

Aware of Damon's keen sense of observation, she faced him and leaned against the counter. "Yes, I meant that." She was proud of her steady voice, but the words themselves didn't have the conviction Cassandra would have wanted.

Damon nodded, as if having expected her answer, and also stood. She tensed, fearing he would corner her again, but he kept a distance between them. "What if I were to tell you the real reason I'm here is to get you back?"

Cassandra gaped at him, her heart thundering with those few simple words. "You said you were here on business!" Her accusation didn't shake him, and she gripped the counter for support, dizzy from a rush of emotions.

If he's here for me....

But the hurt of the past....

Still, what if....

All possibilities ran through her mind, and she shook her head at the assault. When she next looked at Damon, his composed face was at odds with the whirlwind tornado he'd thrown her in.

"You... That's a lie." Cassandra cleared her throat, straightening up. "You're here for Viktor, and I'm just collateral damage. Whatever this is," she gestured to space between them, "you're using it to screw with me."

Emotions flashed on Damon's face, too sudden to be interpreted properly. He took a small step closer, but stopped when Cassandra tensed. "Viktor is an excuse, but not the reason to my presence here."

"You're here for *business*!" There was almost desperation in the way she said the word, and Damon picked it up.

"Repeating it multiple times won't change the facts, Cass. My business is *you*." He paused a beat, then added, "But you didn't answer my question."

Cassandra stopped avoiding his gaze and met it. "If that's true, then I would offer to pay for your plane ticket back home, wherever that is for you."

She tried to move past him, but was not quick enough. Damon's voice reached her, and the confidence in his words threw her for another loop.

"Home was always where you are, Cass," Damon said. "You should remember."

♥∞♥

Cassandra whirled around to face Damon, her eyes searching his for proof he meant the statement. He could read her like an open book, and it was so he noticed both the fear and hope in her expression at his words.

Damon knew his departure had hurt her, and it was a subject he'd avoided long enough. If he told her the truth, then it should be enough to regain at least a semblance of trust from Cassandra. And if he had that…. The possibilities boggled his mind.

It was imperative she know more, at least about that one thing. Before he could change his mind, Damon closed the remaining distance until they were once more chest to chest.

"Cass, we need to talk about why I left. You need to know–"

The ring of a doorbell had him growl. He gripped Cassandra's wrist when it seemed like she would go answer it, rather than hear him out. "Let it ring."

She glanced between him and the door, torn. The following loud banging was the deciding factor – against him.

"Cass, it's me. I drove your car over."

Cassandra pulled her wrist out of Damon's grasp gently, then said, "Later. Renzo brought me my car from the other night at the club."

She walked to the door, and Damon had no choice but to trail her. He didn't trust the Mafia spawn, and there was no way he planned to leave Cassandra alone with him.

When she opened the door, Lorenzo was leaning against the frame and smiling like a little boy. All Damon wanted to do was punch him, but he settled for clenching and unclenching his fists.

Car keys dangled from the other man's hands. At the look of utter delight on Cassandra's face, Damon kicked himself for not picking it up himself. He did his best to push down his annoyance and instead moved into the light, noticing with some satisfaction that Lorenzo's gaze narrowed on him. The laughter in his eyes died and their conversation stalled.

"What are you doing here?" Lorenzo was scowling now, glancing between them as if trying to figure out the mystery of life.

"Renzo…" Cassandra groaned, looking like she wanted to be anywhere but between the two of them.

"I slept the night," Damon said. Lorenzo's eyes widened in response, this time focusing his attention on Cassandra.

It didn't take a genius to figure out he wasn't happy. But did he have feelings for Cassandra? That, not even Damon could tell. So he did the next best thing and turned the focus on the Mafia kid. "Your turn. What's with the visit?"

Cass made a noise of frustration, practically stomping her foot. "That's it! If you two think I'm going to stand for this, you've got another thing coming. I'm going for a run, and you can have your pissing contest without me."

Before either of the men could move, Cassandra put on her sneakers, kissed Lorenzo's cheek and took off on a sprint.

His reaction time affected, Damon could only stare at her shape getting smaller in the distance until she turned a corner. *I should go after her.*

Before he could, Renzo faced him, levelling his gaze onto Damon's. They assessed each other for a beat, mirror images of arms crossed over their chest and feet spread width apart.

Either this'll end in a fight, or bonding. There's no other feasible option.

Damon was about to voice his thoughts aloud, but Renzo exhaled steadily and stepped inside, beating him to it. "Listen, we started off on the wrong foot. The only thing I have against you is the fact you broke Cassandra's heart once upon a time. Aside from that, you seem like an ok enough guy."

Damon couldn't help his snort. "High praise coming from a mafioso's son."

Lorenzo grinned at that. "Friends call me Renzo."

"And you count me one?"

"No…" Renzo's gaze was speculative. "But I will if you cut the bullshit and tell me what's brought you back into her life."

Damon weighed his options, not really keen on trusting the kid. Then he remembered how his dad had watched out for Cassandra earlier that day. Information from Cassandra's file trickled in his mind on the newly reformed Fabrizio Moretti, and he decided against his original impulse.

"Alright, but you're in for a long–"

Damon trailed off, noticing the car across the street. They hadn't yet closed the door and were both standing in the entrance. Back into a corner across the street was a black vehicle with heavily tinted windows. At first glance a few minutes earlier, he'd thought it empty. But now the front window was rolled down, and a shadow moved within.

A flash of a reflective surface within caught Damon's attention. He turned to Renzo to ask him the same, and noticed the red dot on the side of his head.

"Get down!" Damon tackled him to the ground, then dragged him by the arm into a corner of the living room.

Renzo edged away, eyes wide as they listened to the rapid fire of a sniper's rifle hitting a wall.

"What the hell!?"

Damon threw him a look to keep immobile, then crouched to the couch where his bag was lying. He pulled out a handgun and added a silencer. If someone was willing to take a shot in the middle of the evening, and in a residential neighbourhood, they'd need to be as sly as he was.

| 137

To Damon's surprise, when he turned Renzo was next to him, seemingly over his initial panic. "What do you need from me?"

Damon glanced around, hesitant to put him in danger, but knowing he'd need a diversion if he wanted to take out the threat before Cassandra returned.

An idea formed in his head, and he said, "I need to you take a punch. Can you do that?"

Renzo nodded, and before Damon could give him further instructions, he stepped backwards and stood up again. He was back in the line of fire of the assassin, and Damon knew it only gave him a few moments to act. "Watch yourself, kid."

He took off to the back, exiting through the yard and the side of the house. After hopping a few fences, he ended up on the street behind the car. Damon took a deep breath, recalling his special ops training and keeping each step as light as a feather as he approached the car.

The sniper was too busy firing on his moving target – Renzo was doing a good job playing the rabbit to his hunter. By the time Damon opened the door and shot him in the back of the skull, it was too late.

Blood spattered over the windows and car seats, but it didn't faze Damon. He pocketed his silencer and moved his hands over the body, patting him down and trying to figure out who had sent him. The answer came from the cell call log: Cassandra's dad.

"Shit!"

Damon turned behind at the curse, noticing Renzo's widened gaze. "There were no more bullets, so I figured you got him." He gulped, eyes on the body. "You killed him? How are you going to explain this to the cops?"

"I won't," Damon said and pocketed the car keys. "I'll take care of cleaning this. Can you keep an eye on Cassandra until I come back?"

Renzo met his gaze, concern for the girl they both cared for etched on his face. "You got it. Should I call my dad for reinforcements?"

Much as the offer was appealing, Damon shook his head. "No, and don't tell him about this yet. I'll fill you in when I get back."

With Renzo's help, Damon moved the body into the backseat of the car and covered it with a ragged-looking blanket. Then he got in the driver's seat and started the car.

One foot above the accelerator, Damon hesitated and poked his head out the window. Renzo was walking to Cassandra's house. "Hey, kid."

He turned to face him, his shirt now covered in blood.

"Get changed and wait for Cassandra, and keep your eyes peeled, all right?" Once Renzo nodded, he added, "I know you have no reason to trust me, but I'm going to fix this."

Without waiting for an answer, Damon peeled across the cement, tires squealing and smoke hovering behind.

♥ *Chapter 14* ♥

The second run of the day did what it was meant to: exhaust Cassandra's body. It was with a heaving chest she returned home, eager to drink cool water and hop in the shower. She wondered what she would find, and was only slightly disappointed to see her door closed and no sign of the guys.

She was about to slide her keys in when the door flew open and Renzo pulled her in, his arms wrapping around her. His embrace muffled her cry of shock, and it gave her pause.

When he let her go, she peered up at him. "What's going on?"

Renzo glanced behind her instead and closed the door. Then locked it.

"Ok... Now I'm worried." When Renzo turned to her, Cassandra's eyes widened at the blood on his shirt. She also realized something else. "Where's Damon?" On a breathless chuckle, she added, "Please tell me you didn't kill him."

When Renzo froze, Cassandra's heart dropped in her stomach.

"No, *no*! God, no. Cass, you know me better than that," Renzo hurried to add. "I didn't kill him, he's off... Umm..." The way he paced rather than talk, running his hands through his hair in frustration, clued her in that something happened.

"What's going on?" Cassandra asked.

Renzo stopped mid-step, his mouth opening and closing like a gaping fish. When he finally spoke, his answer was not what she expected.

"Damon saved my life."

♥∞♥

Damon pulled in the warehouse by the marina after triple checking he wasn't followed. It figured that Sean wasn't a genius, but considering his previous interactions with the cop, better to be safe than sorry. It wouldn't do to be found with a dead body in a stolen car.

Not bothering to park properly, Damon jumped out of the car and rapped twice on the door. When no one answered, he pummelled the door with his fist, then waited. Moments later, it opened to reveal one of his teammates.

"Zak." Damon nodded in greeting, then motioned with his head to follow.

A head shorter than him, but twice his weight in bulk alone, Zak moved like a tank. He'd been trained not to be surprised, and obey orders without question. Yet when Damon opened the passenger door and showed him the dead body, he whistled in appreciation.

"Clean kill, D. Someone hit on your girl or something?"

Damon growled. "If only. This was a trained sniper, and he tried to kill Fabrizio Moretti's son. In front of me."

Zak's whistle halted, and he narrowed his eyes. Despite not being a field agent, even he knew that a sanctioned hit was the opposite of good news. "Shit. All right, I'll pull Paco in on it. With all the tech mumbo jumbo, he might find something out."

Damon nodded, then reached in his back pocket and held up the assassin's cell. "See what else Paco can get off this thing. And try to get rid of the car, too. In the meantime, I got someone to see."

"No more dead bodies, I hope." Zak's grin said he

expected the contrary.

In spite of himself, Damon returned it. "I'll try. No promises."

♥∞♥

Damon stared up at the skyscraper Viktor now worked in, whistling appreciatively to himself. *Who said money doesn't buy you nice digs?*

He stepped in and found the receptionist desk. "Hey there," he started, putting on his best charming smile.

It must have worked as the young blonde stopped what she was doing and looked up –really looked up. The minute she stopped ogling his biceps displayed on the top of her desk, she met his eyes. Damon could have sworn her pulse fluttered, or perhaps it was his imagination.

If only Cass would... He bit back a sigh, trying to stay in role. *Focus.*

"Would Mr. Beauchamp be available?"

The receptionist blinked a few times, then seemed to snap her out of her daze. "I, um, am not supposed to be giving out that information."

Damon's smile froze, and she jumped in response to his shift of personality. He willed himself to cool off, before he scared his only chance to get in. "Would you please make an exception? I've known him since I was young and am only in town for a few hours. I would love to buy him a drink."

The receptionist gulped, then nodded slowly. "Well... I'm sure he won't mind, if he knows you?"

The last bit came out as a question, and Damon grinned as he nodded. "Oh, he does. Most definitely."

"Ok, well, let me check." She took a second to look

through Viktor's calendar, then nodded. "It seems he's having lunch in the lobby restaurant. Would you like me to show you where it is?"

"I can find my way," Damon replied, grinning to soften the blow when she pouted.

Aromas of a well-priced menu assailed him as he strode off towards the spot. The bar was on his way and he paused by to place an order for takeout. Following the adrenaline pumping in his veins and the close call with death, he was starved enough to eat a horse. Plus, he was probably not the only one who needed sustenance.

Damon wondered if he should have told Renzo not to breathe a word of their little misadventure to Cassandra. *Nah,* he decided. *We have enough space between us as it is and don't need more secrets.*

Movement out of the corner of his eye drew his attention to the pudgy man sitting in a chair by the window, overlooking the water. Whoever he'd been speaking to got up and left in a fuss, so Damon took his chance and walked over.

"Bad business deal gone sour?" His opening line lacked subtlety, but it got the reaction he expected. He towered over the table, blocking the only way out.

Viktor stopped with the fork halfway to his mouth, and his eyes nearly popped out of their sockets.

"You!" he sputtered, almost too loud.

Damon dropped in the chair next to him and discreetly placed his gun under the tablecloth. "Me indeed, Viktor. Now be a good buddy and behave, I have a few questions."

He nodded towards the gun, and Viktor gulped, sweat

building on his brow even as his cheeks reddened. Damon's gaze shifted to the plate, and the unfinished steak now cooling off.

"You should be more careful with what you eat, Vic." A dry chuckle, then he dug the gun into Viktor's knee. "I'm in town because you've gotten involved into some shady dealings with some terrible people. Old habits die hard, and I know from past encounters that you have no trouble getting your hands dirty. So, what's the deal this time?"

"What do you care?" Viktor tossed, a failed attempt at bravery – or plain stupidity.

Damon nudged the tip of the gun deeper into his knee. Viktor jumped in his chair, nearly falling backwards in an attempt to get away. "Don't piss me off, Viktor." His threat was delivered in the coolest tone, and the man shuddered. "When you forced me away ten years ago, you must have known I would come back."

The man glared at Damon, disgust etched on each line of his weathered face. "I should have put you back in jail where you belonged when I had the chance."

"With *lies*," Damon leaned forward, his expression darkening. "Don't forget that. Meanwhile, what I have on you will put you in jail with the truth. So cut the bullshit and tell me how deep in you are."

Viktor gulped, breaking eye contact. "Deep."

"Is Cass in danger?"

Viktor met his gaze again, almost as if attempting to figure out his play. A slow grin appeared. "You still have a soft spot for her."

Damon gritted his teeth and strongly fought the impulse

to shoot him and be done with it.

"Answer me."

"Maybe she is, and maybe she isn't."

Stupid man.

Memories of what Viktor had done, of his shameful departure, crossed in his mind as vivid as if they had happened the day before. A steady wave of anger built inside him, and Damon's hand clenched over his gun.

He wanted nothing more than to shoot the bastard and save Cassandra from his influence. At the thought of what Viktor had put her through, with all his manipulations and control-freak behaviour, keeping a lid on the rage became almost impossible.

Still, Damon forced himself to. He dug deep in his military training, slowing his breath until every cell in his body was attuned to the other. A quick glance around confirmed two security guards patrolled the area.

No matter what he wanted to do with Viktor, if he attracted their attention, it would be all too easy to set him up. And while Derek might have had some leeway with the border cops, he doubted the same applied to the local cops.

Damon leaned an inch closer, his mouth close to Viktor's ear. With his free hand, he wrapped an arm around the pudgy bastard, pressing into his shoulder.

"I'll say this once, so take heed. Clean up your shit and stop sending snipers. Else I'll make an anonymous tip to Moretti. The guy may be retired, but how do you think he would react if his own son was in danger?"

All color drained from Viktor's face at Damon's words, delivered in an icy tone. Without waiting for the rest, Damon got to his feet, placing his back to the security guards.

"You think you can–"

Viktor should have shut up while he had the chance. Swifter than any observing eyes, Damon's hand shot out and grabbed him right between the shoulder and the neck. To an outsider, it would appear as though he was giving him a clap on the back. Instead, he was hitting a pressure point that had the man roll his eyes to the back of his head.

By the time Damon reached the bar to grab his takeout, Viktor was passed out in his chair. It was less than the bastard deserved, but far better than what Damon truly intended to do to him.

At least it'll be enough to put fear in the spineless prick.

Cassandra knew staring with her jaw open was unladylike, but she was past caring. After a few moments of incredulous sputtering, she formed a coherent sentence. "How, exactly?"

Renzo shifted from foot to foot, finally motioning for her to follow him. She walked into her living room, not noticing anything out of the ordinary. Until Renzo pointed to the wall.

"Are those… bullets… in my *wall*?" Her voice broke on the last word, and she stared at her friend, expecting him to deny it.

Instead, Renzo nodded – then the story came out in a rush. How they'd been talking, him and Damon, when Damon tackled him before he was shot. How he then went to take care of the shooter and disappeared with his body.

By the end of the tale, Cassandra moved to the couch, her knees wobbly. Her mind could not grasp exactly what was going on, but she also couldn't get past the daze of one thought: *Damon killed someone.*

It kept going on a loop in her head, shattering any and all illusions she might have had of him. *Who did I really let into my house?*

With a huge effort of will, Cassandra pushed away the judging idea. Damon had wanted to tell her more, but they'd been interrupted before. On some subconscious level, she might have been doing avoiding the reality without realizing it, afraid of what she would hear.

"Cass?"

Cassandra glanced back up at Renzo, chewing on her bottom lip. "I don't know what to say. I'm glad you're alive, obviously. But, shit! Renzo, who would want to kill you? And why?"

He shook his head, at a loss. "Hell if I know, but I need a drink. Do you have anything strong?"

Cassandra nodded and pointed to the fridge. "Vodka in the bottom shelf of the fridge."

He left her in the room, but she could not sit still any longer. She moved about, pacing as she listened to the sounds of the fridge opening and closing, then a bottle being uncapped.

Aikido had taught Cassandra awareness, and she'd never quite snapped out of old habits, though she no longer practiced the martial art with as much dedication as before. In the wake of Renzo's revelations, she reverted to breathing exercises, each meant to calm her and increase her awareness all at once.

Those teachings saved her life. There was a brief noise, impossible to describe. Cassandra's first instinct was to yell for

Renzo, but after what he'd told her, she stayed silent.

Her senses, sharpened by years of martial arts training, were telling her to make herself invisible, and she gave in. She took off her sneakers and moved on tiptoes to the door.

From her new viewpoint, Cassandra had a clear view to the open concept kitchen. She couldn't locate Renzo, at first… Then she stifled a gasp when her eyes fell on Renzo's feet, stretched past her island.

"Don't move."

♥ *Chapter 15* ♥

Damon swore under his breath, hitting the steering wheel with his fists as his eyes took in the never-ending throng of cars piled on the highway. He'd been stalled, advancing with the speed of a snail for the past twenty minutes, and his patience was wearing thin.

He hadn't meant to be gone from Cassandra and Lorenzo for so long, but it seemed time was not on his side. Not taking his gaze off the road, he reached for his phone and hit a button. The wireless connection in the car rang twice, then Paco answered.

"Yeah, boss?"

"Kid, I'm stuck on the freaking highway, and I need to get back to Cassandra's. Can you pull up some back road options?"

"Sure thing." The clicking of a keyboard filled the silence, then Paco said, "I can see your GPS tracker. Get off at the next exit, then turn right onto the boulevard. If you keep going straight, it should bring you to Cassandra's neighbourhood."

"Thanks." Damon switched lanes and took the exit, then said, "Did Zak fill you in?"

Paco didn't even pause. "Yes sir, and no updates yet. I'm trying to crack your dead guy's identity, but it's as if he was reborn a year ago."

Damon's eyes narrowed on the road. "That's no good. Did Zak dispose of the body?"

"And the car. As for the guy, don't worry, I'll keep digging."

Curses escaped Damon, but he regained composure. It wasn't Paco's fault that his impatience had skyrocketed in the last minutes and he wanted results – yesterday. "Do your best, kid. I need to nail the people behind this, and fast."

"You got it, boss." A hesitation followed, and Damon picked up on it.

"What is it?"

"It might be nothing…"

"Spit it out."

"Okay, well you know how you said this guy was a sniper?"

Damon thought back to what he'd observed in the car. "Yeah, he was trying to shoot at Renzo with a rifle only made for the military."

"Well, that's the thing: there's *no* record of this guy in the military. I tried the Navy, Marines, freaking SEALs – or what I got off their files. Nada."

Damon grunted impatiently, and Paco got back on point. "What I mean is he doesn't seem the type. His muscle mass was less than impressive, and I may be no doctor, but I lifted one of his eyes and it looks like it's damaged."

"How would you even know that?"

"Before I got drafted into this hacking business, I was studying for med school."

Damon's jaw dropped. "Would've been nice to find that out firsthand, but good on you. So maybe the dead guy was aiming with his other eye."

"All due respect, boss… I doubt it. He had arthritis in one hand, early onset. He could only shoot with one hand."

Damon was struck dumb this time. "You're telling me

there is no way he could've made that headshot?"

"Exactly."

The car ahead of him hesitated in moving when there was space, and he hit the horn. "Damn drivers," Damon growled. "Move already!"

Damon's agitation increased with the news. If he had misjudged the scene, and the threat… The only thing that made sense was how *little* sense everything made. And yet, he needed a second opinion.

"Put Zak on speaker."

There was shuffling, then both men were on the line. "Yeah, D?"

"Did you hear what Paco was telling me?" Damon asked.

"Yup."

"And?" Zak was a man of few words, and sometimes it was like pulling teeth.

"I think the kid's right. Someone wanted you to think this guy was pulling the shots, but it wasn't him."

"But the shots came from his rifle, Zak," Damon pressed, undaunted. "How would that be possible?"

"Hold on."

Static entered the line for a second, followed by the noise of a murmured conversation, then an appreciative whistle.

"Holy shit!" Paco whispered, shock coating his voice.

"Guys!"

Damon's impatience must have gotten through even over the bad connection as Zak returned on the line.

"You're not going to believe this, D."

Somehow, I doubt that.

"The gun's automated. Remote-controlled. It could have been operated from a distance, and this guy was set up to be a pawn."

Damon hit the brakes furiously, ignoring the alarmed honking behind his car. His encounter with Wraith, Viktor, and the attack on Renzo all sped through his mind. Pieces fit together like a puzzle, and others were left on sidelines.

Was it really Viktor who had hired Wraith?

If yes, that could only mean he was done with Cassandra, for good. Which begged another question – where had the slime ball gone after calling her?

If the shooter was a puppet, someone was pulling his strings, which means…

"Fuck. It was a set up!"

There was only silence on the other end of the line as his team absorbed the news. Then movement confirmed they were on the move. Though he guessed what they were doing, Damon still said, "Zak, Paco, get the hell out of there. Blow everything and haul ass to a safe location. Whoever is behind this did it for one of two reasons. Either to have me reveal my team, or to get to Cassandra while she's unguarded."

A pause for a moment, then Zak came on, "We're out of here, activating explosives as ordered. No civilians around, the base is secure. We're gone, D. Text you the new location."

"No. Wait for my call."

Paco was next, breathing heavily as though having run. "Boss, I checked the cameras from Cassandra's street one more time before destroying everything. You better hurry, your girl may have trouble on her hands."

Damon threw the phone to the ground and hit the gas –
hard. He checked his rear-view mirror once, but there was no
cop in sight. *Sean better stay out of my fucking way right now.*
He couldn't be sure he was still being tailed, but he wouldn't
have put it past the guy.

Gunning the engine harder, Damon's hands clenched the
steering wheel. He had only one priority, and it was Cassandra's
safety.

♥∞♥

The voice behind her was deep, almost superficially so,
as if modified by some device. And he was male, judging by the
faint spice of his cologne. Cassandra's every muscle froze, but
still she focused on Renzo's immobile form.

"What did you do to him?" she asked, trying to gain
time. To show her good faith, she kept both hands up, palms
facing away from him.

"He will survive."

"Then let me check on him." Cassandra's plea fell on
deaf ears, and she knew it was the wrong thing to say the
moment she sensed movement behind.

The intruder shoved her against the wall, and it was only
her flattened palms that saved her a bruise on her face. Still, he
moved in closer, his breath on her neck. "Don't do
anything stupid."

His hands moved over her almost surgically, patting her
down to make sure she had no weapons.

"You do realize it's hard to hide a weapon in this
outfit?" Cassandra was well aware of the shorts and tank top she
was wearing, which didn't offer much coverage. *I'll be
damned if I let this bastard intimidate me.*

The man chuckled low, and the hairs on her neck rose. "Oh, I know. But why deprive me of the pleasure?"

His hands slid over Cassandra's front, this time no longer surgical. He passed over her breasts, lingering briefly. When he reached the end of her shirt, he moved to her back and patted from one foot up her leg. His hands reached close to the apex of her thighs, and Cassandra saw red.

With her free foot, she angled and kicked behind. Her heel connected with something, and without the sneakers the impact was lesser than she'd hoped – but it was something.

Cassandra whirled around without pause and, palm angled, hit towards the intruder's nose. Or rather, what she thought was his nose. Her first face-to-face look at him revealed a ski mask covered any features. A satisfying crunch resounded, and he staggered behind.

"Son of a bitch!" Cassandra's shout echoed in the house, but she was beyond mad. "You treat all women this way? Cause unless you're missing my cue here, you decided to rob the wrong damn house, buddy."

It was all rhetorical, not that Cassandra intended to wait for a response. Since he was still cursing under his breath and holding his nose, it gave her free rein to act. She moved in closer and lifted her right elbow, digging into his collarbone. Her knee was next, straight into his crown jewels, and he dropped to the ground.

"Who sent you?" Her breathing came out in short pants, but she kept her fists clenched just in case.

The man muttered something, but she didn't catch it. Cassandra leaned forward, ready to repeat her question, but he lunged upwards and slammed her into the wall. Pure hatred burned in his dark eyes when they connected with hers. His hand was on her neck, but before he got a grip, Cassandra ducked under and punched him in the solar plexus.

There was an inhale of breath, then a muttered curse in some Slavic language. Cassandra moved out of his way and got her hands on a statue from the side-table.

She turned around and threw it at the intruder, catching him in the shoulder. He moved away, and she could have sworn feeling his glare across the distance. A groan from the kitchen made her itch to go by Renzo's side.

The man looked past her to the kitchen, as if guessing her thoughts. For a scary moment, she thought he would go finish her friend off.

Instead, tires hitting the gravel and Damon's voice yelling her name seemed to have the desired effect. With a mocking salute, the attacker took off for the back door and disappeared.

By the time Damon walked in, Cassandra was in the kitchen by Renzo's side. "Help me, he got hit on the head!" She tried to grab Renzo's head in her hand, but found herself barely supported by her own muscles.

"Cass..." Damon's soft voice got through and a beat later he was there, caressing her cheek, eyes filled with worry.

His gaze moved upwards and his hand came away with blood on it. It was the last thing Cassandra saw before everything went black.

♥ *Chapter 16* ♥

Damon caught Cassandra before she passed out and picked her up bridal style, then carried her to the sofa in the living room. Movement in the kitchen drew his attention away from her, only to see Lorenzo struggle to stand.

Though he knew he should be checking on the younger man, Damon's entire focus was on Cassandra. Once he'd located her first aid kit in the powder room, he cleaned her wound and checked her for a concussion.

Luckily for Cassandra, she seemed to be well – for the most part. Bruises on her light skin had him clench his jaw, cursing all hells for not being there for her.

If this was Wraith or Viktor's doing, they'll pay like they've never paid in their lives.

A groan in the kitchen distracted him. With a last check on Cassandra, Damon moved to the island. Lorenzo held a pack of frozen peas to the back of his head, and nursed a glass of vodka with his free hand.

When Damon moved closer, Renzo looked up. "That mother*fucker*! What happened?"

"You tell me." Damon glanced outside in the backyard, but noticed no one lurking nearby. He moved back to the counter and poured himself a shot, downed it and followed up with another. "Cassandra said you got hit by an intruder?"

At his prompt, Renzo frowned. He paused in rubbing his head, trying to remember. "Some dude in a ski mask. I was getting vodka from the fridge, trying to figure out with Cass why someone would try to shoot at me. He blindsided me when I came in here."

"So he was already in the house?"

Renzo paused with the vodka glass halfway to his mouth, and grimaced. "Honestly, I don't know. After you took off, I never left, just waited for Cass to return from her jog. When she did, I was at the front door for a bit. He could have snuck through the patio backdoor."

Damon moved to the door, sliding it open and checking the lock for signs of tampering. At first glance, nothing seemed out of the ordinary. He would have missed the silver reflection, if not for a trick of the light that illuminated the aluminum stuck in the hole.

After fumbling for a bit, he managed to dig the aluminum out and showed it to Renzo. "Someone was waiting for you guys, and he took measures to make sure he'd be able to get in." Almost to himself, he added, "He must've been casing this place for a while."

"Wanting what, exactly? Is this some random robbery or something else entirely?"

Damon met Renzo's gaze over the kitchen island, and tried to figure out a way to tell him the truth, without actually mentioning who Wraith was. The last thing he needed was Fabrizio Moretti out sabotaging the entire operation for the sake of revenge.

"I wouldn't say *random*, especially considering someone tried to kill you a few hours ago." Renzo paled at the reminder, and Damon pushed the shot glass closer to him, waiting until he'd drank before continuing. "It's all my fault. That shooter, the sniper, he was a pawn. A decoy. Meant to draw me away, and I fell right in it."

"Wouldn't you say it's my fault, considering it seems to

be someone who's after me?" Renzo's head was bowed, and something about his countenance struck Damon as extremely vulnerable. He had to remember the kid was only half a year younger than Cassandra, but in that moment he seemed much more.

"No." He tapped the table to get Renzo's attention, then said, "Because whoever is after you isn't doing so for *you*. It's all tied to Cassandra."

"What makes you say that?"

Damon opened his mouth to tell him everything, then closed it. "Call it a hunch." He sipped the last of his vodka shot, then locked the patio door and crossed the kitchen towards the living room.

Renzo's voice stopped him mid-way. "How's Cass?"

"Looks like she fought him well, but she's injured." At the reminder, Renzo rubbed the back of his head again and winced. Damon moved closer once more. "Let me check your head."

Before he could protest, Damon moved his hand out of the way and checked through the strands of brown hair. There was no blood residue, not even a cut, but upon closer inspection he could feel a bump growing.

"What did he hit you with?"

"The vodka bottle." A wry chuckle escaped Renzo when he pointed to the still-intact bottle.

"Well, either you have a very hard head, or that's a very strong bottle. But you're good. If you get any dizziness, go to a doctor or something. This is the extent of my first aid knowledge."

Renzo rolled his eyes. "Sure, I will."

Damon moved back into the living room where Cassandra was fast asleep. He crouched by her pale and bruised form, clenching his fists. *I could have avoided all of this, if only I hadn't fallen for Wraith's games.*

There was no doubt in his mind the assassin was behind both the attack on Renzo and this latest intrusion. Only someone of his calibre could have disarmed the alarms he'd set up in the house and rearm them without leaving a single trace.

Damon recalled Derek's warning words, of keeping his head in the game. *Look how well that turned out.*

A stomach's growl pulled Damon out of his thoughts, and he glanced up at Renzo. The younger man was still holding the peas to the back of his head, and he shrugged. "What? I'm hungry."

Damon snorted with laughter, then tossed him his car keys, recalling the takeout from Viktor's restaurant. "There's food in my car, back seat. Grab whatever."

Renzo nodded and took off, returning only minutes later with the bags and displaying them in the kitchen. Damon didn't budge from his spot, all thoughts of hunger forgotten. He pulled a chaise by the sofa and stretched out his legs, pulling the gun out of the waistband of his jeans.

From his vantage point, he had a view of the front door, the patio and Cassandra's sleeping form. *Come try something now, Wraith. I fucking dare you.*

♥∞♥

Cassandra's return to consciousness proved to be difficult, as expected of someone who'd hit the wall head-first, then still tried to be a heroine.

Her head pounded, and an ache spread through her

bones with dogged determination. The image of her masked attacker burst into her mind, jolting the remainder of her groggy self. She would find this man and get answers. *Eventually.*

Though her eyes were closed, she could sense someone was in the room with her. Damon's voice somehow got to her fuzzy brain, flickering in and out as if through a bad connection. And was it her imagination, or did he sound worried out of his mind?

"Renzo, I'm telling you, I have to take her to a hospital!" The shout had Cassandra wince, but her eyes were too heavy to open.

Some of the conversation cut off, and Damon must've missed her wince, as he next said, "I don't care if she hates hospitals! I'm not about to lose her because of her stubbornness!"

Instead of taking offense at his take-charge attitude, Cassandra let out a faint chuckle. She regretted it when the vibration increased the pressure in her head, feeling like it would explode.

Damon moved closer, still seemingly unaware of her awake state. He lifted Cassandra off the surface she'd been previously on, and his arms held her close. She would've enjoyed the sensation, if not for the nausea engulfing her and the sudden roll of her stomach.

A few deep breaths later, Cassandra had a lid on it and was able to speak. "Damon," her voice was strained as she whispered, "please, whatever you do, don't move me, and don't yell."

Cassandra continued to inhale deeply, aware of the sound of a cell phone being shut off. They moved in the house,

Damon's hold on her still tight. A few seconds later, a ring started off somewhere in the house, and a weak groan escaped her.

"Shh, it's ok. I'll take care of it."

At the strained sound of his voice, Cassandra forced her eyes open, worried she was too heavy for him. But what greeted her was not an expression of exertion, rather of pain. Guilt filled Damon's sharp green gaze, as well as contained anger. His mouth was downturned, and he was frowning hard enough to give himself wrinkles.

"Damon..." Cassandra trailed off, at a loss on how to continue.

He shoved his shoulder against a door, then entered a familiar room. Next thing she knew, Damon set her down on her bed. He fumbled with her pillow and blanket, avoiding her gaze. When she was finally settled in, he had no choice but to look at her.

"I..." Damon cleared his throat, then stood. "I'll be back. Please don't move, okay?"

Cassandra nodded, unable to do anything else but stare at him in amazement as he left the room.

She settled for turning her head from one side to the other, taking in her surroundings. Damon had brought her up to her room, and she was grateful for the familiar bed. Murmurs from downstairs brought up faint echoes of another male voice – Renzo's.

Satisfied she knew her location, Cassandra closed her eyes, letting the whispers of their conversation lull her to sleep.

♥∞♥

"Cass?"

A soft voice by her ear was insisting she wake up, and no matter which way Cassandra moved her head, it wouldn't let go. She groaned as the pain between her temples returned, stronger than before.

Cassandra opened her mouth to say something, to stop the torture, but all that came out was a whimper. Sharp, insistent bursts of lightning flashed behind her closed eyelids, and no amount of willing them away helped.

"I know it hurts," the same voice said. "It'll be fine. Open your eyes, Cass. I have something for the pain."

Almost afraid to do so, Cassandra listened and found Damon's gentle green eyes – for all of two seconds. The overhead light became agonizing and she held up a hand to block it, then rolled over and covered her head with a pillow.

"Shit." Damon moved around the room and she heard a click. "It's okay, I turned the light off. Wake up, love."

When Cassandra didn't move, he pulled the pillow off her head little by little. She blinked at him, and it took her a few seconds in the darkness to locate him. Once she did, she noticed his extended hands. One held a glass of water, the other two pills.

Without questioning, she swallowed the pills. Exhausted by the simple movement, Cassandra let her head fall back on the pillow, and shut her eyes again.

"I swear, when I get my hands on that guy, I'll bloody kill him!" It was Damon again, but all softness had vanished from his voice, replaced by pure anger.

"Would you calm down?" Cassandra wasn't surprised to hear Renzo. "Seriously, Damon, you've been like this since you found her. Relax, all right? We'll find the guy. But we have to make sure Cass is okay."

As if to prove his point, Renzo moved closer, speaking gently. "Cass, how are you feeling?"

Cassandra blinked again, noticing he'd changed his clothes to some sweatpants and a t-shirt. He looked so different from his regular self, that she arched an eyebrow. "Change of style?"

Renzo chuckled, then perched himself on the edge of her bed. "Funny. I just figured I'd better be comfortable for the next few hours, is all."

He paused, glancing at Damon who was leaning against the wall. His arms were folded over his chest and his eyes shifted from the bed to the window, scanning the outside. "We good?"

Damon nodded, and Renzo focused his attention back on Cassandra. "Seriously, how are you?"

She gave herself a mental once-over, trying to figure out how the fight with the intruder had injured her. Little by little, Cassandra tried to move each muscle. Her right shoulder was in pain, but it was diminishing as the pills kicked in. Her head wasn't pounding anymore, although more painkillers would be needed later as the effects of the first ones wore off. Though her right cheek stung a little, she felt capable enough to stand up.

Feeling the guys' gazes on her, Cassandra cleared her throat. "I'm great. Just… great." She grimaced and despite their dubious looks, sat upright in the bed.

She noticed Damon's disapproval first. He was quick to voice it out loud, too. "Cass, I don't think you should try anything right now. Maybe you should just lie down and sleep."

He's only trying to help.

Cassandra tried to get her brain on board, but his authoritative tone was enough to set off her hackles. "Damon, I'd rather you don't tell me what I should be doing. I'm an adult, remember?"

Rather than argue with her, Damon dragged his eyes away and seemed to step farther into the wall. Cassandra frowned, noticing his bleak expression and something akin to regret and guilt flash before he turned his head away.

She turned to Renzo, asking with her eyes what was going on. He shrugged, then cleared his throat. "We're both really sorry this happened...when we should have been able to protect you." *Especially Damon.*

The words were left unsaid, but Renzo's meaningful look completed the sentence. Cassandra glanced back at her ex-boyfriend. *How could he think this is his fault, when he's done nothing but try to keep me safe since he got back here? Maybe if I'd listened instead of fighting him on everything...*

Oddly, the fact he was taking the attack so hard served to open Cassandra's eyes. No matter what she'd accused Damon of, he cared enough to be there when it mattered. And if he hadn't shown up when he did, who knew what would have happened?

Something built in her chest, causing her throat to tighten. Cassandra fought back tears, eyes glued to Damon. "Renzo, give us a minute, please."

He nodded and stood, then kissed her cheek before retreating from the room. Cassandra waited until she heard his footsteps fading down the stairs before speaking.

"Are you keeping an eye out in case someone else tries to shoot down the house?"

Damon started at her words, and grudgingly turned to Cassandra. "Maybe." He frowned when he realized she was trying to get out of bed. "Please don't. Stay in bed, for your own sake."

She lifted her gaze to his and smiled. "I will, if you join me."

Surprise flashed in Damon's eyes, but it didn't stop him from moving closer. He sat on the edge of the bed, back ramrod straight. Cassandra moved her hand closer to his, their fingertips barely touching.

Damon stared down at their hands for a long moment. His voice, when he spoke, was roughened by emotion. "Cass, I'm so sorry…"

"For what?" When he didn't answer, she decided for another approach. "Damon, this wasn't your fault."

He met her gaze then, jaw clenched and eyes narrowed. "You don't know that. This was meant as a warning – to me."

"That may be true. But had I listened to you more since you returned, this could have been avoided. I should be the one apologizing – and I *am* sorry." Cassandra paused in her well thought-out speech, reading Damon's expression and realizing she wasn't getting through to him. *Guess I should humour him.* "Fine. Explain what you mean, I'm listening."

"Renzo told you he was shot at. But the guy was a pawn. The real guy hired to get you is behind this, and I made it so damn easy for him to get in here."

Someone's really after me? It wasn't the first time Damon had mentioned the possibility, but she'd thought it was a tale designed to keep her dependent on him. Unfortunately, everything about the last few attacks screamed reality.

| 165

"So who is he?"

"A psycho," Damon said. "Hired by a madman."

There was something else, a bitterness behind the statement that eluded Cassandra. In her current state of mind, and with the headache looming, she stuck to the easy questions. "What happened to the body? Renzo said you… killed him."

Something must have tinged her voice because Damon narrowed his eyes. "I *have* killed people before this, Cass. You must know that."

"I do, I just…" Cassandra reached further, placing her hand above Damon's and intertwining their fingers. "It's hard believing it, even though I see all… this."

Damon's eyes glittered at her comment, and the way she gestured to encompass everything about him. "And you like what you *do* see?"

Cassandra's mouth dried when he leaned in closer, and all thoughts flew from her head. She could only stare at him, even as he bent his head and touched his lips to hers, ever so gently. The tenderness was so at odds with the restrained passion in his eyes that any idea of resistance evaporated.

Cassandra melted against him, kissing Damon back and wrapping her arms around his neck. He moved closer still, his torso hovering just above hers. His biceps were corded as he held himself off her, refusing to crush her.

After the briefest seconds of kissing, Damon pulled away. Conflict was etched on his expression, and he opened his mouth to speak. Before he could say a word, Cassandra held up her index finger to his lips.

"Hear me out, please. Aside from this very amazing kiss that I wouldn't have allowed yesterday, you need to understand one thing. Nothing of what happened was your fault, and I don't blame you for it." Cassandra hesitated, but the words were too heavy on her tongue to be left unsaid. "There may be other things I fault you for, but not for this."

Damon sighed and pulled off her, allowing distance between them. Cassandra reached out for his hand again, sighing when he allowed the touch. "I don't know what just happened and honestly I could say it's because I don't have full control of my faculties right now. But the truth is, we've been dancing around this since you came back, haven't we?"

Damon nodded, "Yeah, we have. So where does that leave us?"

"I have no idea. But right now, I need you to understand that you shouldn't be blaming yourself for something that was out of your control."

The slight smile disappeared off his face. "Was it? If I hadn't left, I could have stopped that guy from ever hurting you."

"No."

Her denial was strong as her voice. "You would have gotten hurt somewhere along the way, and I don't want that. I'm through having people bleed in order to save me, Damon. I've lost enough already. You should remember that, if nothing else, from our time together."

Damon's eyes darkened to an obscure green. "I remember everything of our time together, Cass. *Everything*. I was a fool to leave, and I know it wasn't simple for you afterwards."

Cassandra's throat constricted, and words wouldn't get past. A lone tear slipped her control and she wiped it with her free hand. Damon's gaze was unwavering from her.

"I'm *sorry*, Cass. I never intended to hurt you. And I'm sorry for having walked out back then, when I should have stayed to protect you."

Cassandra shut her eyes for a few seconds, then opened them and smiled. Damon's eyes reflected wariness. She raised her free hand and allowed herself to caress his cheek for just a split second. "Damon… There's nothing to forgive."

The Earth could have split open right then, and neither of them would have noticed it. Cassandra was only aware of their touching hands, her breathing changing, and the fast-beating of her heart.

"Oh, yes, there is, Cass," Damon said, breaking the spell. "So many things I have to apologize for… And I'll spend years trying to make up for them."

Cassandra frowned at the determined tone in his voice, not knowing what to make of it. "Does this mean you're staying?"

Damon's arms pulled her closer and he whispered in her hair, "It means I'm staying. And telling you everything – the full story – as soon as you feel well enough to hear it all. It's not for the faint of heart."

Sparks flamed in her chest, but Cassandra willed them away. Yes, she was happy in that moment, more at peace than she had been in a while. And Damon's arms around her felt a little too right…. But none of that meant things were truly all right between them, at least not while they still had secrets.

Before she could ruin her own mood, Renzo came knocking on the door. "Um, Cass? There's an Alain on the phone for you…."

Damon's arms let go at Renzo's announcement, and Cassandra pulled out of his embrace. He stood and moved to the door as if to leave, but hovered around instead. The tension was back in his countenance, and before she could ask about it, her friend cleared his throat.

"Cass…" Renzo's voice was urgent as he held out the phone.

With a small shrug, she took the phone out of his hands and leaned back against the headboard. She glanced from Damon to Renzo, arching an eyebrow. "If you'll excuse me?"

Renzo shrugged and left again, but Damon refused to budge. He stood in the door, leaning against it, following her every movement with hooded eyes.

Cassandra held the phone to her ear, biting back a sigh. "*Alain*. To what do I owe this wonderful surprise?"

♥ *Chapter 17* ♥

Damon could taste metal on the inside of his cheek from the force he was applying to his molars. He eased up somewhat on grinding his teeth, though his blood boiled hotter with each second Cassandra spent on the phone with Alain – *Wraith*.

For the first time since knowing Derek, he wanted to disobey orders. Go against the grain and keep his woman safe, at any cost.

His phone rang as though the devil himself read his thoughts. Damon glanced at the caller ID, and it was Derek. He met Cassandra's intrigued gaze, and moved into the hallway.

"Yeah?" His tone was harsh, uncaring of social etiquette.

"Still miffed I told you to keep your precious in the dark?" Derek chuckled, then said, "Watch yourself, Damon. For better or worse, I made you who you are. You owe me at least a semblance of respect, no matter how much you'd like to disagree with my orders."

Damon sighed, knowing full well his former boss was correct. "Sorry, Derek. This whole thing has me on edge, and Wraith keeps playing games." He softened his tone and said, "What is it?"

"I was calling in to check on you and the team. Amy's worried, rang me to say the safe house exploded and they received no word since. She couldn't reach you directly, as per your express orders."

Damon stepped down the stairs, and after ensuring Renzo was out of earshot, said, "I told Zak and Paco to take off, go underground and wait for me to reach out. It's a temporary situation until I make sure I'm no longer being played."

"Played? By whom, exactly?"

"Wraith." Damon passed by the windows, throwing a quick glance over the yard to ensure no one was lurking in the shadows. Satisfied, he lowered his voice. "That bastard tried to get Lorenzo Moretti shot."

Derek was silent for a moment. "What makes you think it was him?"

After Damon related Paco's findings and Zak's assessment, he added, "Also, Cassandra was attacked while I was on this wild goose chase. Well, her and Renzo."

"And you believe Wraith is after the Mafia man's son to cause a distraction, and perhaps even credit you with his death?" Derek's voice had shifted from the polite to the business tone Damon knew and appreciated. In that moment, he counted his lucky stars for having someone who understood the world he lived in.

"Yeah, I'd bet my hand on it. To top it off, I got the cops on my tail."

Derek made a brief sound of impatience. "Let them chase their *own* tails, for now. You made the right call for your team. What of Cassandra?"

"What about her?"

"How is she faring with everything?"

"As well as she can, I suppose." Damon ran a hand over his face, trying to wipe sleep from his eyes. "She's on the phone with Alain." He rested his head on the couch next, weary of the day's events and what was to come.

"Alain?" The confusion in Derek's tone reminded Damon his boss didn't know everything.

"That's the current alias Wraith uses with Cassandra, but I heard him use Anton before."

"Yes, as far as old research goes, it was his real middle name. I suppose even monsters keep something from their past life." Derek was silent again, then said, "What last name is he using for this alias?"

"Valois. Why?"

There was a swift intake of breath, and Damon stood straight, his fatigue forgotten. "Derek?"

"The file you have on Cassandra. Can you recall what you read, about her parents?"

"That they died in an accident, a stupid high-speed chase by the press. She was in the back seat."

Damon could imagine Derek nodding, so he waited. He didn't have to for long. "The police report investigated one journalist they caught. He was said to be working for some local paper –Alain Valois."

Damon's gut churned. "And let me guess, the paper had no record of such a stellar employee."

"None," Derek confirmed. "When the team dug it up, I thought it an anomaly, but only that. Perhaps it was an independent contractor, selling his stories to the highest bidder. But if Anton is using this same name, it cannot be a coincidence."

"Nothing is a coincidence with that guy." Damon sighed, running a hand over his face. "I fought him, Derek. I could read him as easily as you can read me. He's evil to the core, and worse, he *likes* it. I'm sure he was Cass' attacker earlier."

"Then you must be careful, Damon. If he is as cold-hearted a bastard as you say, then he needs to be caught. Perhaps investigating further on this would be worth it."

"You got it, chief." A resounding beep in his ear alerted Damon to another call. "I have to go, got another incoming call."

"Be safe."

Damon hung up with Derek and stood, pacing about the living room. He hit another key and answered the waiting call.

"Boss!"

"Paco?" Damon frowned, stopping in his tracks. "I told you guys not to contact me until I reach out first."

"Heard you loud and clear boss, but there's trouble afoot. I looked more into the dead guy's background and found ties to an old branch of the Albanian mob. When I dug deeper, it turns out they've re-established operations under different shell corporations in North America."

"What operations?"

"Drugs, gambling… women." The last was a hush, and Damon knew what he was getting at. Human trafficking was too much of a plague these days, one his group could only lend a helping hand in eradicating.

"What about this guy?"

"Until a week ago, he was on their pay as some kind of bouncer at one of their clubs. Then he was offered better money."

Damon's thoughts whirled around. If he was as shady as Paco had discovered, could there be a link between him and Viktor? Wraith wouldn't be caught dead in the spot, it would be like leaving a neon trail to follow. Viktor was not as cunning.

"What's the location?"

"Désirs Noirs," he answered. *Dark desires. Figures.*

"Hack into the security cameras, anything in the area. Try to find me shots of Viktor Beauchamp going in and out, how long he stayed, anything."

"You got it, boss."

"And, Paco? Thanks for keeping me up to date. You guys stay safe."

Damon hung up, sighing as dropped his head in his hands. The situation was getting worse by the minute, and if he didn't tell Cassandra soon....

"Who's Paco?"

Damon started and turned around. Only a few feet away, Cassandra was watching him, with Renzo in the background. *How much did they hear?*

♥∞♥

One look at Damon's face confirmed, without a doubt in Cassandra's mind, that he hadn't intended her to hear any part of his conversation with the so-called Paco. Right on the heels of that realization was the recollection of a promise to tell her everything, once she was well enough to hear it.

Straightening her back, Cassandra moved into the living room and took a seat on the couch opposite Damon. Renzo leaned against the wall, listening in.

"Who's Paco?"

Damon clenched his jaw, then mumbled, "He's my teammate. He and Zak help me by running background checks, security and IT needs for this operation."

"Assigned by your private security company?" Damon nodded at her question.

Out of the corner of her eye, Cassandra noticed Renzo

standing up straighter. "That's how you knew how to take care of the shooter. I wasn't sure if you were military or more like my..."

Damon chuckled at that. "No kid, I'm no Mafia man. But that doesn't make me any less dangerous." His sharp gaze turned on Cassandra at the last bit.

"Well, glad we got that settled." Her smile was wry, and she tried to quiet the anxious butterflies in her stomach. "But you promised me a story once I felt better, so let's start with the easiest. What happened ten years ago?"

Cassandra could tell her question took Damon by surprise, but he, too, remembered his promise. He leaned forward, elbows on his knees, eyes on her as he told his tale.

"When you and I met, I was nothing more than a troubled kid from juvie, only out by your father's grace. It was a dream come true interning at his firm. And meeting you...was the best part of that dream."

Cassandra tried to steel herself against his words, but her heart refused to. Perhaps it was her recent tryst with the intruder or a new awareness of her mortality... Either way, she listened to Damon without judgement.

"A lot of my interning was getting documents signed, fetching stuff for them, the usual. It started off well, but within a few months – as you and I grew closer – I paid more attention. I discovered some deals taking place between lawyers and their clients went unnoticed by upper management. Stupid as I was, I brought my suspicions up to Viktor – with hard evidence." A pause, and the hardened glint was back in his eyes. "I took Viktor at his word when he asked me to leave all my research overnight with him. Then I came to see you, for your gift."

"It was the night of my birthday?" Cassandra's whisper was barely audible, but Damon nodded nonetheless.

"Yup. And after the kiss that night, and Viktor walking in…. I thought it best to go see him and ask for his permission to date you." Damon broke eye contact then and stood up, walking to the window.

As he looked outside, his clenched fists told Cassandra the rest of the story before his words did.

"I headed to his office that day and was surprised by the two security guards posted outside. Viktor explained that if I told anyone about the details of those transactions, he would tell the security guards I tried to rape you, and they'd call the cops."

Cassandra gaped at his back for a long moment, then turned to Renzo. His expression was equally shocked, and he could only shake his head.

"Are you *shitting* me?" She exploded, standing up and walking to Damon, forcing him to look at her.

"No," Damon said. "Viktor also added that it would only take a suspicion for me to be thrown back into adult jail, especially with the same judge from before. He wrote me a cheque, telling me to take off. I ripped it to pieces in his face and planned to come to you, but I left through the parking garage… And was attacked. I don't know why they didn't kill me, maybe they hoped the journey would. Either way, they dumped me into the basement of a cargo container, and left me for dead. I arrived in the UK illegally and swore to myself I'd get money and come back to you. I haven't been able to keep that promise… until now."

Cassandra's heart thudded in her throat at the thought of so many lost years, opportunities…. "I… I'm so sorry, Damon."

"No offense," Renzo interrupted, "but that Viktor guy is a bastard, Cass."

Before he could add anything, his phone rang. Renzo answered it, frowning. "Dad?" A pause, then the frown deepened. "I'm at Cass', stayed the night."

Cassandra reached out, touching Damon's hand. He glanced down at their fingers intertwining, and a smile tugged at his lips. "Some story, huh?"

"You could say that."

"Wait, you want me there *now*?" They turned to Renzo just as he hung up, rolling his eyes. "Gotta bounce, dad needs me for something. See you guys later?"

Cassandra let go of Damon's hand and stepped back, biting on her lip. "Oh, crap." The words escaped her as she recalled promising Alain to meet him that night.

Stupid as it was, she'd agreed more out of courtesy than a true desire to be in a club after the attack. Considering what was brewing between her and Damon, she fully intended to let the Frenchman down easily that night.

She eyed Renzo, then Damon, but the latter's intense gaze clearly hid an underlying frustration. "Umm…" Standing her ground wouldn't be easy, especially since her ex-boyfriend seemed to have quite an aversion to putting her in the path of danger.

Which was exactly what would happen that night. After all, going out in a crowd after a shooter had tried to take out her best friend was not the best cover. Especially considering she was heiress to one of the biggest empires in the world.

"Go on, Cass," Damon said, though it sounded more like a growl than anything else. So he'd known – or suspected – the

| 177

reason for Alain's call and was waiting for her to remember it.

Damn him, for being so perceptive!

In a rush of arrogance, Cassandra raised her chin up, and answered Renzo's question, rather than Damon's command. "You'll see me at the club. I promised Alain I'd do my best to be there tonight."

Renzo's eyes widened and he darted a glance towards Damon. Cassandra refrained from doing the same, knowing fire would blaze in his eyes, since he no longer bothered to conceal it.

Renzo, now clearly expecting another row between her and Damon, cleared his throat and said, "All right then. Later." With the parting words, the front door closed, and she was left alone with Damon.

Cassandra took a deep breath and turned to him. "I'll be upstairs changing."

Damon stepped in front of her before she could move, and with his free hand lifted her chin up. "So did it meet your expectations?"

She couldn't pinpoint the tone of his voice, somewhere between bitter and hopeful. "What do you mean?"

"My explanation for leaving." Damon searched her expression, then his own shuttered as if he'd found a disappointing answer. He let go of her and stepped back, releasing a pent-up breath. "Or did it only serve to make you hate me more?"

"I don't..." Cassandra cleared her throat, in an attempt to forcefully get past the stubborn lump that was choking her. "I don't hate you, Damon. And I don't get what you mean by meeting my expectations, but your story did answer questions

I've needed solved for a while now."

Damon's expression didn't change, and she couldn't figure out what to say to bring back the connection that had been lingering between them earlier. At a loss, Cassandra added, "I just need time, D. To wrap my head around the bastard my adoptive father is, and to figure out where I stand on this."

Rather than argue, Damon nodded. His countenance made her even more wary, if that was possible. Not sure if his quick acceptance was good or bad, Cassandra swallowed past the lump in her throat and climbed the stairs back to her room.

♥ *Chapter 18* ♥

Less than thirty minutes later, Cassandra emerged from her room. A dark purple wrap dress hugged her body, displaying her curves. The silk whispered against her skin, paired with three-inch-high stilettos. She hadn't bothered with much makeup, other than her usual mascara and lip-gloss.

Though she was still shaken by Damon's confession, there was nothing she could do for the time being. She'd meant what she'd said. Time was key. And still, part of her wanted nothing more than to run to Damon and admit all was forgiven, if only they could start anew.

Lost in her thoughts as she walked down the hallway, Cassandra nearly jumped out of her skin when Damon walked out of the kitchen. Freshly showered – presumably in the basement shower – and changed, he was clad in a pair of blue jeans and a dark t-shirt. A leather jacket was slung over his left shoulder.

To her further confusion, rather than start a heavy conversation Damon's eyes raked over her body from top to bottom, then slowly made their way back to meet her gaze. A blush burned in her cheeks, but Cassandra willed herself to remain composed.

As the outfit he was wearing implied he wasn't staying home, she frowned. "Where are you going?"

Damon shrugged, seemingly unwilling to answer, and she rolled her eyes, about to leave. "You can order pizza if you're hungry. Later, Damon."

His hand shot out when she passed by him, blocking her way. Without a word, he reached for her palm and took her car keys out of her hand. He then placed them on the small table near the door.

Cassandra glared at Damon, tapping her foot. "What do you think you're doing?"

"I'm coming with you." Only the slightest smirk accompanied his announcement, which further irked her.

"I don't need a bodyguard, Damon! Haven't we been over this already?"

He looked her up and down again, the distinct burning in his eyes sending a shiver down her spine. Cassandra gritted her teeth, determined not to let him see it.

"Oh, I think you do, Cass," was all he said. Engulfing her hand in his larger one, he led her out the door and to his shiny car.

Despite everything in her that wanted to start a scene, Cassandra bit her feelings down. *He's impossible, there's nothing more to it. And the more I show him this gets to me, the more he'll do it.*

When Damon slid in the car and turned the engine on, still wearing that satisfied smirk, Cassandra had to sit on her hands. The impulse to slap him was too strong.

♥∞♥

An hour or so later, Cassandra's fury had abated. Damon was with her every step, either behind her or ahead, predicting her every move. Despite his earlier demeanour, the way he kept an eye out for trouble and manoeuvred them away from drama had its perks.

So although it still irked Cassandra that he saw her like someone in need of saving, she gave in. No rescue arrived from Alain, as the charming Frenchman was nowhere in sight –

something Damon was all too happy for.

As he returned by her side with a drink, Damon scanned the crowd. He pointed to a booth away from the bar, and Cassandra followed him there.

"Remind me why we have to be in this forsaken place again?" His scowl had more than one girl scurrying away. "Because I really don't see the point."

"Well, let me enlighten you. A, I had a date tonight, but it seems to have fallen apart – and I'm pretty sure you had something to do with it." Damon opened his mouth to protest, but Cassandra held up a second finger. "And B, me and Renzo like the music, and he wanted to hang out."

Damon muttered something under his breath, but the conversation stalled when a shadow loomed over the booth. He tensed, turning his body halfway to hide Cassandra's. They both relaxed when their eyes fell on Renzo – grinning and carrying a tray with drinks.

"I thought your dad wouldn't let you out," Cassandra said, reaching up and helping her friend set the tray on the table.

Renzo bent to kiss her cheek, then took a seat on her free side – she was effectively sandwiched between them. *Well, I bet no one's going to try anything now…*

Renzo's laugh pulled Cassandra out of her thoughts. "Old man's getting weirder by the day. He was asking about you, Cass."

Damon's attention zeroed in on Renzo's words, and Cassandra sensed his body taut with tension once more. She wanted to smack her friend for throwing coal onto the fire.

"What was he asking?" Damon probed.

"Just how Cass is doing, if she's seeing anyone… I

asked him about his visit at the club the other night, and all he said was that I had everything under control."

Damon didn't answer, instead glancing out at the mass of people moving on the dance floor. He reached blindly for one of the glasses Renzo had brought and took a sip, but his eyes remained fixated on some unseen threat.

Cassandra sighed and reached for a drink, leaving the last for Renzo.

"How are you?"

Renzo's question surprised Cassandra. She glanced towards Damon, then back to her friend, knowing he was alluding to Damon's earlier revelations. "I'm okay. I... It feels good to have questions answered, you know. Not wonder anymore, thinking I had something to do with..."

She trailed off, and Renzo nodded in understanding, reaching for her hand.

♥∞♥

Damon tried to keep his expression blank, though it killed him inside. Cassandra thought he hadn't heard, but he wouldn't have missed her words for the world. He'd hoped at least his explanation would have fixed part of the distance between them, but it didn't seem it had helped – not if Cassandra's attitude was anything to go by.

The wayward thoughts were enough to distract Damon from his vigilant watch – at least until another man pushed through the throng of people.

His muscles tensed despite his best efforts to hide it, and Cassandra stopped whispering to Renzo, turning to him instead. "What is it?"

"Not what, *who*. Alain." The words come out through

gritted teeth, but already Cassandra stood and exited through Renzo's side. Damon was too late to stop her. Yelling would have only drawn attention.

He watched with narrowed eyes as Cassandra sashayed to Wraith – Alain. They chatted for a bit, his lips way too close to her ears for his liking.

As a way to distract himself from the raging tornado that demanded he go and rip the assassin's head off, Damon focused on assessing him. The lighting was dim in the club, but to his trained eyes it played no tricks. That's how he noticed the purple skin under Wraith's eyes, from where his nose must have been broken.

"What's wrong?" Renzo asked, moving within hearing.

Damon clenched his fist under the table, and jerked his chin to Wraith. "That guy is what's wrong."

Renzo followed his gaze and his eyes landed on Wraith. "My dad warned me about him."

His words were enough to catch Damon's attention, and he turned away from Cassandra and her dancing partner. "What about him?"

"Dad said the guy's bad news, known in their circles." Renzo frowned, his eyes set on Damon. "He's hiding something. What's going on? Why his sudden interest in Cass?"

Why, indeed... It might warrant a closer chat with Mr. Moretti.

Rather than answer Renzo, Damon said, "Why didn't you tell Cass any of this?"

The younger man gave him a look. "Because you don't trust this guy and yet haven't told her anything. So how about you tell me the truth, and nothing but the truth?"

Damon sighed, then glanced at Cassandra again. Only, she was gone – as was Wraith.

"Shit!" He jumped to his feet, drink forgotten on the table, scanning the crowd wildly. *Not this again!*

"They're over there," Renzo pointed out, now by his side. Damon shifted his gaze to a corner, where Wraith was leaning a bit too close to Cassandra.

He was about to stalk there and rip him away from her, when Renzo gripped his forearm. "Tell me." His gaze was insistent, jaw clenched in determination.

Damon let out an annoyed breath, then wrenched his arm away. "He's a hitman, all right? From what my team gathered, Cassandra's dad hired him to kidnap her, so he could get his hands on her money. I'm here to protect her, but was ordered not to tell her and grab dirt on the guy instead to put him in jail."

There was a long moment of silence as Renzo stared at Damon, then he exploded. "Are you *kidding* me?" His eyes were near black with anger. "I thought you loved her, man! But you're using her as bait?"

Damon saw red. He grabbed Renzo by his shirt and slammed him into the wall, with no care for the attention he'd be attracting. "I *do* love her, dammit! But I was given orders."

"And you listened like a good little puppy?" Renzo spit in his face, sneering. "I thought you'd protect her, man. That you were some big shot guy with a security firm. But you're just another coward who takes orders, aren't you?"

Damon's fist punched the wall with enough force to put a dent in it, but still he didn't let go of Renzo. "You don't have a fucking clue, kid. None at all. This guy's not going let her go, even if I take her away. I need to make sure he's going to be somewhere he can't get out of. But he's a ghost! And yeah, to keep an eye on him, I have no choice but to let Cass do whatever the hell she pleases." He threw a glance over his shoulder, his voice softening. "Even if it means getting close to him."

"And you're letting him dance with her!"

"I don't want to!" Damon roared, slamming his fist in the wall again. "But it's my best bloody chance to get something on this guy. Do you know the kind of monster he is?"

One-handed, he pulled his cell out of his pocket and scrolled through until he loaded the pictures. When he pointed the screen towards him, Renzo went slack under his hand, paling.

Cassandra chose that moment to walk in, without her suitor.

"What the hell is going on here?"

Before Damon could answer, she shoved him away from Renzo and grabbed the device.

"Cass, no!"

It was too late to pull the images away, Damon knew it as soon as her eyes dulled and filled with tears. She held a hand to the table, as if unable to stand up any more, and leaned against it. With her free hand, Cassandra continued to scroll through the pictures for long moments.

Damon knew what she was seeing: dismembered bodies, mutilated children, decapitated women. Wraith had tortured anyone and everyone for money. Jack the Ripper had nothing on him, and even after all this time he couldn't get the images out of his head.

He didn't want them in Cassandra's. With a look to

Renzo warning him to stay put, he pulled the gadget out of her hands.

"You don't need to see this," he said.

Cassandra looked up at him then, but it was pure fury he read in those eyes. "What kind of monster does that?"

Damon hesitated, glancing at Renzo. The kid kept his mouth shut, but he could see in his eyes the disapproval over keeping silent. He glanced down at the pictures, and right then and there, he decided enough was enough. *No more secrets.*

"Your new admirer."

Cassandra's eyes widened, and she glanced over her shoulder to where she had presumably left the assassin behind. "Alain? But…"

"That's one of his aliases, but his middle name is Anton. He's a ghost, known through international policing circles as Wraith. Interpol has warrants galore on him, as does every police force in the world. None have been able to catch him. I wanted to kill him the minute he contacted you, but was told to bring him in – legally. With proof that would put him behind bars for the rest of his life."

"Why not kill him?"

Damon searched her gaze, unused to Cassandra's harsh tone. Realization dawned on him that the pictures had shaken her more than she would admit.

"Because they want the information he can give."

"As if a monster like him would give that freely!" Renzo said.

"He wouldn't, but there are ways…" Damon pocketed his cellphone, shrugging. "Once he's behind bars, nothing stops the country that has him from getting whatever they need out of him through any means they see fit."

"You mean torture," Cassandra whispered.

Damon met her gaze, and nodded. "He doesn't deserve mercy."

"No, he doesn't," she agreed. "But why him? Why does he have his sights set on me?"

Here comes the hard part. "Your dad set him on you. Alain is also the one that attacked you, in your home."

Cassandra's eyes hardened, and she lifted her chin that bit higher. "Then I want to help you catch him."

"Cass…"

Renzo's plea fell on deaf ears, as Cassandra stepped closer to Damon. "What do you need from me?"

And while the soldier in Damon was fist-punching the air in victory, his heart squeezed.

♥∞♥

The restaurant was beautiful, cozy and romantic, and the company was agreeable. It would have been a perfect first date, were it not for the psycho opposite her. All Cassandra could think of were the pictures from Damon's phone, and his tortured expression as he'd filled her in on the operation.

She'd been angry at first that he hid all of it, but it had faded with the realization she could help nail the monster. And now, sitting across from Alain in a demure black dress, she willed herself to breathe evenly.

"Relax," Damon said in the earpiece.

The device he'd given her was hidden behind her cascading hair. Cassandra tugged on her earlobe, the signal they agreed on for her to confirm she was all right. If she was not, and wanted to get out, all she had to do was cough into her elbow. Not that she planned to do that, after having spent the better part of the previous evening and morning convincing Damon to let her be his field agent.

I'm getting what I came here for.

"Something on your mind?" Alain – Anton – asked as their waiter left to bring their food.

"I'm sorry," Cassandra smiled, sipping the last of the wine from her glass. "Old drama, is all."

With a smile that made her skin crawl, he poured them more wine. Cassandra held the glass to her lips for an extra moment, inhaling the aroma. *Could he have slipped me something?*

She didn't want to forget she was sitting across from a psychopathic monster. That alone should have sent her running for the hills, and the fact she wasn't was worrisome.

To distract herself, Cassandra took a sip of the wine and said, "So, what brings you to Canada, Alain?"

He threw her an odd look, and she forced a smile. "Your French is much too flawless for you to have been born in Québec. And your style is easy enough to pinpoint as French."

Alain glanced down at what he was wearing, then around them, noticing the less than classy looks men sported. A surprised laugh escaped him. "I suppose so!"

Damn, but he's a good actor.

"Don't fall for it," Damon whispered in her ear. With the gadget doubling as a microphone, he could hear the entire conversation. "His entire profession revolves around being a chameleon. Stay on your guard."

Cassandra took a larger gulp of her glass, and Alain was quick to refill it.

"Business mostly, although I'm hoping to get pleasure out of it, too." He smiled, his eyes connecting with hers. "What about you? I thought the DiCavalier family was Italian. That seems a long way from your home."

Cassandra made a face, remembering how much her family's name had been in the news.

"My parents wanted me to have a normal upbringing, and Canada was their choice."

"Ah, yes. They died when you were young, didn't they?"

"Yes."

"That must have been very hard," he probed, but she couldn't force herself to open up to him.

Rather than allow the disgust to show in her face, Cassandra pretended to blink back tears. "If you don't mind, I'd rather not talk about it."

"Of course. I apologize. Here I am, supposed to apologize for my rather rude disappearance from yesterday to you, and instead I'm making you sad. I'm very sorry, Cassandra."

Cassandra dabbed at her eyes with the napkin and sniffed delicately, for good measure. "It's all right. And my friends call me Cass."

"Cass it is, then."

"Speaking of last night, what *did* happen? You left pretty abruptly from the club."

"Ah yes." Alain broke eye contact and took a sip of his wine, then said, "My parents' estate in France had problems, and I had to direct the workers on how to fix them. All boring work, but time-consuming. I envy your freedom."

"Freedom?" Cassandra laughed. "Hardly. I'm in constant fear of my identity being found out, and ending up a media magnet like my parents. That fear rules some – most – of my choices, from who I pick as friends to where I go for dinner. So freedom... No, I wouldn't say so."

Alain nodded as if understanding her, then smiled and raised his wine glass. "Then how about a toast to almost-freedom, and the hopes of more!"

Cassandra raised hers, and took another sip. The conversation continued on useless topics, and she was getting frustrated. Right when she was about to interrupt with a personal question – that Damon had specifically said to avoid – her ex-boyfriend whispered in her ear again.

"We're good. Got what we needed, Cass. Time to put an end to it."

"What?" She hadn't realized she'd spoken out loud until Alain stopped in the middle of what he was saying. "I'm so sorry," Cassandra giggled, pointing to the wine. "This must have gone to my head, and I have to admit I lost track of the conversation."

Alain smiled, but this time it was thin, and there was a feral look in his eyes that caused her to shiver.

"Not at all, *cherie*. Perhaps it's time to call it a night."

Cassandra ignored the *darling* endearment and nodded, barely hiding her relief. It took Alain only moments to pay the bill, then they were exiting the restaurant. She was trying to figure out how to avoid getting in a car with him, when Renzo's voice called out.

"Cass!"

Cassandra turned around in time to see Renzo get out of

his pickup truck, and head over. He didn't bother hiding his hostile look from Alain.

"Renzo, what are you doing here?" she asked him, baffled.

"I need to talk to you. In private."

His words were clear and his gaze demanding, so she turned to Alain and smiled. "*Merci encore* for a lovely dinner, Alain. See you soon?"

The assassin smiled, just as surprised at Renzo's unexpected presence. "Of course." With that, he walked around to his car, and drove off.

Cassandra waited a beat until he disappeared around a corner, then headed to her friend. "What's up? And what the hell did Damon mean you guys got what you needed?"

"Not me," Renzo scowled. "His team. One guy broke into Alain's car and was able to pull data from the GPS tracker. The other guy used it to pinpoint his last locations and figure out where his lair was... They went there and found enough proof to put him away, including collectables."

"Collec..." Cassandra trailed off, eyes widening as she caught onto his meaning. "He kept parts of his victims?"

Renzo's grim expression was enough of an answer. "I'm glad they got what they needed, because no way in hell I'd let you do this again. It's too damn dangerous to be playing with the likes of him."

Worry poured off him, and Cassandra's frustration at being kept out of the loop eased off. She wrapped her arms around his strong torso and hugged him tight, whispering, "I'll be okay. You guys have my back."

Renzo returned the hug, then pulled away after a few

moments. "Damon said something about new information that came to light."

"Is he inside?" She was looking at the car, as if expecting him to step out.

"No, I'm supposed to bring you to his hotel."

Cassandra followed Renzo to his car, and within moments they'd pulled in front of one of the more chic hotels of the Old Port. She whistled low, impressed at the luxurious place that looked like a remodelled castle. "He's staying *here*?"

"Just for the night. Apparently, it's a good cover."

Cassandra nodded and stepped outside. Before heading in, she leaned through the open window and winked at Renzo. "Be safe."

♥∞♥

Damon could have burned a hole in the carpet with all his pacing. After Zak and Paco had confirmed getting the information from Wraith's lair, he'd asked Paco to set up an encrypted transfer to Derek and his team back home.

Soon as that's completed, Wraith is done for. With the data they'd recuperated, they could track his movements, his aliases and usual hangouts. Paco had already developed an algorithm to sort through the information and start predicting where Wraith would be next based on previous patterns.

Still, through it all, Damon's thoughts were on Cassandra and the risk she was taking. If she slipped up, and Wraith realized she was there as a distraction...

There was a knock at the door, and he yanked it open. His eyes fell on Cassandra, looking delectable in a black dress that reached mid-thigh, and her hair loose around her shoulders.

He reached for her at the same time she reached for him.

The minute she was in his arms, Damon pinned her to the wall and kissed her.

Cassandra answered like she always did, melting in his arms, and it made the separation that much more painful. When he tried to pull away, however, she grabbed his belt and yanked him closer. "No stopping," she urged, kissing him back.

Damon groaned in her mouth, wanting to give in to what she was offering, but dreading the reasons that were pushing her to it. He knew the adrenaline of a successful mission could cloud the mind, and it was not what he wanted to justify their first time together.

Despite his internal admonishing, he picked her up in his arms and she wrapped her legs around him in a vice grip. His mouth angled over hers, even as one hand dug into her hair, pulling her head back so he could kiss her neck.

Her intoxicating scent engulfed him. It was a perfume he should have been able to name, because it'd been in his dreams for ages… And, ultimately, it was his undoing. Also, his wakeup call.

With a superhuman effort, Damon pulled back, and forced Cassandra's legs back on the ground. Her eyes shone with passion, and he touched her cheek. "I will be everything you want me to be tonight, but no more secrets. There is still something I need to tell you."

Cassandra opened her mouth to speak, but he pressed his index finger to her lips. "Just hear me out."

When she nodded, he grabbed her hand and sat on the couch, pulling her in his lap. "Anton is not only the monster responsible for those pictures. He is also the man who orchestrated your parents' murder."

There was no gentle way to announce it, so he chose bluntness. In his arms, Cassandra stiffened, and pain crossed her features. "What?"

Damon inhaled and interlaced her fingers with his. He hoped, if nothing else, that he could be an anchor for her in this time.

"Anton comes from France, that much is true. His father had a prominent winery in the south. It wasn't as prosperous like the larger ones, but it made money. Anton had three siblings. His father and yours knew each other. When your father opened his resort, Anton's father lost everything in bad investments. Lost to rage and insanity, he killed his wife, Anton's siblings, and took his own life. Anton only survived because he was away at school."

Cassandra's eyes widened in shock, but Damon rushed on before she could intervene.

"Anton looked into what put his family in such deep debt and blamed it on your father. He resolved to take from the DiCavalier family what was taken from him. So he followed your parents, and clashed into their car, causing the accident."

"Why didn't he come after me?"

Damon thought back to the information they'd found, and gulped his rage down. "Because he wanted you to grow up, and really understand the torture he'd be putting you through. Over time, Anton lost track of where you were, because you were so well-hidden. Your adoption records were sealed, too. He made more enemies and staying hidden was more of a priority than finding you. But then your dad gave him you on a platter, and he couldn't refuse."

Damon paused, waiting for it all to sink in. "Cass... No

matter what happens next, Anton is done hurting you. We have enough to put him away for life, and I swear to you that I don't plan to let him touch a hair on your head."

Cassandra let out the breath she'd been holding, then wrapped her arms around his neck. She buried her head in his neck and her soft sobs broke his heart. It was a testimony to her strength of character that she was still standing after the revelation.

When she'd calmed down, long moments later, Damon caressed her back. "Let's order food?"

Cassandra nodded, and he reached for the landline to place a quick order for room service. When the knock sounded at the door after ten minutes, they shared a surprised look.

"That was fast..." Cassandra laughed and got off him.

Damon stood, tucking the gun in the waistband of his jeans. He was not taking any chances. The peephole was obstructed, which alone served to raise his hackles.

He glanced behind at Cassandra and gestured for her to move to the side, out of sight. Once she did, Damon opened the door a smidge. "Yes?"

The wooden frame was slammed into him, and four cops stormed into the room. One of them held up his badge and a paper that warned of nothing good to come.

"What the fuck is all this?" Damon asked as the cops moved in on him.

"Damon Voight, you're under arrest for assault."

The bastard delivering the news was none other than Sean, the cop who'd been tailing him since the club incident. And he was smiling like a damn cat going in for the kill.

♥ *Chapter 19* ♥

Cassandra tapped her foot, aware of the hard dig of the chair in her back. Her eyes hadn't strayed from the guy at the front desk in the last two hours while they interrogated Damon. No amount of her confirming his alibi this time stopped Sean from arresting him.

When Sean had barged in, Cassandra had wanted nothing more than to rip him a new one. But Damon's hard look had silenced her, and she'd listened to him. Following them to the station in a taxi was a no brainer, and she'd hoped to at least get more information on the so-called assault charges.

All they would tell her was that there was an ongoing investigation.

Near growling, Cassandra jumped to her feet and marched to the front desk. They'd changed shifts ten minutes earlier, and the new officer looked up with a bored expression on his face. "Yes?"

"I want to see Damon Voight."

He typed something on his computer, then shook his head. "No can do. He's in questioning."

"He's been in there for two hours!"

A shrug. "It can take a while."

Cassandra pursed her lips, trying to calm her fervour. "What are the charges?"

His blank gaze narrowed in on her. "You family?"

"I… no. I'm his girlfriend." The words sounded right, even if they were said in the heat of the moment. *But then again, aren't I?* Cassandra set that question aside for a better time.

The officer sighed, as if he couldn't be bothered, and

said, "The man from the club *Fire & Ice*, stabbed a few days ago? They say your boyfriend did it, lady. That's all I can tell you."

Cassandra slammed her palms on the edge of the counter. "That's *bullshit*! Damon didn't do anything, it's Sean who's trying to make him go down for something he's innocent of!"

The officer only arched an eyebrow, nowhere impressed by her outburst. "Don't shoot the messenger."

Cassandra took a deep breath, then chose to switch tactics. "Can I post his bail?"

After a quick look at the computer screen, he said, "Your guy's here on a tourist visa, isn't he? Makes him a flight risk."

Cassandra narrowed her eyes. "My boyfriend is a Canadian citizen, dumbass."

He looked back from his paperwork to her. "All his documents are marked as from the United Kingdom."

Cassandra could have screamed her frustration at the world in that instant. But someone called out, and she turned to see Renzo rushing forward. She'd woken him half an hour earlier, unable to stand the wait by herself.

She went into his arms, aching for his familiar hug. Renzo didn't disappoint, but not even the warmth of his arms was enough to reassure her. Cassandra pulled away, pursing her lips. "We need to get Damon out of here. They won't let me see him and they've been interrogating him this entire time without a lawyer!"

Renzo glanced behind her at the officer, then met her eyes. "How long has it been?"

"Two hours!" Cassandra lowered her voice, dreading to

ask but willing to cross any lines at this point. "Can your dad pull any strings?"

To his credit, Renzo didn't even blink. His slow befuddled smile raked her hard. "Funny you should mention him... That's why I'm here. He wants to see you."

"Now? Renzo, I can't!"

"Damon will be in there for another hour, at least. And with his military training, I've no doubt he's able to handle himself. Plus, my dad's outside waiting in the car, so it won't take long."

Cassandra sighed and followed him out.

"So did Damon get to tell you anything new, before being arrested?"

"Yeah," she muttered. "This Alain/Anton guy is the same who murdered my parents." Cassandra went on to summarize the story, and through it all Renzo held her hand, an anchor to her grief.

Soon, they were outside the dark stretched limo, and he opened the door. Cassandra stepped inside and took a seat on the leather interior. Renzo joined her within seconds and closed the door. Fabrizio Moretti was sitting opposite them, nursing a glass of vodka. It was odd seeing him so forlorn, considering he rarely drank anything stronger than wine.

"You okay, Uncle Fabio?" she asked, throwing a confused glance to Renzo, who shrugged.

"No..." Fabrizio glanced from his glass to her. "I haven't been entirely honest with you, Cassandra. After my wife's death, I swore to stay on a righteous path, and no longer see innocents hurt. While I've done my best in this, I failed to some extent. I should have warned you the moment it happened."

"The moment what happened, dad?" Renzo's tone had a hard edge to it, and it seemed to get Fabrizio back on track.

He downed the rest of the glass, then stood straighter and fixed his suit. "Your father came to me, first. He asked me to handle your kidnapping. You see, Viktor gambled his fortune away. The millions he got each year for taking care of you, all gone."

Cassandra's jaw dropped at the revelation. Damon had alluded to as much, but to hear Viktor was completely broke…

"He gambled it all to the wrong people, and then some," Fabrizio said. "Unfortunately, this meant when they came collecting, Viktor didn't have anything to pay them. But he knew about your trust fund."

"I can't touch that until I'm twenty-five," Cassandra frowned. "Why would he kidnap me?"

"Because he was aware if he ransomed you, the people in charge of protecting your parents' estate would pay up. The money would be enough to get the sharks off his back for the time being, after which he planned to force you to sign over the rest of the fund to him."

"As if I would have!"

Uncle Fabio ran a hand over his face, sighing. "Which is why he came to me. But when he told me his plans, and what he wanted to do in order to break you…and get you to comply…" He grimaced, looking repulsed. "I wouldn't have done it, either way. But once he mentioned all that, I wanted to kill him."

Cassandra's frown deepened as she recalled the last time she'd been in the same room with her stepfather. At the time, he had dark circles under his eyes and he'd been sporting a nasty black eye and broken nose. "That was you, the broken nose?"

Fabrizio's eyes darkened. "I wish I'd done more, but it was a line I didn't want to cross after my promise to my departed wife. Sadly, my refusal drove him into the hands of a worse man."

"Anton."

Fabrizio leaned forward, reaching for Cassandra's hand. "I hope by now your friend Damon warned you, and you're aware of everything."

Cassandra nodded, squeezing back. "He did, and he also collected enough information to put Alain behind bars."

Fabrizio's gaze shifted to Renzo, then back to Cassandra. "Let me offer you protection. A man like this Wraith, as the coppers call him, he's not to be trusted to remain behind bars."

Cassandra shook her head and removed her hand. "Thanks, Uncle Fabio, but I'll be fine, honestly."

The former Mafia enforcer sighed, then leaned back against the seat. "Suit yourself."

Renzo spoke in the silence that followed, his voice tense with anger. "Dad, why didn't you mention any of this before? We could have both been seriously hurt."

Fabrizio exhaled a heavy breath. "Because I didn't realize what the fool did until I saw Cassandra the other night with that man. I'm terribly sorry, Cassandra."

In a surge of sympathy, she leaned over and hugged him. "This is by no way your fault, Uncle Fabio. But there is something you can do to make it up to me."

As he listened to her plan, he let go of his drink, and the

glint of danger washed out the glaze of alcohol in his eyes. "Consider Viktor handled."

♥∞♥

"You have nothing on me."

It was the fifth – or tenth – time Damon made the same statement, to no avail. Sean meant to destroy him, and he'd been circling the interrogation room, playing games he wasn't fit to.

A square four by four, the room barely held a table and two chairs. Damon was cuffed to the table, and while he could have broken free, he preferred not be in a high speed chase with the police.

Not when there are better uses for my time. His thoughts went to Cassandra, and what had been interrupted in the hotel room.

"We have witness accounts," Sean said, "and your prints at the scene."

Damon leaned back in the chair as far as he could, and shrugged. "All circumstantial, which is why I refused a lawyer, dumbass."

Sean ignored that last part. "So how do you explain what happened? A mysterious other man, that's your story?"

Damon stared at him point blank and nodded. "Exactly."

Something about his countenance must have annoyed Sean, as he got all red in the face. "You think you're God's gift to women, don't you?"

Damon refrained from rolling his eyes. The guy had serious issues and the time was not right to address them. No matter how appealing the idea was, assaulting a cop for stupidity would only result in further questioning.

"You have nothing to hold me," he repeated.

"I'll find something." Sean leaned back against the wall, crossing his arms and shooting a smug grin.

Damon kept his gaze levelled on him, but the door to the interrogation room opened and in walked another man, dressed in a suit. "This interview is finished, officer."

"Detective–"

"I said it's *over*. You have no cause to hold this man." The newcomer turned to Damon, palms open in silent apology. "You are free to go, Mr. Voight."

Once he'd un-cuffed him, Damon rose from the table. He rubbed his wrists and took his time walking to the door. He stopped right in front of Sean, towering over him. For long moments, he stared at the cop, his fist itching to be put to use.

Rather than give in, Damon smirked and saluted him. "Told you. Next time, learn to listen, *boy*."

Leaving a red-faced cop behind, Damon walked out and signed for his things. He'd have to call Derek and thank him for putting in a good word – they must have been monitoring the local police stations.

Seeing Cassandra waiting for him in the waiting area derailed his thoughts. She was sitting on an uncomfortable-looking bench, leaning forward with her elbows on her knees. As if sensing him, she looked up – then she was in his arms.

Damon held her tightly, never wanting to let go. He inhaled the scent of her hair, then allowed some space between them.

"How did you get out?"

Damon glanced back, noticing the detective in a corner. He saluted him, then disappeared back to where he presumably worked. He glanced back at the beauty in arms, and grinned.

"Sheer good luck, I suppose?"

Cassandra punched his arms lightly. "I'm serious!"

Damon wrapped an arm around her shoulder and turned her towards the exit. As they walked out, he whispered, "I've got my former boss to thank, no doubt. He tends to come in handy in tight situations."

"I'd say…" Cassandra trailed off, and he sensed she was holding back something.

Once they were outside the police station, Damon turned down the street and stopped. "What is it?"

She bit her lip, then said, "Uncle Fabio says Viktor went to him first to kidnap me. When that didn't work, he got Anton."

Damon's eyes narrowed at the revelation. Exactly how many people did the contract get to, in Viktor's desperation?

If there's more than one assassin out for her… It would explain the attack at the club. After all, the two goons they'd fought had none of the finesse Wraith did. Damon felt an ice grip get hold of his heart, and he pulled Cassandra tighter against his side. He needed to take her away – *far* away – to a place he could arrange twenty-four-hour protection.

He cupped her cheek with his free hand and searched her eyes. "Come away with me."

Cassandra's eyes widened. "What?"

"Let's get out of Canada for a bit. Go to Europe… Maybe even see your parents' estate."

"Why the sudden urge to do that?"

Damon kissed her softly, then said, "Because, Wraith will be in jail soon. And while that takes care of him, and the information I have on Viktor ensures he'll be put away for good too, I don't want to take any chances. If Moretti's telling the truth, then Viktor might have gone to even more people. And if that's the case…. Isn't it better to get away for a bit, avoid the storm?"

Cassandra looked at him for a long time, then smile. "Okay. Let's."

♥∞♥

As Damon pulled into her parking spot, Cassandra noticed Renzo leaning against his own car. She jumped out of the passenger seat before Damon had fully parked and ran to hug her friend.

Renzo returned the embrace, tightening his grip before releasing her. "All good?"

"Yep. They let Damon go."

The smirk on Renzo's face tipped Cassandra off, even before Damon asked, "It was you?"

"Not me. My dad." He shrugged at their confused glances. "What can I say? Turns out Fabrizio Moretti still has connections in the local police force."

Cassandra turned to Damon to see how he was taking the news, but he seemed to be over his shock. He took a step closer to Renzo and held his hand out for the younger man to shake. "Tell him thank you."

"Will do." Renzo's gaze shifted between them. "So, what's the plan?"

"We're leaving for a while," Damon said. "I don't know how many people Viktor contacted in his stupidity, and it's best Cass is away from this while it all blows over."

"Blows over?" Renzo frowned, missing the link.

"My team pulled enough footprints Viktor left behind in his illicit affairs. They've already contacted the police, and the proof will get him behind bars – for good. Zak and Paco will stick behind to make sure the cops have anything they need, and once he's officially arrested and put in jail, they'll take off and return to the UK."

Cassandra was silent for a beat. Had she expected Viktor to get away with it? Did she even want him to? *Not really.* And yet, part of her felt guilty for causing harm to the man that had accepted her in his house as an orphaned child.

"Cass." Damon's hand on her shoulder brought her out of her ruminations. "You don't owe Viktor anything."

She gaped at him, surprised he'd read her thoughts with such accuracy. Damon kissed her forehead, then said, "And if you want to stay, we can. No pressure."

Cassandra shook her head and pulled out of his arms. "Hell, no! Let me pack a quick bag and we can take off."

Damon nodded and stayed behind with Renzo, while she stepped inside the house. It was only once she closed the front door that she had the uncanny sensation she was not alone. Damon and Renzo hadn't checked the house to make sure it was empty…and neither had she.

"No hugs for your dad?"

Cassandra let out the breath she'd be holding, almost in relief – but not quite. *So daddy came to visit.* She stepped into the kitchen, where Viktor loomed over the countertop. The lights were off, but the glint in his hand was hard to miss even in the darkness.

Yelling for Damon and Renzo was no longer an option. *I can't afford either of them to get hurt, not this close to the end. Besides, I've handled daddy more than once before.*

Cassandra moved closer, lifting her palms up so he'd

realize she was unarmed. The gun made Viktor dangerous, but no more than usual. She took in his dishevelled state, the bloodshot eyes and ripped suit, and the opened bottle of liquor sitting on the counter. By the looks of it, half of it was gone.

Images of a drunken Viktor beating his wife, and attempting to hit her, ran through her mind. After her first cut lip from his fists, Cassandra had increased her martial arts training until she could hold her own. Viktor had never put his hands on her again – not for lack of trying, especially as she grew older.

Eyes narrowed, she took in the monster of her childhood, the proverbial boogeyman. Other kids in school had been afraid of fictional creatures, but she'd had evil living in her own household.

Cassandra cleared her dry throat. "What are you doing here?"

"What, a father can't come for a surprise visit to his daughter's house?"

"Not when he's breaking in and pointing a gun at her," she retorted.

Her eyes were on the weapon in Viktor's hand, even as she moved the last few steps. Only the granite island stood between them. Now that she was closer, Cassandra caught sight of the crystal glass and the stench of vodka pouring off it.

"Some things never change, eh, daddy?" She sneered at him, her gaze locked on the alcohol. "What are you doing here, Viktor?"

He stared at her for a beat as though not quite recognizing her. "You always had a mouth on you," Viktor finally said, drinking some more.

"Whatever you say. How about we do this without the alcohol?"

Viktor glanced at the glass in his hand, then downed the whole thing. He set it back on the counter gently, at odds with his harsh words. "You ruined everything, you little bitch."

"No, I think you did when you decided to kidnap me, then sell me to highest bidder, *dad*."

Viktor's eyes shot pure venom. "You don't even need that money."

"Doesn't mean it's yours for the taking." Cassandra leaned over the counter, staring him in the eyes despite the gun's nozzle mere inches away. "What did I ever do for you to hate me this much? Why did you even want to adopt me?"

Viktor laughed, cold and bitter. "Sophie always wanted a child, wouldn't stop yapping about it. Then when they showed her the figure amount, how could she refuse? Didn't know you'd be such a handful."

Cassandra gritted her teeth at his callous answer. "So it was all about the money?"

"Poor little princess," Viktor cackled. "Haven't you learned yet? Money makes the world go round."

It happened so fast, Cassandra didn't realize at first what happened. Viktor froze, his eyes opened wide. The gun dropped out of his hand, clattering to the ground. His massive body followed in the following second – and that's when she saw it.

Blood poured out of the back of his head, staining the floor with its ruby tinge. Cassandra was paralyzed at the sight, mouth opened in a silent scream of horror. Then her eyes fell on the reason for his untimely demise: the knife protruding from his skull.

Out of the corner of her eye, Cassandra saw a shadow move. She whirled around towards the living room, in time to catch Alain – Wraith – walk in.

Gone was the softness he'd exuded as Alain, replaced by a blank expression. His eyes were cold, filled with hatred and a feral rage she could almost feel across the distance. And in his hand was a gun with a silencer, pointed straight at her.

"Don't appear so surprised, *chérie*. I thought you were done with your questions and brought the interrogation to its inevitable conclusion."

Cassandra gulped, ready to scream for help. Damon's warning was clear in her head, and she wasn't about to take any chances with the psychopath. Before she could, Alain lifted his free hand, which held a rectangular object with wires. Atop it was a blinking red light.

"Make one sound, and I'll explode your car. It's rigged with enough C4 to bring this entire neighbourhood down – and your two bodyguards with it."

Cassandra dropped her hands to her side, knowing a lost cause when she saw one. "What do you want?"

"Right now, for you to turn that pretty ass around and walk out your backdoor without a noise. After… Well, I'm sure we can come up with something fun for the both of us."

His sinister laugh gave her goosebumps. Possibilities ran through her mind at warp speed, but one certainty overpowered her desire to fight. Alain was a trained assassin, and not her usual partner for sparring. And considering how their last fight had gone, the chances of triggering the explosives were too high.

Shoulders slumped, Cassandra nodded. "I'll do what

you want, just let them go." Fighting tears back, she walked out, feeling his presence at her back.

They exited through her yard into a back alleyway. Parked in a corner was a car, engine still running. Alain opened the passenger seat, and waited until Cassandra got in.

Once she was seated, he lifted a wet towel from the dashboard. She smelled something sweet, but before she could identify it, Alain shoved it in her hand.

"Time to say night night," he grinned.

Cassandra stared up at the man she had once thought handsome. There was nothing in his expression, only an eagerness that was bordering on maniacal. For a second, she wondered why he hadn't just shoved the cloth in her face and forced her to pass out.

Then the glint in his eyes clued her in: Alain wanted her to do it. By obeying his command, she was surrendering. And for a psychopath bent on playing games, there was no better aphrodisiac.

He wants revenge, and he's going to take his sweet time breaking me. I've got to be strong, because there's no way in hell this demon's going to have my soul.

Gritting her teeth, Cassandra put the cloth to her mouth, and inhaled. The hum of the engine roaring to life was the last thing she heard before falling into a blackout.

♥ *Chapter 20* ♥

Something's wrong.

The thought was sudden, but unyielding, and Damon had learned not to ignore such instincts.

As he raised his gaze to Cassandra's upstairs window, Renzo said, "She's taking too long."

The younger man's words oddly echoed his own unease. "What makes you say that?"

"Cass is not your girlie girl. If she said it's a quick pack that means less than five minutes. We're going on ten, now."

That was all the incentive Damon needed to storm into the house. Even before he'd inspected the entire area, the eerie silence was enough to convince him – Cassandra was gone.

"Cass!" Undaunted, he ran upstairs, checking every room only to find them all equally empty.

Her bedroom was more telling than everything else. No suitcase on the bed, not even a rumpled bed sheet. *She didn't even make it upstairs!*

Damon rushed back down and headed to the kitchen. He found Renzo crouched by Viktor's body. The knife handle jutting out from the back of his head was enough to tell him whose handiwork it was.

"Wraith."

Renzo stood, swallowing hard. "He took Cass. So how do we get her back?"

Damon pulled out his cellphone and dialled his team, putting them on speaker. Zak answered and he gave him a rundown of the situation. In the background, he heard keyboard typing and assumed Paco was already trying to pull a digital footprint.

"I'll send someone to clean up," Zak said, "and we'll arrange everything into a plausible story for the cops. What do you need from us besides that?"

"Two plane tickets to London, first class for the earliest morning flight you can find."

"London, as in *UK* London?" Renzo frowned. "You think you'll find Cass that quick?"

At Damon's dark expression, Renzo ducked his head and muttered an apology. He set about wiping his prints from the counter.

"I also need you to run a search for all aliases of Wraith," Damon said. "It's a long shot, but something may pop up."

Zak barked something in the background, then returned on the line. "You got it. Where are you going?"

"*Désirs Noirs*." Damon walked to the couch, where he still had a gym bag stashed. He rummaged through it and pulled out a gun, then slid it in the waistband of his jeans.

"The club your first dead shooter used to work at?" Zak sounded confused.

"Yeah. If Viktor picked up the Albanian from there, there's bound to be a trace of Wraith somewhere. Could very well be someone in there connected the two."

"Okay, boss. We'll work on it on our end."

Damon hung up, then headed to the door. "My guys will send someone, but you may want to get out of here. Cops will come at some point or another."

"Hell, no." Renzo followed him outside, and to the car. "I'm coming with you."

"This could be dangerous, kid."

Renzo's jaw clenched and he jerked his chin. "I'm well aware."

Pressed for time, Damon didn't bother arguing. Each second spent on logistics was another moment Cassandra was with Wraith.

"All right, let's go." He gestured for Renzo to get in the car, then started the engine.

The drive to the club took less than ten minutes, and he was thankful traffic was light this time of day. Since it was still early morning, the business was closed to the public, but staff was working inside.

When they entered, the bartender, a pretty blonde girl with an easy smile, greeted them. "Gentlemen, you're here much too early. The fun doesn't begin until tonight."

"I need to see your manager," Damon cut across.

Her eyes widened and her smile became more forced. "Just one moment."

She returned from the back with a man in a suit, too much bling everywhere. Damon realized this was a guy he could make squeal if only given enough time.

Which he didn't have. So, he did the next best thing and pulled out his gun.

"You're not serious," the man scoffed. "Robbing me in daylight?"

"This isn't a robbery." Damon walked closer until the gun was mere inches from the man's face. He levelled his darkening gaze on him, scowling. "I want information on a man named Wraith. You may know him as Anton, or he also runs by the alias Alain Valois."

"Never heard of him."

Damon took off the safety of the gun. "How about Viktor Beauchamp?"

The boss scoffed. "Haven't seen that guy in a while, but he owes me money. Be sure to tell him, would you?"

Renzo threw Damon an impatient look he could easily interpret. The entire affair wasn't getting them anywhere, and time was ticking by.

Damon took a step closer to the owner. "You had a bouncer. Someone who left a while back. Glaucoma in both eyes."

"Nicky, yeah. Boy left me high and dry. What of him?"

"Did he ever come in here with anyone?"

"No, but now you mention it, he hung out by a warehouse with a bunch of Albanians."

Damon dropped his gun. "Give me the address, and we'll be out of your hair."

The man was only too happy to oblige.

♥∞♥

Cassandra stirred from the deep fog of sleep, her senses returning one by one. Smell was first. A damp, mouldy musk permeated the air. There was a slight chill, artificial enough in summer it implied an air conditioner. The sounds were next – scrapings, as though someone was dragging a chair on the floor.

She cringed at the noise, and a laugh echoed around her.

"Ah, you are awake. Perfect."

It wasn't until Alain ripped off her blindfold that Cassandra realized something was stopping her from seeing. She tried to swallow a few times, hating the pasty taste. Her senses felt foggy, and she had a feeling standing up would be impossible, even if she hadn't been tied up.

There goes my plan of escape.

Panic was settling in, but if she showed it, it would make Alain that much happier. *Speak of the devil...*

He moved closer, facing her. "Now, Cassandra, how about you tell me how you know Mr. Voight, hmm?"

She yanked her chin out of his hand, turning her head to the side. He laughed, then gripped a handful of her hair and pulled on it – hard. Cassandra's head was forced back and a cry escaped her lips. When she noticed his savage grin, she tempered it down.

"Don't stop," Alain hissed close to her ear. "I *want* to hear you scream."

When Cassandra only bit her lip and glared at him, he let go and stepped back. She followed him with her eyes, determined to fight the drowsiness and watch his every movement.

Alain walked behind her, then reappeared to her right. It was then Cassandra noticed the side-table. To her horror, it was not the scrape of a chair she'd heard earlier. The monster had been sharpening a large hunting knife with a rugged blade.

Rather than reach for it, Alain passed by the table that held the knife. He walked a few more meters, then disappeared behind a plastic curtain and into the darkness beyond.

Cassandra took advantage of his inattention to inspect her surroundings, hoping to find an escape. The mix of adrenaline and fear for her life had been enough to force her senses into full-blown awareness.

Judging by the rectangular shape and large walls, she was in a warehouse. Paint peeled off them, and the only windows were tiny and place high off the ground, near the ceiling. The area itself seemed to be split into sections, with thick plastic curtains separating each side. Cassandra was in one corner of the building, and Alain had vanished towards the other side. There were no other voices, nor any landmarks outside.

She tried to wiggle her hands, but Alain had tied them with a zip tie. The more she tried to move, the more they dug into her wrists. Cassandra hissed at the sharp pain – she was trapped.

As though sensing her despair, Alain returned. "Now, you *will* talk," he said, emphasizing each word as if savouring it. His walk was slow, purposeful, like a cat playing with its prey. On his way to Cassandra, he picked up the hunting knife, and knelt in front of her.

"You will tell me *everything* I wish to know, including where Viktor stashed the money he owes me. If you don't cooperate, we may have to start our little party earlier than intended, *chérie*."

Cassandra hated the way he used the endearment, sullying it with his bitterness. Yet her attention was otherwise drawn when the knife's tip pressed against her knee cap. She gulped, but the lump in her throat was still choking her.

"Do you know how much pain you would be in, if I press just the right way, and cut the right strings?" Again, that savage grin. "Speak. *Now*."

Cassandra didn't intend to lose her leg, nor did she plan to give Alain more satisfaction than she already had. *But first things first.* "If I tell you, will you untie my hands?"

He laughed at that, and it echoed in the cavernous walls. "You think you can negotiate?"

Despite what she really wanted to do, Cassandra tried to

keep calm. "What's the matter, *Alain*? Or should I call you Wraith? Scared I'll run away?" She paused, assessing the glint in his eyes. Testing him was fragile ground, but her instinct warned to push a little more. "I thought you liked the chase."

Alain's expression remained blank, and the tip of the knife dug further into her skin. A sharp pain erupted when the metal pierced her skin, but he stopped before it got too deep.

"You are correct," he sneered. "I enjoy the chase very much. And with you, it will be all the better savoured."

Alain stood and came behind her. Cassandra felt a tug on her wrists, then release as the restraints fell away. She pulled her hands forward, massaging the wrists.

The assassin then pulled another chair and sat facing her, twirling the knife in his fingers. "Now, speak."

Damon, hurry…

"I met Damon when I was in my teens. He interned at my father's firm…."

♥∞♥

They were still on their way to the warehouse when Damon's cell rang again. "Talk to me."

Out of the corner of his eye, he saw Renzo fidget on his seat, one leg bouncing up and down. He knew the kid was as anxious as he was to get Cassandra back safe, yet they weren't any closer to it.

They'd been driving around for hours checking potential areas. Paco had pulled up his map of Wraith's footprints in the city, but all they'd seen so far were empty housings.

Damon hit the steering wheel in frustration, then threw the phone at Renzo. "Hit the speaker."

Once he did, Zak came on the line. "I might have something,"

"Tell me."

"This last warehouse you're heading to, I pulled a satellite image. Paco combined it with our infrared something-or-other. It's empty, except for two heat signatures in one corner."

"Which?"

"South-west."

Damon glanced at Renzo, nodding. "Thanks, Zak. I'll take it from here."

"Also, the tickets you wanted are ready. But, boss?"

"Yeah?"

"There's been a recent shipment of C4 to that warehouse. More than enough to make it explode – and then some."

Damon thanked him again and hung up. "Fuck me," he bit out, and Renzo threw him a look.

"Explosives?"

Damon didn't answer. Instead, he gunned the engine until the GPS tracker showed they were a few minutes away. He slowed down and the only sound from the car was the softest of purrs. With a flick of a switch, he turned off the lights and they neared incognito towards the warehouse.

The building was located at the end of a cul-de-sac. It was surrounded by several industrial places, all as badly maintained as this one. They got out of the car, and he signalled Renzo to be quiet.

"Follow me, step only where I do, and be ready for anything." Damon pulled a second gun out of the trunk before closing it. "In case you need it." He then handed Renzo the car keys. "And this is for a quick getaway."

Renzo met his gaze, understanding the unspoken agreement. He nodded, then tucked the gun in the back of his jeans like a pro.

He might be a kid, but he's quick. I guess growing up with the Mob has a way of teaching you street smarts.

Damon turned away from him, forgetting everything except the mission. He had his gun out and ready, his body coiled with anticipation.

Wraith had given up his chance of a life spent in jail the minute he'd kidnapped Cassandra. Regardless of what Derek or any other agency in the world thought, Damon planned to make sure the assassin was taken care of – permanently.

Silent as ghosts, they moved through the shadows and slipped in through the back door.

♥∞♥

Alain was staring at Cassandra, and it was oddly disconcerting. She was not comfortable with his look, as it seemed he was ready to explode. Her knee was bloodier than before thanks to his constant picking at it, whenever she didn't give him a satisfactory answer.

For the last few hours, Cassandra had told him her life story, but there was nothing she could say for Viktor's money. Alain had gone suspiciously quiet when she'd admitted what Uncle Fabio had revealed – that Viktor had been completely broke.

Alain leaned forward, lifting the knife towards her chest. "This isn't working, so evidently I shall have to get more creative."

He grabbed the front of her t-shirt and yanked upwards, forcing Cassandra to her feet. Resistance would have been futile and only led to her being in a more vulnerable spot than she was already. And the last thing Cassandra wanted was Alain's cold gaze on her naked body.

She was yanked out of her thoughts by his brutal shove, straight into the wall. Her back hit the cement with force, and Cassandra gasped at the pain. Then Alain was in front of her, hand on her throat.

"Now, let's see if you can sing for me, pretty bird."

The knife's tip rested against her throat, and Cassandra tried to quiet her breathing for fear of stabbing herself by mistake. Alain only smirked, his eyes roaming over her face, taking in her terror and getting off on the control he exerted.

Once Cassandra clued in to his game, her laboured breathing returned to normal. Alain's eyes glinted dangerously, but it didn't stop her. "You're going to have to do way worse if you want to break me."

Silence extended around them, until the air was thick with his anger. Then he dropped the knife, and smiled. "I thought you'd never ask."

She didn't see his movement coming before he'd back-handed her so bad, she found herself on the floor. Cassandra tasted metal, and a check-up with the tip of her tongue confirmed her lip had split.

I'm not going to die here, at his *hands.*

She tossed her hair back and rose to her feet, staring down Alain. His jaw was clenched, and he was breathing heavily. A vein throbbed on his right temple, and Cassandra had the confirmation she needed – he was losing it.

Just one more push.

"Is that the best you got?"

Roaring with fury, Alain grabbed her by the shoulders and slammed her back against the wall. Her head throbbed from the impact, but Cassandra tried to focus and raise her knee to hit him. Before she could, Alain reached for her throat, gripping it and squeezing.

"You've outlived your usefulness to me, *chérie.*"

Cassandra tried to scratch at his arm, attempting to pull away. But Alain only hoisted her higher until her feet were dangling off the ground. "It's about time you pay for daddy DiCavalier's mistakes."

The murdering intent in his eyes was clear, and tears of helplessness rolled down Cassandra's cheeks. *Damon…*

Alain brought his other hand to her throat, ready to snuff out her life to good. But a shape burst out of the curtains behind and tackled him. Cassandra dropped to the ground, inhaling deep breaths of air into her deprived lungs.

She glanced at the two men rolling over, her vision blurry from the temporary lack of air. When the assailant threw a punch, she recognized Damon's tattoo.

"Damon!"

He came for me.

Renzo was by her side next, pulling her up. When her weight fell on her injured leg, Cassandra started to fall. His arm around her waist anchored her, and he started dragging her away, back the same way they'd appeared.

Cassandra glanced behind, her eyes glued on Damon as he battled with Alain. The sight of the two of them fighting was enough to give her pause, and she slowed down.

Damon was quick, dropping punches and avoiding the knife that sliced through the air like a sword. But Alain was a panther on the prowl, ruthless and with nothing to lose. He clocked Damon under his jaw, sending him flying into the wall.

Damon shook his head and faced him, a bloody gash on his forehead. He no longer had a gun in his hand, and Cassandra saw it lying not far away.

"We have to help Damon!"

Renzo looked at her like she was crazy, then tried to drag her away. "He can handle himself."

As they were stuck arguing, a loud bang resounded. Cassandra looked back again, in time to see Damon strike Alain, and the two tumbled into the plastic curtains. Next to where they'd disappeared, fire sparked, and quickly engulfed the area.

"Damon!"

Through the curtain, Cassandra saw a shape stand and look towards them. "Get her out of here!" Damon's voice was hoarse with emotion – and smoke.

Cassandra reached out to him, but Renzo was relentless in dragging her away. His grip and her injury made it impossible to fight him. They got to the car and he pulled out a fob to unlock it, then dropped Cassandra on the backseat.

He slammed the door shut, then rushed to the driver's side. When he started the engine, Cassandra punched the back of his seat.

"We can't leave him there! *Renzo!*"

Renzo's eyes met hers in the rear-view mirror, and she read hesitation in his expression. "Damon said to get you away, Cass."

"And I'm telling you we can't leave him!"

After another beat, Renzo nodded and reversed until the car was by the exit they'd come through. "If anyone but Damon comes out of there, I'm taking you far away," he warned.

His gaze dropped to her injured knee. "We need to stop that bleeding." Out of the corner of her eye, Cassandra saw him reach into the side door pocket and pull out a Swiss army knife, using it to cut a wide bandage from his shirt.

She didn't speak when Renzo moved through the two front seats and managed to wrap it around her knee, effectively stopping the bleeding for the time being. Her eyes were glued to the exit door, praying against all hope, but only smoke escaped from within.

Cassandra wrung her hands, leaning her forehead on the window. Her breath fogged it within seconds, and the outside became blurry.

"Here."

She glanced at Renzo and the box of tissues he was holding out for her. It was only then Cassandra realized her tears were part of the reason her vision was so blurry. She wiped her face, then blew her nose. Grabbing another handful of tissues, she wiped down some of the blood from her leg.

Renzo let out a breath. "We need to take you to a doctor."

"Not yet, Renzo. Please, I –"

An explosion rocked the car, and Cassandra turned to the door. She reached for the door to storm out, but Renzo locked them inside before she had a chance to.

Cassandra glared at her best friend, hating him in that moment. "Let me out!"

"No! You're not thinking straight."

Hot tears cascaded down her cheeks, and before long Cassandra curled onto herself and let the sobs out. "Damon…"

Another explosion sounded, and her sobs only grew louder. Then she felt a light touch on her shoulder, and looked up to see Renzo staring out the window.

"Cass…" He trailed off, but his hand moved to unlock the doors as if by reflex.

Cassandra straightened up then, wiping at her eyes and trying to figure out what had her friend's attention. Smoke surrounded the entire area, and the warehouse she'd been held captive in was in flames. But through the thick grey condensation, a shape appeared.

The locks snapped open, and she knew it was Renzo's doing. Hands trembling, Cassandra opened the car door and stumbled out. She barely dared to believe her eyes – yet the confident stride was unmistakable.

"Damon!"

Half-limping, half-dragging her leg, Cassandra moved towards him. At the sound of her voice, Damon picked up his pace and within seconds she was in his arms, surrounded by the scent of his skin and smoke.

Damon was holding her tightly enough to suffocate as he kissed her cheeks, her eyes, and everywhere he could reach. She held on to him, thanking the fates and the entire universe for allowing him to escape with his life.

When Damon finally pulled away, a grin lighted his face, dirty with blood and soot. "I reckon we'll need a shower before hopping on that flight to Europe."

♥ *Chapter 21* ♥

A thumb was caressing her cheek, the touch as light as a butterfly. Cassandra's eyes cracked open and met Damon's gentle green gaze. He was watching her through half-lidded eyes, and it took her a moment to realize they were both lying in bed.

"Hey there, sleepy. How are you?" Damon's question was whispered, as if not to scare her away.

"I..." Cassandra's voice came out hoarse, so she stopped and cleared her throat, frowning.

The hand that was caressing her cheek moved away as Damon produced a bottle of water off the night stand. He opened it and handed it over, watching as she drank most of it.

With her throat no longer scorching, Cassandra handed back the bottle, then snuggled closer to Damon, resting her head on his chest. His arms effortlessly pulled her closer against him, and he rested his chin on the top of her head.

While Cassandra wanted nothing more than to enjoy the moment of peace, she couldn't help but think about how they'd gotten there. And at the source of all her worries was one question: *where do we go from here?*

"Damon..."

Before she could finish, Cassandra found herself on her back, Damon hovering over her. His face was close, green eyes flashing. "Stop it."

Cassandra pouted, more than a little miffed at his commanding tone. "Stop what?"

"Stop overthinking it," Damon said, his tone more gentle the second time around. "I never should have left back then, and we both know we belong together. Now that Viktor and Wraith are taken care of, what's there to keep us apart? Who are we to fight fate? You rolled into my arms last night, Cass, and it was the best night's sleep I've ever had." He paused, nuzzling her neck, then moving his way up to her mouth for a kiss. "This is *right*, and I dare you to say otherwise."

Despite the confidence shining in his voice, Cassandra saw the wariness in his eyes. That, more than anything, eased up all her worries. Because if he was willing to show his emotions, then she had nothing to lose.

She wrapped her arms around his neck and smiled. "In that case, I'll decline on the dare, because I'd lose."

Victory flashed in Damon's eyes as her words registered, and his grin lighted the room. "I knew you'd see it my way." All talk ended when his lips descended on hers in a blissful kiss.

When Damon pulled back, his eyes sparkled with that contained happiness Cassandra had witnessed only a few times before. She returned his grin, a happy buzz warming her core.

Realizing she still had no idea where they were, Cassandra pulled back enough to really see his face. "Where exactly are we?"

Last she could remember, they'd landed in London and had rented a car. Tired from their ordeals, she must have fallen asleep.

"We..." Damon repeated, and she couldn't help a delighted shiver. He seemed to be enjoying the sound of the word as much as she was.

Cassandra focused her wandering thoughts on what her boyfriend was saying, in time to hear the end of his explanation.

"… so the guys had tickets for London ready. I only ever intended it to be a pit stop on our way to somewhere much more romantic."

Cassandra gaped as the full meaning of his words sank in. "We're not…"

"Oh yes," Damon smirked. "We're in Paris, in my little apartment a few minutes from the Eiffel Tower."

A long silence followed, as Cassandra tried to figure out if he was joking or not. Before she could stop him, Damon dropped his mouth on hers once more, and he was kissing her like the world was ending.

Cassandra gave in to the sensuous touch of his lips, wrapping her arms around his neck and returning it full-force. His hands roamed her sides, then held onto her hips. The kiss continued for longer moments, but Damon never pushed for more, seemingly content with the PG-rated action.

"Damon…" She tried to speak around his kissing, to ask if he was serious about Paris, but he wasn't giving her a chance to.

When the nagging voice in her head wouldn't stop, and curiosity got the best of her, she pushed Damon off and rushed to the window. In her eagerness, she'd pushed him off the bed, but his oomph of surprise barely registered as she stared at the incontestable truth.

In plain view for all to see, and dazzling her eyes, was *la fameuse* Tour Eiffel. Cassandra gasped and whirled around, unable to contain her delight.

"Damon!"

His expression softened, and a warmth Cassandra wasn't used to showed in Damon's eyes. "You like?" There was vulnerability, an openness to his question that got to her.

"I love it! Damon…" Cassandra moved back to the bed, kneeling next to him. "This is amazing."

She leaned in to kiss him, and he reached for the back of her neck, pulling her closer. As their lips connected, Cassandra finally let the remainder of her walls down, and embraced their joint fate.

There was no room for thinking or decisions between them. She reached for Damon's shirt, and pulled it off with his help. His hand cupped her cheek, thumb caressing it. "Are you sure?"

Cassandra nodded, then ducked her head to nibble at his throat, jaw, and back to his mouth. "Never been surer in my life," she whispered against his lips.

Damon's arms wrapped around her waist then and lifted them both up, before dropping her on the bed gently. Piece by piece, he removed her clothes, until there were no barriers left between them.

Murmurs of appreciation left his lips as he trailed them down her body, then up again. Cassandra squirmed under his attention, panting for more. When Damon licked around her collarbone area, then moved to her breasts, and down her stomach, she couldn't recognize the sounds coming out of her mouth.

"Damon…"

She shattered around his questing fingers, sobbing her pleasure and begging for more at the same time. As if reading her mind, Damon moved over her, his body as naked as hers was.

Cassandra glanced down, noticing he'd put on a condom

before she even had to suggest it. She met his green eyes, sparkling with amusement. "Did you doubt I'd take care of you?" he said.

She chuckled, then lifted her head to bite his shoulder. "Not a bit. It was worth the wait."

Surprise flashed across Damon's face, but he had no time to voice anything aloud. Cassandra lifted her hips, at the same time pulling him closer. He entered her in one swift stroke, and she gasped at the pain, closing her eyes.

♥∞♥

Damon stilled, feeling the tension in Cassandra's body. He waited until her beautiful eyes opened again, searching her gaze. Bit by bit, her body relaxed under his, though her expression remained wary.

When she nodded, he moved within her. It took all his willpower to hold back, but he managed it. *For her, I'd do anything. And to think she waited...*

Damon stopped thinking when Cassandra angled her hips and her mouth opened in surprise, then she flushed. He bent over and sampled her lips, then kissed each cheek. "Are you ready for more, love?"

Her eyes widened as if wondering what else there was that could top it. Damon only grinned, then changed the pace of his strokes. He moved one hand between their bodies, touching her centre of pleasure.

Cassandra's soft gasp, followed by a longer moan, was music to his ears. And it would not be the last of the night.

♥∞♥

"Where do you think you're going?"

Cassandra laughed at the sleepy mumble. Damon's arm

tightened around her, and he pulled her even closer. They'd fallen asleep their exerting activities and brunch in bed, and she'd woken up spooning with him.

"Damon, come on," she tried for a scolding tone, "I need to go to the washroom…" Cassandra trailed off, wondering if he'd fallen back asleep and if she could sneak off.

She got her answer when he nuzzled her neck, sending delicious shivers down her spine. "What for?"

"Damon!" Cassandra's indignant whine was broken up by her burst of laughter. "I'm serious, I really have to go. *Now.*" After a pause, she mock-pleaded, "Let me go, please?"

"Never!" Damon growled and pushed her on her back, hovering on top. He gazed at her through hooded eyes, a soft smile playing on his lips. The hardness of his body distracted her, and Cassandra found her mind wandering back to…

"Fine. You have…" Damon made a show of trying to decide, "… 5 minutes. So hurry up, love."

Cassandra laughed and scurried from under his arm as soon as he moved it. She reached the bathroom and glanced over her shoulder, smiling when she saw him asleep. After all the nights he'd spent keeping an eye on her in Canada, was it any wonder the man needed his beauty rest?

She rushed through a shower, wondering how long they'd be staying in Paris. Now that the stress of Viktor and Alain was over with, nothing stopped them from taking their time enjoying Europe together, and getting reacquainted.

Cassandra made a mental note to ask Damon if his company could do without him for a bit. About fifteen minutes later, she walked out of the washroom, pleasantly sore in all the right places from his previous ministrations.

To her – slight – disappointment, Damon seemed asleep again, an arm thrown over his face to block out the sun.

However, as soon as she got closer to the bed, he rolled towards her. With incredible accuracy for someone supposedly half-passed out, he reached for Cassandra's hand, and pulled her back in bed.

"That was over five minutes," Damon reproached.

Cassandra laughed, snuggling in his embrace. *This, a girl could get used to.*

"Cass."

She smiled at the unmistakable annoyed tone in his voice. "Hmm?"

"Stop laughing. Sleep."

She chuckled against his chest, then quieted down. "Sweet dreams, Damon."

He made a sound of approval at the back of his throat, then his breathing slowed down and Cassandra knew he was gone to dreamland. She did the same, intending to enjoy her time with Damon to its fullest.

If she'd known then what was to come, perhaps she would have avoided repeating past mistakes.

♥∞♥

They'd been out having dinner at a small restaurant in Paris, and decided to end the evening with a walk through the cobblestone streets. Despite the later hour, people still filled the streets, and their chatter disrupted the night.

Reading her mood, Damon pulled Cassandra into a deserted street, and she sighed in happiness at the quietude. They walked hand in hand, in companionable silence, and the moon shone on them in approval.

After a few blocks, Damon tugged on Cassandra's hand and went to cross the street, when he heard an engine revving. Out of the corner of his eye, he caught a car speeding towards them. Reflexes kicked in and he pushed Cassandra out of the way.

With no time to get out of the way, he chose the second-best option besides dying and jumped towards the car. His shoulder hit the hood of the car, then he knocked into the windshield. He caught sight of two men in leather jackets inside, before falling off to the other side.

The car sped away, and Damon hit the ground full-frontal. Cassandra yelled his name, and all he could think was, *Don't let me be dead, I still need to protect her.* He'd been wrong thinking all the danger disappeared with Wraith and Viktor's deaths.

"Come on, Damon. Don't do this. Don't you dare let go…" Cass cradled his head in her hands. The heat from her palms permeated his skin, and he winced.

With a struggle, he opened his eyes. The lampposts' light was sensitive and he had to blink a few times. His first instinct was to check for the car, but it was long gone. "Looks like they're gone for good."

Cassandra helped him to his feet, and half-leaning on her they edged out of the street. After a few steps, Damon paused. Something was floating in the street, carried off by a soft breeze. He'd missed it at first, but he was pretty sure it hadn't been there before the car had crossed them.

"And it appears they left a message." Clenching his fists, Damon limped to the offending paper. He scanned the words, his jaw clenching with each passing second.

Cassandra joined him and read over his shoulder. "Mademoiselle DiCavalier, your father left unpaid debts behind. You should transfer the money to our labeled account, unless you wish to pay in *other* ways."

Which, translated, meant that either she paid whoever it was all of her inheritance, or they'd kill both of them. *Great.*

"It must be the Albanians. They're the only ones we haven't taken out." Damon crumpled the paper, and Cassandra looked up at him. "This has gone on way too long," he said.

"I know. And I'll end it, Damon. If all they want is money, I just need to go to my parents' estate in Italy, sign the documents with their lawyer and access my trust fund earlier. Piece of cake."

Damon scowled at her, trying to rein in his disagreement. "Hardly, love. You forget how many branches of the mob exist throughout Europe, never mind Italy. Either could have been contracted to kidnap you. And there's no way I'm letting you go in there alone." He glanced at the crumped paper in his hand, then met Cassandra's gaze again. "Paying them off won't solve this, trust me on it."

Cassandra opened her mouth to no doubt argue her point further, but blinking lights and sirens stopped their conversation. A string of cop cars pulled over, apparently alerted by some bystander or other of the accident.

Damon and Cassandra were each questioned by separate officers, and their statements taken down. After a lengthy discussion with the French police, where they gave as vague details as they could about the car, Damon and Cassandra were allowed to leave.

They got back into the hotel and Damon headed to

shower, needing a minute to figure out how he'd talk some sense into Cassandra. *Without causing a fight that could ruin this entire vacation.*

♥∞♥

Someone knocked on the hotel door, interrupting Cassandra's ruminations. She hesitated answering, considering the recent attack, and glanced towards the bathroom door. With Damon still showering, she headed to the door and looked through the peephole. An elderly, distinguished gentleman in a full on suit was there, flanked by a younger man.

"*Qui c'est?*" She asked who it was in French.

"My name is Lucien Montagnard, Ms. DiCavalier. I am with Interpol."

Cassandra pulled back from the door, frowning at it in confusion. *Interpol?*

"How can I help you?"

A slight chuckle echoed from the other side. "Would you mind opening the door so we may speak face to face?"

Cassandra glanced over her shoulder, biting her lip. She knew Damon would probably be upset over her taking risks, but her curiosity was too strong. Before opening the door, she slid the chain barring it in place.

In the small open space, she met the elderly man's open expression. "Show me some ID."

He slid his badge and his partner's through the opening, and Cassandra locked the door in their faces. After perusing the IDs for a few minutes, she opened the door fully and handed them back.

"So you're not lying. Which brings me back to my original question: what do you want?"

Lucien shared a look with his partner, then said, "I was hoping you would walk with me."

Cassandra was surprised by the request, but not enough to be duped. "Not until you tell me what it's about."

His hazel eyes twinkled with mirth, and he said, "You remind me so much of your mother, Ms. DiCavalier. I received wind of the report from earlier, the car striking down your companion. I knew your mother long ago and wanted to speak with you. It need only take ten minutes, nothing more."

Cassandra's curiosity increased tenfold, but wariness still lingered. She threw a meaningful look to his partner. "We can go, but alone."

Lucien nodded and turned to the younger man, waving him off.

"Let me write a note to Damon."

Cassandra headed back into the hotel, grabbed her wallet and left Damon a note saying she was going by the convenience store down the street to grab snacks. Then she followed the Interpol cop in silence, until they were a few blocks away from the hotel.

After her recent dance with danger, she kept an eye out to make sure they were staying in a public space. Despite the late hour, tourists filled the streets, and she relaxed ever so.

"What brought you to Paris?"

It was not the question Cassandra expected, but she saw no harm in answering it. "We – me and Damon – needed a vacation."

"And have you been together for a long time?"

This time, she found the question incongruous. "What is this all about?"

"You have to forgive an old man's curiosity, *ma chère*. Affairs of the heart are my favourite treat."

Lucien's kind demeanour put her at ease, despite the pointed questions. But his next one brought Cassandra to a dead stop in the middle of the street.

"So your departure had nothing to do with a certain Anton?"

Lucien must have read the wariness on her face, as he lifted both palms up in a universal sign of peace. "I mean no harm, Cassandra. Word travels among our circles, and when I dug deeper..." A sigh, then, "I should best start from the beginning. While I do not blame you for mistrusting me at the moment, I beg you to hear me out. My intentions are only good towards you. Here, let's take a seat."

Cassandra trailed behind him, heading to a bench on the side of the road. They sat down, facing each other while pedestrians kept an ongoing stream of traffic.

"Thirty years ago, I was a young officer in the French police. I did a stint in the military, but settled for being a regular officer of peace. In my third year, while responding to a call of domestic violence, I visited the victim at the local hospital. That is where I met your mother, Elena."

Cassandra really looked at him then, trying to envision the meeting. Back then, his receding hairline wouldn't have been so prominent, and with his square jaw and gentle eyes, Lucien would have made a striking young lad, she bet.

"How was she?" she asked.

The light shining in Lucien's eyes told her enough, even before the words poured out. "Elena was a ray of sunshine. She worked as a volunteer at the hospital, helping with victims and counselling when needed. Despite a degree in psychology that makes most people jaded, she had a huge heart. I was smitten with her, and a friendship developed over the next months."

Lucien's smile fell off and he paused, collecting his thoughts. "I found out Elena was running away from someone. During a summer in Italy, she fell in love with the local mob boss, Vittorio Castelloni. At the time, she did not know what he dabbled in. Thiers was a consuming passion, and when she found out, Elena left him. But Vittorio was in love with her and kept trying to win her back. He was never abusive, only persistent."

Cassandra frowned, unsure whether to believe him or not. Could her mother have hidden that much? Then images of a dark-haired man showing up at their estate floated through her mind, fleeting and unfocused. She tried to keep her attention on Lucien. "Was she hiding from him, here?"

"Yes. But beautiful as your mother was, she did not pass long unnoticed. Anton's father was one of her many admirers, as was Jean-François, your father. It turned… ugly, for lack of a better word." Another pause. "Anton's father would not let go, even after Elena made her choice. Your father begged her to arrange protection, but my hands were tied by bureaucracy. So Elena called the one person she did not want to."

"Vittorio."

"Yes. It seemed fitting. And he handled the issue the way men of his station do. I didn't ask what happened, but I did make sure my regiment's attention was turned elsewhere. Afterwards, your parents moved to Italy and established their business. Vittorio left them alone, and Elena was safe…

Though I missed her terribly in the years that passed."

Cassandra let the tale sink in, then voiced what was on her mind. "Thank you, for sharing. I... I didn't spend much time with my parents, as they died when I was young."

"Terrible accident..."

There was something in his eyes that warned Cassandra there was more to come. "Anton had a hand in it. As he did with what happened in Montréal, yes."

Lucien nodded, as though having expected such a revelation. "There is something else you need to know of. The car that struck your companion yesterday, it is registered to the Albanian mob. I am afraid they were the ones that put your step father in touch with Anton. With both gone, they expect payment."

The news did not come as a surprise, and it confirmed Damon's theory. But Lucien's carefully chosen words implied something else. The last piece dawned on Cassandra, and she glanced at his badge. "And you cannot arrange protection."

Lucien's eyes were sad as he answered. "There is nothing I wish for more, but I am no longer a *policier* as the rest, a field agent. I am close to retirement, and Interpol's upper management does not listen to an old man's tales. My administrative access enabled me to use Interpol's resources to follow the trail and find out what I could from recent events, but if I put this information to my supervisors, they will call Damon in for questioning."

"What? Why?"

"There is a warrant out for his arrest from Canada."

Cassandra swore under her breath, cursing Sean. "I thought that was handled."

"I am sure it is something he can easily get out of, but with Damon in custody, it would leave you unprotected."

Cassandra tilted her head to the side, feeling like she was missing something. "So how do you suggest I handle the mobsters?"

"The way your mother did. Go to Italy."

"And ask Vittorio for help? He doesn't even know me!"

Lucien laughed at that. "*Ma chère,* you are a copy of your mother. He cannot deny you, no matter what."

Cassandra glanced back towards the hotel, but Lucien seemed to read her mind. "It is best to leave Damon if you want to get into Italy without issues. The warrant is international, and he might get nabbed at the border. I know you do not want to, but he will be safe here. The mob will follow you."

Cassandra nodded, knowing in her heart he was right. Much as she disliked leaving her boyfriend behind, especially considering what they had survived, his safety would be assured. *And at the end of the day, I don't want him to pay for something that's meant for me.*

They walked back to the hotel in silence. Cassandra stopped for a brief moment at a store and picked up some croissants, then followed Lucien back to the front entrance.

When he dropped her off, she hugged him. "Thank you for the advice, Lucien."

He smiled when she pulled back, and grabbed her free hand in his. Cassandra started when she felt him slip something into her palm.

"Do not look at it until you get in, away from cameras," Lucien said. Nothing about his expression changed, but his eyes spoke volumes. "Interpol has eyes everywhere. But that is the contact you will need for Vittorio."

Cassandra kissed his cheeks and headed into the hotel, feeling like her entire world had come crashing down in a few moments. A few hours earlier, she'd been enjoying a romantic dinner with Damon. Then he'd been run over, their lives had been threatened, and she'd found out her mother had a different life before marrying her father.

She stopped in front of her hotel room, pausing. *Can I really do this? Leave Damon? And more importantly, is there another option?*

Before she could decide, the door opened and Damon rushed out, nearly colliding with her. His hands reached out to steady her, and he ran his eyes up and down her frame, checking for injuries. "Dammit, Cassandra! Why didn't you wait for me?"

Rather than answer, she buried her head in his chest, hugging him tightly. After a moment of surprise, Damon's entire being relaxed and he wrapped his arms around her, holding her in silence for a few moments.

When Cassandra drew back, the words were on the tip of her tongue. She wanted to tell him everything Lucien had, and decide together. But then Damon's expression softened, and he tucked a strand of hair behind her ear. "I was worried, love."

There was so much unsaid in those words, Cassandra's throat tightened and the truth wouldn't come out. If she told Damon, he'd come with her and would be focused on keeping her safe, rather than himself. He'd treat the entire thing like one of his missions, and she'd seen how much he was willing to risk.

He barely survived fighting Wraith. There is no way in hell I'm risking his life for a bunch of mobsters, not when I just got him back.

"Hey, are you okay?"

Damon's index finger under her chin reminded Cassandra that she'd been silent for too long. She nodded, pasting on a smile. "Yeah, I just needed air. Plus, I was hungry for something besides room service."

She held up the paper bag with fresh croissants, their enticing smell wafting around them. Damon grinned and pulled her inside the room, then took the goodies away from her hands. "I've got a better idea."

His mouth was on hers in the following breath, and Cassandra kissed him back. His every touch, every kiss, could be their last, and she wasn't about to waste a single moment of it. She allowed his love to wash over her, healing her pained heart.

And when they tumbled into bed, she made love to him like it was the last time. Their joining was fierce, almost raw in its passion. Damon tried to slow it down, to be gentle with her, but Cassandra was having none of it.

For each slow pace he attempted to set, she demanded more. When Damon seemed unwilling to give her the intensity she craved, Cassandra took matters in her own hands.

She rolled them over and straddled him, kissing him to stop any questions from rising. His hands moved to her hips, groaning as he pulled her down on him. Cassandra enjoyed feeling his hard-on through their clothes, but she needed more.

Muttering in frustration, she pulled down his boxers, then discarded her own underwear. Damon watched her too closely, almost as if trying to read beneath the surface.

Can't have that.

Cassandra crawled over Damon, positioning herself above him. In one swift move, she took him inside. She threw her head back, exposing the long expanse of her neck as she rode his length. Damon trailed his hands from her collarbone to her breasts, then started toying with her until she was pleading for more.

"How much more?" he asked, his eyes dark with desire.

"I want everything."

Damon rolled them over, then lifted one of her legs, creating a deeper angle. Cassandra moaned at the new sensations, and tried to close her eyes.

"Look at me, love. I want to see it when you shatter."

Dazed and close to the brink, Cassandra found his gaze – then gave in to the ecstasy. Damon was quick to follow, dropping his head to her chest.

Once Damon was exhausted and asleep, Cassandra slid out of bed and showered quickly. She got dressed in the dark, then wrote him a note explaining everything. She kissed his cheek one last time, holding back her tears and praying she'd see him again.

Then she snuck out like a thief in the night, heading for the airport.

♥ *Chapter 22* ♥

Present time

"What the *hell* do you think you're doing?" Damon's voice growled in Cassandra's ear, and she had to move the phone away while he let out some very obnoxious curse words.

When only silence remained, she placed it back near her ear. "Are you done now?"

"Cass…" His voice softened, but there was still a hard edge to it. "Where are you? Why did you leave?"

Me. The word was implied, but Damon kept it to himself.

"Damon, I didn't leave *you.* I, um…" *How do I even go about explaining this?* With a sigh, Cassandra settled on the truth. "When you were showering the other day, I had a visit from a Lucien Montagnard. He's from –"

"Interpol." Damon spit the word like it left a bitter taste in his mouth.

Cassandra frowned. "Yeah, how did you know?"

"We've crossed paths. What did he want?"

"Well, he knew my mom and the story of her and my dad and Anton. He also figured out why the Albanian mob is still after me – because they want their money. You were right, after all." She paused, then said, "So I arranged a meet with some lawyers and set up a trap at my family's estate. There's a contact here in Italy that can help me deal with it."

His silence gave her hope that Damon agreed with her course of action. That hope was shattered the moment he exploded. "So you're in *Italy*?"

Cassandra cringed, pulling the phone away from her

while he cursed some more. *This is so not going like I'd planned.* She glanced again outside, noticing the men were still not moving.

What the hell are they waiting for?

"Yeah, I'm in Italy at the DiCavalier estate."

There was some shuffling in the background, and the sound of a zipper. Then Damon came back on the line. "And did they follow you?"

Cassandra hesitated again, but his impatient sigh wrenched the honest answer out of her. "Yes."

"Cassandra."

The sudden serious tone of Damon's voice had her focus. "What's going on? You seem out of it."

"Who, me? Nah, no way." She attempted to direct the conversation otherwise, but Damon wasn't fooled.

"What's going on?"

Cassandra blew out a breath, risking another peek outside. She thought about faking bad service and hanging up on him, at least while she sorted the mess out. How could she explain to him that not only was she in danger, but she hadn't even had time to meet with the lawyers nor call Vittorio for help?

At the exact moment Damon repeated his question, two of the men moved forward. They had their bodies angled weirdly, and Cassandra inched closer to the window, trying to figure out what they were doing.

By the time they straightened out, it was too late to do anything. Each man had hold of a machine gun, and they aimed them towards her floor. Without hesitation, they started shooting and spray of bullets shattered the windows.

"Those sons of bitches!"

Cassandra ducked to the ground, swearing as she tried to get out of the line of fire. *They must be doing this to force me outside.* Damon's worried flow of questions echoed through the phone, but she couldn't focus on that. Not when she was about to be turned into Swiss cheese by the same men destroying her parents' house.

"Cassandra, answer me!"

She'd managed to get into a corner away from the windows, and she lifted the phone to her ear again. "I'm fine."

"Fine? That sounded like you're in the middle of a shootout! What the hell's going on, Cass?"

"I swear it's nothing big, Da—"

Damon interrupted before she could finish, rough with emotion. "Stop lying to me." Softer, he continued, "I can help, you know I can."

"Not with this, I won't let you. I love you, but it's for the best." She hung up on him, then crawled in the area least littered by shards of glass, until she was under a window again.

Cassandra reached for the gun tucked in the waistband of her jeans, and took the safety off. She'd had shooting lessons a few years back, and only hoped her aim was like riding a bicycle.

The volley of bullets had stopped, presumably while they recharged or waited to see if the attack would flush her out. Cassandra poked her head to identify some targets. She knew shooting the attackers directly was her best option, but they were small targets. So she aimed for the cluster of them near cars, and pulled the trigger.

Her arm vibrated with each shot, and shouts echoed

from below as the men took cover. Cassandra shot until an empty click resounded, then pulled her hand back. She risked a glance to see she'd caught two of them – fatally or not, she couldn't tell from so far away.

Either way, it was enough to get their attention elsewhere. Crawling away from the window, she pulled her cell back out.

♥∞♥

Damon was shaking with anger, and panic for Cassandra's safety. He knew the sound of bullets as well as he knew the sound of his own breathing, and there was no way his girl was safe.

Damn her, but doesn't she realize how much danger she put herself in? And she expects Vittorio to pull her out of it?

When Cassandra has said Italy, he'd known what had drawn her there. He knew about the mobster, and Paco had filled him in on the connection with Wraith on the plane from Canada, while Cassandra had been asleep. But there was no way he was letting Cassandra suffer for her parents' mistakes.

The tightening in his chest almost suffocated him, and he hit the wall in rage. A deep breath later, he was dialling a number.

A French-accented voice answered in English. "Yes?"

"Lucien, what the fuck did you tell my girl?"

There was a pause, then the Interpol consultant sighed. "Only what she needed to know." After summarizing their conversation, Lucien added, "There's a warrant out there for your arrest, I did you a favour."

"Last I recall, I didn't ask you to. As a matter of fact, after your last *favour*, I'm pretty sure I told you to stay the hell out of my way next time I'm in your country!"

"Damon, I couldn't have known Interpol would act on the information so quick and they'd ruin your operation. Those girls dying, it was collateral damage, yes. But we got the bad guy, in the end."

Damon's hand tightened around the cell with enough force to break it. "You're full of shit. Is Cassandra collateral damage too, then?"

Lucien sighed. "No. I meant what I told her. Vittorio will help, and she can get the mob off her back once and for all."

"Except she never got a chance to call him apparently, since she's stuck in her parents' estate and being shot at! And I'm not even in same country to save her!"

There was a stunned silence, then Lucien whispered, "What?"

"You heard me, you French bastard. And now you're going to help me. I need a plane to get to Italy, and the clearance so I'm not asked any questions at take-off and landing."

"I can't do that."

"I don't *care*!" Damon's hiss in the phone had nothing polite about it, and his tone took on a harsher edge. "Do this, and I won't fuck you over when I return – if Cassandra's unharmed. But if you don't help me, I will personally hunt you down and kill you."

There was a gulp on the line, then Lucien said, "I do not wish Cassandra to come to any harm, either. Give me an hour."

"You have five minutes."

Damon hung up and threw his remaining equipment in a gym bag, then zipped it closed. By the time five minutes had passed, he was already out of the hotel and in a taxi.

He dialled Lucien. "Well?"

"It's done. Go to this address, the pilot's name is Didier. He'll get you where you need to go."

Damon wrote down the coordinates and hung up. He handed the information to the taxi driver, then sat back and did something he hadn't done in ages. He prayed – for Cassandra's safety, and to get there on time.

♥∞♥

Commotion outside caught Cassandra's attention once more. Three new cars joined the pile, and this time a well-dressed man hopped out of the back of one of them. Even from afar, Cassandra could tell the other men responded to his authority, and a shiver ran down her back.

He must be the boss.

She glanced at the paper she'd been holding crumpled and inhaled deeply. *It's time.* She couldn't delay it much longer. And if she was wrong, and Vittorio didn't pick up... Cassandra tried to ignore the sinking in her stomach.

The line rang and rang, then someone answered in Italian. "Ciao." The word was clipped, unwelcoming, and the words got stuck in her throat.

"*Chi sei?*" Cassandra knew enough of the language to translate. *Who are you?* When she didn't answer, a string of Italian followed, none too amicable.

"I don't speak Italian," Cassandra finally said, and the rant stopped.

There was a heavy silence, and when the man spoke again, his voice was hoarser. "Elena? How... How can this be?"

Cassandra gulped, almost tempted to lie since her voice was so like her mother's. But she pushed back the unwelcome idea. She couldn't lie to Vittorio, not when the unspoken emotion in his tone told her everything she needed to know. Mobster or not, he'd loved her mother, and that love had never died.

"It's not Elena," Cassandra whispered, "but her daughter. My name is Cassandra, and I... I'm in trouble."

She'd imagined a variety of ways the conversation could go, but nothing went as expected.

"Where are you?" was Vittorio's immediate response, almost panicked.

"At my parents' estate," Cassandra said, realizing only after that he might not know where it is. And she hadn't bothered to note the number of the place before getting there.

"Villa Manzoni?" Vittorio asked, and she blinked in surprise. There had been a faded golden plaque on the outside gates with those exact words. But how did he know?

Rather than bother with questions that could wait, Cassandra nodded. "Yes."

There was a scuffle on the other side of the line, and orders barked in Italian. Sounds of engines starting followed, both smooth and harsh. Guns being loaded, and more background echoes. The rapidity of it stunned Cassandra into silence, at least until Vittorio returned on the line.

"What kind of trouble, *cara*? How many men?"

Cassandra glanced out the window again. "Albanian mob kind, and if I was to guess, about thirty."

More barked orders resounded, then Vittorio was back. "Stay inside the house, I will be there soon." Cassandra's stomach dropped in relief, but she didn't get to speak her gratitude. "Stay inside, *cara*. Whatever happens."

"Okay," she said, and he hung up.

It was only after the fact that Cassandra realized the implication of her phone call. She'd signed the death warrant of the men outside. They had families of their own – maybe. Did they deserve this? She could not be their judge, jury and executioner. But somehow, it seemed fitting that Vittorio would be.

♥∞♥

The jet got him to Italy in the promised hour, and a sleek Italian motorcycle with a full tank of gas awaited him when he got off the plane. Damon made a mental note to thank Lucien – or at least not go after him for being a foolish old man.

He set all thoughts aside and hopped onto the motorcycle, breaking traffic laws on his way to Cassandra's estate. Thirty minutes of a drive with twice the speed limit later, he still hadn't caught the eye of any cops.

But when he got to the estate, Damon almost wished he had. More cars than he'd counted on surrounded the villa, and from the look of it the men were well armed. There would be no walking free of this.

Without slowing down, Damon reached for his gun. *Since I have the element of surprise, might as well use it.* He revved his engine, and the motorcycle shot forward, as if eager for blood. The men were either not expecting company or too cocky in their own right, as they took too long to turn around.

By the time they did, Damon had already gunned two down, and steered the bike in a semi-circle around them. He zigzagged between cars, the sleek ride too quick for them to catch him. Four more men dropped, but he knew the wounds might not be fatal.

Damon's quick movement and reflexes helped him evade their counter shots, leaning left and right on the bike to duck them. The click of an empty gun didn't slow him down. He tossed it to the side and reached for his spare, continuing the rampage.

"Damon!"

His mistake was looking up, fearing someone had gotten past him and to Cass. He breathed in relief when he saw she was up by a shot-out window, but it was too late for him. The split-second was enough for one of the bastards to shoot out his back tire.

The motorcycle squealed on the sandy pavement, and Damon hopped off it, landing a few meters ahead. A first bullet in his shoulder had him wince, and he gunned down the shooter. He went to aim for the next man, but the motorcycle smacked into him with its last breath.

Damon's gun flew out of his hand, and he hit the ground – hard. Three of the men headed over and pulled him out from under the motorcycle, holding him for a fourth one.

Dressed in a suit, gelled hair and cold eyes, the leader was pulling on his cigar. "Perfect timing. Now we can negotiate."

He turned to the window, grinning towards Cassandra. Then he reached inside his vest and pulled out a gun, aiming it at Damon's head in clear challenge.

Cassandra knew what Damon's gaze was telling her, to stay away and not move. She hadn't expected him to show up, let alone start a one-man crusade against this many of them. And now he was exactly where she'd been trying to avoid.

"What the *hell* was he thinking?" She muttered, running down the stairs. Vittorio's instructions were clear, but there was no way she was letting Damon get killed.

Cassandra glanced at her wrist watch. Vittorio hadn't given an expected time of arrival, but it had been twenty minutes since their call. She could only hope he would be here soon. Tucking the gun in the back of her jeans, she opened the door and walked out.

Her eyes were on the leader, but she couldn't help glancing over at Damon. "Don't do this," he said, before being head-butted with a gun. He fell silent, but his eyes were shooting daggers at his captors.

Cassandra focused on the boss. "Let him go, you have what you want."

"I do not think so. You've been a pain in our ass, Miss DiCavalier. But a chip to bargain with you seems to be in our favour."

Cassandra wanted to wipe the smirk off his face, but she knew impulsive behaviour was the last thing they needed. "You want money, right? Then tell me where to sign."

The man stepped closer, and Damon struggled against his captors. One of them punched him, but it didn't stop him from trying to retaliate. Another hit to his head had him slump in their arms, unconscious.

The violence of their actions stunned Cassandra into silence. *He'll be fine. He has to be.*

When the leader was only a few steps away from Cassandra, he looked her up and down. Then he grinned, and something sparked in his eyes. "I have a better idea. We'll recruit you for our harem, and once you're nice and broken in, then we can talk about your money."

Cassandra willed herself not to react, but still her fists clenched, giving her away. The leader laughed at her expression, then turned to his men. "You can take care of him. No mess. Make it quick, by the water, and dump the body in."

At the boss' signal, his men grabbed the unconscious Damon by the arms, and dragged him to the edges of the lake. Cassandra watched them disappear, her heart thudding in her chest.

She arched an eyebrow at the boss. "And now what?"

He smirked and held out his hand to her, as if inviting her for a dance. "And now, you come with me to my manor, where we can do some private business."

Cassandra nodded, bowing her head as if resigned to the outcome. Inside, she was boiling with anger. She handed the man her left hand, and waited until he turned away, intending to drag her with him.

The moment he did, she used her free hand to reach for the gun at her back. She kicked with the heel of her foot in the back of his knee, and he cried out as a resounding crack filled the air. He fell on his knees, and Cassandra used the momentum to grab his neck in a tight hold, close to strangling him. She pointed the gun at his temple.

Shock and fear radiated in his entire body, and she smirked. The two remaining guys around them drew their weapons and pointed them at Cassandra, but she used the boss' body to shield herself. If they shot, they'd kill their boss first, her second.

Cassandra put her mouth close to his ear. "Tell them to drop their guns. Now."

She felt his Adam's apple move as he gulped. "Drop your weapons!" As the men hesitated, her hold tightened, and she took the safety off the gun. "Now!" He choked, and the men grudgingly threw the guns at Cassandra's feet.

Now what? The clock is ticking.

Damon had disappeared with the men a few minutes earlier. Cassandra knew from her childhood it took at least ten to walk to the lake, but who was to say they'd wait until then to kill Damon?

Rather than take any chances, Cassandra moved the gun and shot at each of the men. At such close range, she hit their knees or shoulders – flesh wounds that would heal. When they were all groaning in pain, she pistol-whipped the boss.

Leaving the unconscious man behind, she took off on a run towards the lake – and Damon.

Please let him be alive.

♥ *Chapter 23* ♥

Cass is still in danger.

That thought had all of Damon's focus when he came to, his head pounding. He was being dragged down a dusty road, and he counted two men's shuffle of feet. After a few more moments, he was tossed to the ground.

"Boss said to do it at the lake."

There was a laugh, and a different man spoke. "What the boss don't know won't hurt him."

Damon heard the tell-tale sound of the safety being taken off a gun, and waited until he felt the cold steel pressed against the back of his head.

"Foolish stranger…"

"Will you hurry up already?" The man's comrade muttered something in Albanian, but the damage was done.

Their banter provided the distraction Damon needed to jump into action. He rolled on his back and gripped the gun, forcing its aim towards the second man. He shot three times, and the poor sucker dropped to the ground, clutching his bleeding chest.

The Albanian who was holding the gun recovered from his mistake and punched Damon. They rolled on the ground, and Damon was able to manoeuvre the gun away. He head-butted the guy with the weapon, and the man went limp.

Stumbling away, losing blood from his shoulder wound, Damon was more aware than ever in that moment of his mortality. But he refused to die without telling Cassandra he loved her.

He cursed the hand of fate that had put them together

only to pull them apart.

♥∞♥

Cassandra ran up the path, appearing to the top just in time to see Damon wrestle with one of the Albanians. She watched as he won and stumbled to his feet, gun in hand.

His tired gaze lifted and he saw her in the distance. Relief spread on his face, but Cassandra screamed in horror.

"Damon, watch out!"

A few meters behind him had appeared a third man, and he was aiming his pistol towards Damon. She pointed her gun and shot at him, but missed. Her movement was enough to clue Damon to the danger.

He whirled around, dropping to a knee and shooting back. In the open field, her boyfriend was too easy of a target, and two more men showed up. *Where the hell are they coming from?*

Only did then did Cassandra realize that the forces she'd seen from the window were not the only ones in the area. It was too late to correct her mistake, but she wasn't about to let Damon be killed.

For a moment, she was distracted by noise in the distance. She glanced towards the villa, noticing the cloud of dust on the path leading to the house. Sounds of a helicopter gave her hope that police had arrived.

Ducking and running with newfound eagerness, Cassandra lifted her gun and shot in the direction of the newcomers, hoping her blind aim nabbed at least a few of them, even if only with nonfatal wounds.

The unconscious Albanian knocked out by Damon got off the ground, reaching for his partner's gun. Cassandra saw the man shoot, and without thinking slammed into him from behind. The surprise attack offered her the upper hand, and Cassandra used it to put him in a headlock until he went limp.

Cassandra then turned to Damon. He was grappling with the last of the newcomers, taking as many hits as he was delivering. A gun went off between them, and Cassandra yelled. She aimed her own gun and shot twice at the guy, then ran over. She kept thinking of the two gunshot wounds she hadn't been able to stop.

She slid to the ground next to Damon's too white face, and her worst fears were confirmed. Blood was seeping from a stomach wound. Cassandra tore his shirt off and pressed it on the wound.

"Damon!" Tears streamed down her cheeks, but she tried to choke them back. "Don't do this, you need to hold on. I'm so sorry for leaving, for not listening to you. I love you, Damon. Please..."

He blinked, staring at the sky for a second before meeting her gaze. The green eyes she loved were clouded and unfocused, but Damon opened his mouth, trying to speak. The effort turned out to be too much, and his head rolled to one side.

For a frightening few seconds, Cassandra was afraid he'd died right in her arms. But then she checked for his pulse, and found it – weak, but consistent. She saw his smiling face in her mind, and his eyes, full of love for her.

I want to look into those eyes again, and I'll be damned if I let him die on me.

"I will not lose you, Damon," she whispered fiercely in his ear. "Not after all we've been through. We deserve another chance."

Heaving under his weight, but pumped with adrenaline, Cassandra managed to get Damon's arm around her shoulders and drag him to the house. She kept the t-shirt pressed to his stomach, trying as much as she could to staunch the blood flow.

When they got back to the villa, she realized it wasn't a helicopter she'd heard – and that was definitely not police cleaning up. It was Vittorio and his men.

Among the many moving about, grabbing bodies and stuffing them in cars, one man in a suit turned to her. He was tall, board shouldered with eyes the color of pure onyx.

He coolly assessed Damon's half-unconscious body leaning over her, and nodded to one of his men, barking an order in Italian. Cassandra tried to protest when Damon was taken away from her, but Vittorio was there, restraining her.

"He will not harm your man, only bring him to the closest hospital. I know the *dottore* there, he will take good care of him. Besides, he is a devil, yes?"

Cassandra stared at him in confusion, and he grinned, his gleaming white teeth shining in the sun. "Damon is his name, no?"

"How do you know…" Cassandra trailed off at Vittorio's amused look. "I guess you had enough time to do research on your way here?"

"Quite the contrary, cara. No research was needed, because only one person alive would have known to give you my contact." He paused, then said, "Lucien filled me in."

"Ah." A second later, a short laugh escaped her. "Then yeah, I guess you could say Damon is a devil." She looked in the distance, where the car carrying her boyfriend had disappeared in a cloud of dust.

"Come," Vittorio said and walked to a black limousine. "I will bring you to the hospital, and it gives us time to talk."

Cassandra followed him to the car, wiping at her face. Sheer exhaustion settled in her shoulders, and once she fell onto the leather seat, her body only wanted to curl up and sleep.

Vittorio seemed to understand this as he poured her a healthy dose of some liquor. "Drink."

Cassandra threw it back with little thinking, and he grinned. In his eyes, she saw recognition and some of the love he had for her mother. She understood why what he did would have scared Elena, but...

"Why did my mom leave you?" Cassandra asked, biting her lip. "Sorry, I don't mean to bring up bad memories. Especially after what you did for me. I owe you a lifetime of gratitude, but..."

Vittorio waved her off. "No gratitude needed. I am more than happy to have been able to help you, Cassandra. As for why Elena left me..." He glanced out in the distance, a wry smile tugging at his lips. "I was a headstrong fool who thought the only way to keep a woman was to boss her around. Your mother may have been scared at what I did for a living, but I am under no illusions. I did not make things easy for her, used as I was to have things my way."

"Damon does that all the time," Cassandra grumbled. When Vittorio laughed, almost surprised, she added, "And I mind it, don't get me wrong. But I love him in spite of it."

"Maybe that was the key, then," Vittorie smiled sadly, "perhaps her love was not enough. But I do not blame Elena, never did. Once I got my head out of my ass, as you Americans say, I only wanted her happiness. It was why I helped her back then, in Paris."

Cassandra nodded, understanding this loyalty. "I *am* sorry."

"What for?"

"For causing you trouble. The bodies, the…"

Vittorio's expression hardened and he leaned forward. "Make no mistake, Cassandra. Those men deserved what happened, and more. This was an easy death compared to what I wish would have befallen them. I may dabble in the occasional gun smuggling and illicit gambling, but these men were perverse to their core. Their deaths do not atone for the evil they perpetrated, but they at least will offer their victims some freedom."

He touched her hand lightly, a brief reassurance. "Do not lose sleep over this. Over *them.* They do not deserve it."

Cassandra searched his gaze, wanting the absolution he offered. Vittorio was a man used to such things, as was Damon, to some extent. But the bodies she'd seen… She looked away, wondering if she'd ever be able to get their images out of their minds, considering she'd had a hand in their deaths.

Vittorio's hand on hers squeezed, demanding her attention. "You still feel guilty, because you are a decent human being. They were not. Half of those men ran prostitution houses across Europe, forcing women to serve under them. Some of those victims were as young as fourteen." Cassandra's eyes widened, and he inclined his head. "Yes, *cara.* Hear me when I say, they are undeserving of your guilt."

Under his powerful gaze, Cassandra could only nod. What he revealed didn't excuse the carnage, but it did make her feel better knowing the men had been as bad as Viktor.

The car pulled to a stop then, and she glanced outside. They were parked in front of a stark white building, which she assumed to be the hospital. The chauffeur came around to open her door, and Cassandra started to step out.

"*Ragazza…*"

Vittorio's soft-spoken word stopped her, and Cassandra glanced back at him. He smiled then, a genuine grin that told her this wouldn't be the last time they would speak. "This may not make much sense, but someone very dear to me once gave me the same advice. Do not let this experience jade you, nor change you. Family may have gotten you into this trouble, but do not forget the healing power of love. *Il sangue lega, ma l'amore lega meglio.*"

Cassandra frowned at the words. Her poor understanding of Italian didn't help, and she only understood the word *blood*. Yet something about the way Vittorio said the words calmed the skittishness inside her.

Impulsively, she threw herself in Vittorio's arms and hugged him. "*Grazie*," she whispered in his ear, thanking him once more.

When she pulled away, she could have sworn his eyes shone a little too brightly. "Prego," Vittorio said, then waved her off.

Cassandra stepped out of the car and when she looked back, his shades were on, his face a blank expression. On an awkward wave, she took off running for the emergency room.

Everything hurt, especially his head.

Damon opened his eyes and inspected his surroundings, only to see walls passing by quickly. He got the impression he was being moved somewhere, but where? Something was over his mouth, stopping him from saying words he wished he would have voiced earlier.

He tried to search for Cassandra, but didn't see her. *Is she safe?*

Steady beeps surrounded him, and words spoken in Italian. *Where the hell am I?* A man in a white mask grabbed his hand and shot a syringe filled with liquid in his vein.

Damon winced at the bite of the needle and tried to struggle, but instead he fell into a blissful sleep.

♥∞♥

After a painstaking conversation with the nurse on duty, Cassandra was told to wait in the reception area. Damon was in surgery, but she was promised the doctor would come and see her as soon as he was done.

She slumped in a corner chair, curling into herself and resting her head on her knees. Fighting the bad guys seemed like a piece of cake when compared to the long wait ahead. The fact she had no control over what would happen was enough to drive her insane, and her anxiety spiked up a notch.

On a whim, she called Renzo. He picked up despite the time zone difference. *"Ciao, bella,"* he mumbled, and after a quick calculation she figured it was past two in the morning in Canada.

"Bet you say that to all the girls," Cassandra teased back – or tried to, but choked on the last word.

Renzo caught on to it, and his voice grew serious. "What's wrong?"

"In a minute," Cassandra said. "Can you translate something for me?"

"Sure."

She fumbled around the words Vittorio spoke, repeating them semi-well. Renzo was quiet for a moment, then said, "It means, *blood ties, but love binds better.*"

Cassandra stared into nothingness for a few seconds, lost in thought.

"Cass? You still there? What's going on?"

"Yeah, I…" Cassandra cleared her throat. "I'm good. My mom used to say that…"

Then, culmination of everything, she burst into tears and told Renzo everything.

♥∞♥

"Cass, he'll be all right." Renzo moved towards Cassandra, touching her shoulder in a wordless gesture of comfort.

After her original breakdown over the phone, he'd taken a red eye flight and arrived in Italy within hours. He'd been by her side when the doctor announced the original surgery had succeeded, and had stayed vigil over Damon for the two days they'd kept him under observation at the hospital.

Renzo had also supported Cassandra when she'd fought with the hospital, convincing them to release Damon in her care after his vitals had checked out. He didn't seem to be waking up, and she had a feeling he needed to be in more comfortable quarters – and away from the sterile environment.

They'd set up in the untouched wing of Villa Manzoni, but still Damon hadn't woken up. Cassandra had been by his side day and night, and a nurse came to check on him periodically. His condition was improved, and even his bullet wounds healed as the days passed by.

The nurse and doctor said the hits to his head contributed to the semi-coma, while his brain swelling reduced. According to them, Cassandra could do nothing but wait.

Despite their assurance it would be a while before Damon awoke, Cassandra refused to move. She'd allowed Renzo to bully her into showering and eating – twice. But she needed to be next to Damon, to make sure he was alive every second of every day until he opened his eyes.

"Cass…." Renzo's tone was concerned. "You should get sleep. No offense, but you look like crap. And you need food. It's been days since you had anything else but coffee."

She shrugged, offering a grimace of a smile. "I'll make you a deal. I'll eat and sleep when Damon wakes up, okay?"

Renzo shook his head, then muttered something about getting food and walked out of the room. Cassandra reached for Damon's hand once more, squeezing it in hers. In the large king-sized bed, after days of only intravenous fluids, he seemed pale and thinner.

Tears welled in her eyes, and Cassandra blinked them away. She stood and walked to the window, her gaze getting lost in the expanse of the horizon.

"Cass…"

She whirled around, almost not believing her eyes. "Damon! You're awake!"

He blinked a few times, then narrowed his eyes as if remembering something. "You threw yourself at me."

Cassandra waved him off, kneeling by the bed. "Forget that. How are you feeling?"

True to his nature, Damon scowled. "Forget that. You

left me behind in a different country, only so you could get yourself nearly killed? Then went and tried to save me, to top it off?"

"Damon…"

"You're awake!" Renzo walked in with good, unaware of what he'd stumbled into. He grinned, setting his platter on the coffee table and nearing the bed. "Man, it was about damn time!"

Damon tore his gaze from Cassandra and a corner of his mouth lifted in a smile towards the younger man. "Few bullets won't kill me anytime soon. When did you get here?"

Renzo shared a look with Cassandra. "A few days ago. You've been out of it for a while." When he noticed the tension between them, he started backing away. "Tell you what. I haven't slept much, so I'm going to go out and find me a nice spot in the shade and pass out. Meantime, you guys can, you know, sort yourselves out."

"Renzo, wait!" Cassandra's call went unanswered, as Renzo exited the room and closed the door behind him.

"Cassandra."

She turned to Damon, biting her lip. For days now, she'd waited for him to wake up – but she hadn't once considered how things would go, especially given his overprotective side. "I had to get you out of the way, Damon. When that guy had his gun on you… I couldn't think of another way."

Rather than yell at her again, Damon only looked her over. With each passing second of silence, Cassandra's throat felt tighter, and tears threatened.

"Why do you look so tired? And…" His eyes raked her up and down as his frown deepened. "Shit, Cass, when the hell was the last time you ate?"

At the genuine concern in his voice, the tears spilled and Cassandra started sobbing. Damon ripped the needles off him and stood, coming to her. One shoulder was in a sling while the bullet wounds healed, and his entire stomach was bandaged. None of that stopped him from wrapping his free arm around her.

"Hush, love." Pulling her tighter against him, Damon inhaled the sweet smell of her hair. "I'm sorry, I was so worried for you... It came out wrong. I should be thanking you for saving my life."

"Damon, I'm sorry," Cassandra whispered in his chest. "For this entire mess. I love you, and I never meant to put you in da—"

He stopped her from apologizing by pressing his lips to hers. Cassandra sighed at the feel of his mouth on hers, as if a part of her had finally been set right. She gave in to the kiss, wrapping her arms around his neck.

When Damon pulled away, he still didn't let go, instead burying his head in the side of her neck. "This is what's been missing, for so fucking long it feels like forever."

His grip tightened enough to cut off her air supply, and Cassandra choked out a laugh. "Need to breathe!" Damon didn't let go, instead started walking backwards until they both fell on the bed.

Since he still held onto her waist, he pulled Cassandra half on top of him, then forced her head to lie down on his chest. "I don't care what excuse you pull, you've obviously not been sleeping or eating right. So now that I'm awake, I'm going to remedy that. Sleep."

When Cassandra gave in and snuggled closer, she was rewarded by a kiss on her forehead. Between her exhausted body and Damon's steady heartbeat under her ear, Cassandra's eyelids grew heavy within seconds.

As she gave in to sleep, her last thought was, *He's safe. He's alive. And he's mine.*

♥ *Epilogue* ♥

Two weeks later...

Damon glanced at the wide expanse of ocean, and wiggled his toes in the creamy sand. As inviting as the water was, the girl by his side made it impossibly hard to leave.

He shifted on the beach towel and moved on his stomach, crawling to the shade where Cassandra was lying down napping. Dressed in nothing but a red bikini, her skin a healthy golden, she was as alluring as Venus herself.

He ran a hand down her back, smiling when she mumbled something in her sleep. Thanks to a good regimen of food and the type of exercise that didn't require a gym, Cassandra had recovered her vigour – as had he.

Barely days after waking from his coma, Damon had met the man whose resort they were currently using – Vittorio. The mobster had offered them some time away from reality, and after a call to Derek to ensure his business would be in good hands, Damon hadn't hesitated.

Where life would take them, he didn't know. But he planned to spend it by Cassandra's side, enjoying each moment as they came.

Unable to resist the temptation further, Damon bent his head and started kissing down her back. Cassandra moved under him, shifting from a deep sleep to a semi-awake slumber. Her whimpers turned into soft sounds of desire, and he chuckled against her skin.

The girl was his, and he'd spend eternity making her happy.

She's safe. She's alive. And she's mine.

Dear reader,

Thank you for reading my novel, Blood Ties, Love Binds. This baby was a few years in the making. I originally started it off when I was still in high school, and the story took a backseat for a while to other books. When I finally got back into it, I'd learned that I'd changed as a person. And, because Cass has a lot of my traits, this meant she had to, as well.

I hope you found some comfort in her strength. What I really wanted to communicate was that a woman can take care of herself without a man to come save her. But at the same time, there's something to be said for the compromise we get into when we fall in love ☺

If you enjoyed this story, please consider leaving a review at your favourite retailer.

Cheers,

Alexa

About the author

Alexa Whitewolf was born in Dracula's country, Romania, a fact which added onto her already creative imagination. These days, she can be found in a Starbucks or *with* a Starbucks coffee, typing away or writing by hand her next novel.

When not at the local Starbucks, Alexa is hard at work trying to get her two furry canines, Achilles and Zeus, to stop digging holes in her backyard, while enjoying nature with her husband ☺

Follow her blog and read more at www.alexawhitewolf.com

Alexa is also excited to interact with each and every one of you via Facebook, Twitter or Goodreads, so don't be shy!

Also by the Author

The Avalon Chronicles series
Avalon Dreams
Avalon Wishes
Avalon Nightmares
Atrox – A Novella

The Sage's Legacy – YA series
The Dragon Medallion
The Dragon Manuscript
Relics of the Underworld

Moonlight Rogues series
First to Fall
Second to Surrender
Third to Tumble
Last to Love
Moonlight Rogues: Origins

Standalone novels
Blood Ties, Love Binds
Unconditional Love
Blazing Ashes (Coming Soon)

Sign up for my readers' group at
www.alexawhitewolf.com/contact and receive a copy of
Unconditional Love for **FREE**, as well as first dibs on cover
reveals, discounts, giveaways, prizes **and more**!